CW00833254

BAD MONDAY

Chris Martin's home life may be looking up now
her two-timing husband has moved out and her
lover in, but her life as a reporter on the local rag
is in the doldrums, condemning her to covering
village fêtes and lost cats. Until, that is, she lands
an interview with Rick Monday, a local boy who
found fame as a rock star in the seventies.

Though the interview itself turns out to be a
major disappointment, the follow-up is dynamite:
Monday is found with an ornamental dagger in his
chest and Chris was one of the last people to see
him alive. Determined not to let the biggest story
of her career get away, Chris defies her editor and
the police by conducting her own investigation
into the murder. Undeterred by close encounters
with a violent songwriter and a deranged groupie –
not to mention the large boot of a corrupt detective
– she pursues the trail as it leads her through the
often seedy world of rock music and into a web
of family lies and secrets. But the price of this big
story could be Chris's life.

BY THE SAME AUTHOR

A REAL SHOT IN THE ARM
A SECOND SHOT IN THE DARK

BAD MONDAY

Annette Roome

HarperCollins*Publishers*

This novel is entirely a work of fiction. The names, characters and incidents portrayed in it are the work of the author's imagination. Any resemblance to actual persons, living or dead, events or localities is entirely coincidental.

Collins Crime
An imprint of HarperCollins*Publishers*
77–85 Fulham Palace Road, London W6 8JB

First published by Collins Crime 1997

1 3 5 7 9 10 8 6 4 2

Copyright © Annette Roome 1997

Annette Roome asserts the moral right to
be identified as the author of this work

A catalogue record for this book
is available from the British Library

ISBN 0 00 232645 0

Typeset in Meridien and Bodoni by
Palimpsest Book Production Limited,
Polmont, Stirlingshire

Printed and bound in Great Britain by
Caledonian International Book Manufacturing Ltd, Glasgow

All rights reserved. No part of this publication may be
reproduced, stored in a retrieval system, or transmitted,
in any form or by any means, electronic, mechanical,
photocopying, recording or otherwise, without the prior
permission of the publishers.

BAD MONDAY

1

'Oh, thank you, Mr Heslop!' I exclaimed enthusiastically, tucking the folder under my arm before he could change his mind and snatch it back. 'I really do appreciate this. I promise you, it'll be the best interview I've ever done. As a matter of fact, I think I've still got a Bad Monday album at home. I was quite a fan, you know. I'll get it out and play it – and I'll get a copy of *New Musical Express* – do they still do *New Musical Express*? – and see if I can work out some proper *in-depth* music questions for him.'

'Hang on!' Mr Heslop looked slightly alarmed. 'What are you talking about? Nobody's going to be interested in in-depth musical questions, for God's sake. Rick Monday was a local boy who made good, went away, ballsed everything up, and finally decided to come back. People aren't going to be interested in his chord sequences – or lack of them, as is more relevant in his case. They want to be proud of him. They want to know about his new record, his new career, and what colour he's painted his bathroom. And they want to know *why* he's come back home. What exactly *is* it Tipping's got that California hasn't?'

There didn't seem to be any answer to this, so I didn't give him one. I felt a bit miffed, but I said, 'Don't worry, Mr Heslop. If there's a story there, I'll get it.'

'Hmm, all right. But just remember that if there isn't, filling a half-page will do nicely.'

I thanked him a few more times, went back to my desk and collected my things. It was Friday evening and my interview with Rick Monday wasn't until late on Sunday. I'd got plenty of time to prepare, but my mind was racing already. What should a forty(ish) housewife-turned-local-reporter wear on an assignment to interview a forty(ish) rock star she had once quite fancied? Discreet shoulder pads and a tailored skirt, or a 'Save our Wildlife' T-shirt and jeans that looked as though they'd been crawled through a cornfield in?

I went downstairs half settled on the jeans, and found Detective Sergeant Wayne Horton waiting in Reception. He was lounging on our leather-look sofa with his eyes closed and his grubby grey trainers on the coffee table. He appeared to have been reading my front-page piece, 'Town Centre Traffic – Council Seeks New Solution'. (I was rather proud of this: it was our big story of the week.)

He opened one eye and grinned.

'Been waiting for you,' he said, removing his feet from the coffee table and dislodging several copies of the *Tipping Herald* in the process. 'I've got something that might interest you.'

Wayne was in his early thirties, and his T-shirt clung interestingly to the sleek bit between chest and waistband where most of the other men I know have a large mound instead of a sleek bit.

'Hallo. You look tired,' I said.

'Tired? Knackered's more like it. I've been on stakeout all night!' he exclaimed, rubbing the stubble on his chin. I felt a little frisson of excitement. It's not often you have conversations with people that include the word 'stakeout'.

Wayne noticed the frisson. He smiled. 'Come on, buy me a drink and I'll tell you about it. Help me up.'

I extended a hand rather nervously, and he took it and pulled himself up.

'I'm afraid I can't buy you a drink,' I said. 'I'm sorry, but I've got to go straight home this evening. You see, it's Friday, and Pete gets home early on Friday, and my daughter has her friend round, and if I'm not there to stop her she'll play Nirvana for hours and eat pizza on the new sofa, and Pete will end up in the pub.'

'Oh.'

8

'Well, perhaps we could make it some time next week,' I suggested. 'We could make it lunch. What's the story?'

'Burglary.'

'Oh. Actually I'm not sure if burglary is worth lunch.'

'No? These ones are. They're all down to one man and they've all taken place late at night. The victims are usually old people or people living alone. Sometimes they're actually *in* the house watching television while their not-so-friendly neighbourhood burglar lets himself in and helps himself to whatever he fancies. Your editor will like that.'

This was beginning to sound better. A serial burglar ought to be worth lunch. 'What areas is he targeting? Do you think he's a local man?'

'Well, he could be a local, we just don't know. He seems to have a good idea of the general layout of the properties, back entrances, vulnerable entry points, etc. He's going for the better-off areas.' Wayne reeled off a few of them.

'I see. Have you got any leads?'

'I wouldn't go that far. Everybody's got plenty of theories, but that's about it. We're co-operating with Tipping. He put an old woman in hospital last week.'

'You mean he *attacked* her?' Mr Heslop had been waiting for ages for a 'Pensioner beaten up in own home' story so we could do a Crime Prevention issue full of burglar alarm ads. I got out my notebook eagerly. 'Let me have her name and address?'

'No chance! The poor old dear's been through enough. She accidentally walked in on him and he threatened her, and now she's had a heart attack. I personally promised her she wouldn't have to talk to anyone like you about it.'

'Oh, thanks!'

'Just say, "a seventy-seven-year-old Hudderston widow,"' suggested Wayne, pausing for me to write it down. 'Anyway, last week my DI came up with this brilliant theory. You see, all the burglaries have taken place between Thursday and Sunday nights, and there seemed to be a definite pattern to them. So last night six of us spent eight bloody hours in two Transit vans waiting for the bugger to strike in the area we'd

9

pinpointed as his next target.' Wayne tilted his head so that he could watch my pencil cross the page. 'Well, of course, he didn't show up, and I've wasted a whole day filling out paperwork to justify the overtime. Oh, and don't say that, of course.'

I smiled, and wrote: 'The police are pulling out all stops to catch suspect before he strikes again, but so far have few real leads.' 'So, could I say that you're advising anybody who lives alone to make sure their doors and windows are properly fastened and to ring you if they see or hear anything suspicious? Is there anything else I could put in my piece?'

'Not that I can think of. Now, isn't that worth lunch?'

'Oh, I should think so!' I decided I couldn't resist telling him my big news. 'Do you know, I'm interviewing Rick Monday on Sunday. The rock star.'

He stared at me blankly for a moment, but then his face lit up.

'Oh, yes, I remember him. My mum used to fancy him. She had that record of theirs. 'Just for the Money', wasn't it? She used to play it all the time when I was about ten.'

I winced. 'Oh. Really?'

'It was supposed to be some sort of rebellion against his father and his middle-class upbringing, wasn't it? Wasn't his father the Labour Councillor who got all those Community Centres built?'

'Two. Two community centres.' I began to wish I hadn't mentioned it. 'Well, I must . . .'

'Yeah, I remember now. *Bad Monday*. There were four of them in the group, but it was really just Rick and that other one, the miserable-looking one who plays with that other group now . . . you know . . .'

'Modus Operandi.'

'Yes, that's them! They had that big hit last Christmas with . . . oh . . . what was it? Er . . .'

'I can't remember.'

'Me neither. Anyway, he lives on my patch now, in a big house near the golf club. I think he was a local boy, too. Weren't he and Rick supposed to have had some sort of

10

punch-up over something? They split up in the middle of an American tour. There was a picture in the paper of them trying to strangle each other, and the miserable one started making death threats. Christ, what was his name?'

'McGill. Will McGill.'

'Oh, yes. Bad Monday did some good stuff – it was a shame they split up. Hasn't Rick got a new solo thing in the charts?'

'Yes. It's called "Reaching out for No one" and it was at number three last week!' I beamed with pride, as though I'd had a hand in this achievement. 'It's been adopted by a children's charity because it's something to do with child abuse.'

'Oh. Really?'

'Well, I think it's supposed to be about loneliness, but you can take it two ways – or something.' I made a mental note to check up on this before Sunday. 'Anyway, Rick's involved with several charities now and they're holding the annual Hatchley Heath fête in his garden this year – that's why I'm going to interview him.' I glanced at my watch. My neighbours had probably already absorbed way beyond the safe dosage of Nirvana. 'I really must go. I'll ring you next week.'

'Oh.' He pretended to look upset. Or perhaps he really was upset; you could never quite tell what Wayne was thinking. 'You mean, I can't tempt you out for that pint? Why not?'

'I told you. I've got to get home. Come on, I'm going to the car park.'

Wayne followed me down the steps to the street. 'You know what your trouble is?' he remarked, turning towards his car.

'No – what?'

'You haven't realized yet that you're a free agent. See you.'

I had no idea what he meant, so I didn't bother to answer.

On Sunday evening I arrived at Tangley House, Rick Monday's new Hatchley Heath residence, in plenty of

11

time for my seven o'clock interview. I parked the Mini in the only space available on the grass verge in front of Yew Tree Cottage. When I'd finished manoeuvring, I noticed that there was a large notice pinned to Yew Tree Cottage's front gate instructing people in angry capitals not to park on the grass, so I hung around for a few moments, hoping that someone official-looking would pass by and tell me it was all right. The annual Hatchley Heath fête had been held that afternoon in the grounds of Tangley House, and the front lawn now swarmed with men and women in tracksuits shouting instructions to one another as they attempted to dismantle a platform and gather up yards of heavy-duty cable. A furniture van with parts of a coconut shy protruding from its rear was painstakingly reversing out of a muddy hole next to the drive. Actually, it looked to me as though claiming, as the publicity posters had, that the fête was to be held 'in the garden of Rick Monday's new home' was pretty misleading, and must have disappointed anyone who thought they might find themselves ducking under his washing carousel on their way to the ice-cream kiosk. Most of the action appeared to have taken place in a field adjoining the front garden. The back garden was screened from view by ivy-clad brick walls, and the door to it looked firmly closed. Tangley House was a rather gloomy Victorian Gothic mansion, the sort of place that might feature in a third-rate haunted house movie. It had a slightly dilapidated look about it, and I couldn't help wondering why Rick had chosen to live in it.

I got out of the car and walked up the drive. I had finally opted for a 'Be an Ele-friend' T-shirt and a pair of jeans that held my stomach in, and I was feeling quite good about myself. I'd rehearsed all my opening questions in front of the mirror, and I muttered through them again as I ducked past a group of canary yellow tracksuits and approached the porch.

'Excuse me – can I help you?' Without warning, a harassed-looking woman of about my own age appeared at a run from behind me and sprang on to the porch steps, barring my way. She was wearing a 'Save the Hump-back Whale' T-shirt and jeans that didn't quite hold in her stomach.

'I've got an appointment with Mr Monday. Chris Martin, *Tipping Herald*,' I said, producing a card.

'Oh, that's all right then. Sorry. We've had all sorts here this afternoon. People have actually been trying to get into the house, would you believe? Sally Beecham,' she added, extending her hand. 'I'm on the Hatchley Heath Society Committee.'

I took her hand and shook it, and remarked that from what I'd heard the fête had been a great success. Sally looked pleased, and said she'd see if Mr Monday was free. I followed her into the porch, which contained a brass bucket full of umbrellas. The front door had been propped open with an old flatiron, and the hall – which was large enough to park a bus in – had a mottle of muddy footprints across its black-and-white tiled surface. We both stopped and tut-tutted spontaneously over this, and Sally mentioned the word 'Flash' several times.

'I think I managed to keep intruders out of the house,' she explained, 'but of course the people who were running the tea tent had to come in to get water for the urn. I'm afraid the weather was against us this afternoon.'

'What did you mean by intruders?'

'Oh, you know – fans, mostly. Apparently we got a mention on Radio One and people have been coming from far and wide. Well, you can't blame them, can you? It's exciting, isn't it? I don't mind admitting I used to be a fan myself!' she enthused, and she blushed slightly, from which I deduced that she still was. 'I actually came across one extremely odd-looking woman in the porch. She said she was looking for the toilets, but I'm afraid I didn't believe her. Not at all the sort of thing we're used to at Hatchley Heath fêtes. Well, I'll just give him a knock for you.'

She tapped diffidently on a door at the rear of the hall, opened it, and disappeared into the room. While she was gone I took a surreptitious look around the hall and peered up the stairs. The house was a big disappointment. According to my notes it had previously been used as offices by a mail-order company, and it looked as though Rick hadn't done anything to improve it since moving in six months ago. Handsome Victorian-style doors remained hidden beneath a thick build-up of chipped and scratched gloss paint, and the walls and ceilings had been smothered in faded white emulsion without any regard for dado rails, etc. On the other hand, there were no signs of rock-star style orgies of bad taste: no tiger-skin rugs, no solid gold telephones – and no glittering chandeliers with discarded fishnet stockings caught up in them. I suppose this was even more of a disappointment.

Sally backed out into the hall.

'He's on the phone at the minute,' she said. 'I think he's talking to the radio people.'

'Ah.'

'I'll keep an eye on him for you. It's about the handover, I think. Of the fête takings.' She peered round the door, shook her head, and slumped back as though exhausted. 'Well, all I can say is I just hope the extra money we took today will make up for all the work we've put in, because if it doesn't some of the doubting Thomases in this village are going to have a field day with poor Rick. After all, he was only doing it for us. Hang on.' She took another quick peek into the room. 'Still talking. Look, don't get me wrong – *I'm* not complaining – I'm all for new ideas, but sometimes you wonder if it's worth the, you know, the *aggro* it causes with certain people. What I – Ah.' She broke off and craned round the door again. 'Yes, he's definitely finishing now. There. As I said, it's the radio people. Anyway, I suppose you're used to all this – famous people and photographers all over the place and everything.'

'Not really,' I confessed.

Sally shook her head. 'Well, I suppose I've more or less got used to being around Rick himself, he's so charming and natural, but I don't think I'll ever get used to rubbing shoulders with celebrities. It gave me quite a shock this afternoon when I ran into Will McGill on my way back from collecting in the raffle money. I mean, what next – Paul McCartney down at the Centre buying some of our organic jam?' she added, with a giggle.

14

I thought for a moment. 'Will McGill?' I queried. 'Are you sure? I thought he and Rick hadn't spoken to each other since the group broke up.'

'Oh, no – didn't you see that story in the *Sun* the other week? I picked it up in the train,' she added, hastily. 'You remember that big charity concert that was on the television? The *Sun* had a photograph of them backstage shaking hands.'

At that moment there was a faint 'ting' from within the study and, without waiting for me to answer, Sally pushed open the door.

'Someone to see you, Rick,' she announced, gushingly.

Rick was seated at a large mahogany desk with his back to us, his head silhouetted against the late afternoon sun flooding in through the French windows.

'It's the lady from the *Herald*.'

He rotated round in his swivel chair and looked at me. He extended a hand, and I walked forward and took it.

'I'll be off then.' Sally departed, closing the door behind her, leaving me alone with my erstwhile heartthrob.

For a moment we studied one another. Or at least, I studied him. It was a bit of a struggle to reconcile the Rick Monday sitting in front of me with the Rick Monday I'd once had pinned to my bedroom wall. The one on the bedroom wall had been lean and sultry; his thighs, tightly clad in worn denim, had been parted provocatively across the saddle of a high-powered motorbike, and his pouting lips had caressed a half-smoked cigarette in the way you hoped he might, well, caress parts of you. He'd had a sensuous tumble of chestnut curls and brooding blue eyes that burned right out of the wall at you. The Rick Monday sitting in front of me now with his legs discreetly crossed was wearing a canary yellow tracksuit that completely obscured all his attractive masculine bits, and his sensuous tumble of curls had been tamed into an unobtrusive ponytail.

'Right, take a seat,' he said, backing the chair round so he could swing his legs up on to the desk. 'I'm afraid I'm a bit rusty when it comes to giving interviews. But I've just

15

heard the *Sunday Times* may be featuring me soon in a series they're doing on celebrities who work for charities, so I can use you for practice.' He grinned disarmingly. 'Do you mind being practised on, Chris?'

I tried not to think of the picture of him on the motorbike. 'No, not at all.' I sat down.

'Right. Good. Your photographer was here this morning. He took a couple of shots of me at the desk, and a few more over by the window with the gold disc behind me. He said that was what your editor would have liked. He said if he'd been working for the *Times* he'd have done something all arty-farty in the garden with a birdbath.' I glanced towards the French window. On the wall next to it was a gold disc in a glass frame, shimmering where the light struck it. 'Well, let's get on with it, then, shall we, Chris? How about if I tell you my story, and then you fire away at me with a few questions. You know – whatever you like. Have to be a bit quick, though. I'm meeting someone for dinner in half an hour.'

I got my notebook out hastily. I was warming to him already.

'Well, I'm a changed man, Chris, that's the story,' he announced briskly, with a most unsettling wink. 'Really. You'd let your daughter go out with me.'

'Oh!'

'I was a bit of a bastard in the past, I admit it, but I've bloody paid for it, and now I know better. I mean, in the end, it's what you leave behind you when you go that counts, isn't it? Pleasure's all very well, but you can't . . . you know, leave it to anyone, can you?'

'No, I suppose not.'

'It's middle age, isn't it, Chris?' He winked again, rather gratuitously, I thought. 'Anyway, I had a good life in California – parties, women, booze, you know the kind of thing – but I've come back now to make something of what's left of my life, before it's too late. The family were on at me to wise up for years, and my only regret is that I've left it too late for my mum and dad. I expect you know they're both dead now. Still, I guess they knew I loved them.'

16

He paused to ponder this remark, and so did I.

'OK? Well, I expect you've got the picture. Let me start by giving you these.' He pushed a handful of leaflets across the desk. 'Don't read them now, they're for later, a bit of background info for you. They explain the work of the Acorn Trust, which I'm sure you know all about – Christ, of course you do. Their *raison d'être* is improving the lives of young people, right? My brother introduced me to them, he's been working for them for years. Oh, and don't worry, I'm not going to get all boring about it and stop having the occasional glass of champagne or the odd . . . well, Chris, let's say romantic distraction. But I'm going to devote as much of my free time as I can to helping the Trust. The Acorn Trust believe that young people are the future. A disadvantaged, alienated youth will grow up to be a disadvantaged, alienated adult – do you get my drift?'

'Yes.'

'Good. John Bradman of the Trust was our guest of honour here today, as you also probably know. I've given you the text of his speech, in case you want to use it. The Trust funded the new short-tennis courts over at Hudderston Sports Centre, and they're putting up the money for the activity centre for children from deprived areas we're hoping to get going just down the road here. The thing is, I think I'm in a unique position to do something for young people, because they respect me. They respect my music, and they know I've *been there*. I'm not just some old fogey preaching at them who's never done drugs or chucked a brick through a hotel window or anything.' He winked again. 'And these days I'm a respected member of the adult community, too. I mean, I'm working hard at that. Did you know I've joined the Hatchley Heath Society?'

'Er, yes, I think it was in my notes,' I agreed, and I blushed, because I hadn't bothered to read the note I'd been given on Rick's involvement with the Hatchley Heath Society. As far as I was concerned – and as far as the old Rick Monday I used to lust after was concerned – membership of the Hatchley Heath Society was pretty close to being a fate worse than death (no pun intended).

17

'Right, well, I got the fête a mention on national radio this weekend, didn't I – when did you ever hear of a village fête getting a mention on national radio? Do you know, we've probably made at least double what they took at last year's fête. With luck we should be able to afford to set up a Christmas tree recycling depot in the village this year.'

Just for a moment, I wondered if he was sending me up.

Rick produced one of his most devastating smiles. 'So, there you have it, Chris, that's little old me for you. I suppose you could say I was pretty . . . well, self-indulgent in the past, but I took a few knocks and it put me in touch with myself. Know what I mean? By the way, what do you think of "Reaching out for No one"?'

'Oh, well, I really liked it!'

'Good. And I think you'll really like the new album I'm working on, too. I'm compiling a list of quotes from insiders in the business, but I haven't quite finished it so I'll have to send it on to you. Feel free to use any of them you want. I'll make sure your paper receives an advance copy of the album as soon as there's one available.'

'Will you sign it?' I asked stupidly. 'For my daughter, of course.'

He laughed, and at this point, the phone on his desk rang.

He lifted the receiver. 'Ronan, hallo . . . Yes, yes, it is, I'm in the middle of an interview . . . Ah. Well, I'm sorry you had to find out like that, but I've been trying to get in touch with you for weeks . . . Come on, what're you talking about?' His expression turned suddenly to a scowl. 'Look, the truth is you've been too busy with that new band of yours to give a toss about me, so I decided . . . Yes, you have . . . Well, that's up to you . . . Yes, I do know exactly what I'm doing . . . No, all right, if that's what you want – fine. I never go to bed before midnight. See you just after eleven.'

He banged down the receiver angrily.

'My manager,' he remarked, sullenly. 'My *ex*-manager, as a matter of fact. You might like to know – you can put this

18

down – I'm going to be managing my own career from now on. And my brother will look after the financial side.'

'I see.'

'Bloody managers. They bleed you dry for years, then cry their eyes out when you do the obvious thing. Oh, well, who gives a shit. What were you saying?'

'Er . . . I was going to ask you about "Reaching out for No one". I read in the *Independent* that it's about a child-abuse victim who is haunted by his or her past experiences.'

'Ah.' He got up. On the far side of the room was a reel-to-reel tape deck, a keyboard, a monitor, and a bank of equipment displaying red and green lights, and he went over to it, deftly flicked a few switches and turned the monitor off. 'It's basically about loneliness, actually,' he said. 'About coming to terms with being on your own and not having someone else to warm your feet in bed at night. That's what the song's about.'

'Yes. But –' The song and Rick's plaintive singing voice began to echo tunefully at the back of my head. '"Reaching out for no one, touching in the dark . . ."' I repeated, resisting the temptation to imitate the tune. '"Lost before you loved me, losing all to you . . ." I wondered if it was based on anyone in particular – someone you've come across in your work for the Acorn Trust, perhaps?'

'No. Look, let's just leave it at that, shall we? I'm sure you know how the creative process works. You bang around for ages with an idea and then it suddenly comes together. Sometimes it's hard to pin down your original influences. I put the finishing touches to it here as a matter of fact, at this very keyboard.'

'Did you?' My son Richard had been whistling 'Reaching out for No one' only the other day when he called to collect his washing: I couldn't wait to tell him I'd sat in the very room where bits of it had been composed.

'Yes. I did. And I'm telling you, when you hear the new album you'll be even more impressed. I reckon there are at least two number ones on it, you wait and see.'

'I will!'

19

He smiled.

I smiled back. 'I've got just a couple more questions, if you don't mind.'

'Shoot,' suggested Rick, his pouting lips sending a small shiver down my spine.

'Well, I'd like to ask you about the break-up of Bad Monday. For a start, why *did* the group break up, do you regret it, and is there any possibility you might ever get back together with Will McGill?'

There was silence for a moment. 'Actually, that's three questions, Chris,' remarked Rick, a touch sullenly. 'No, I don't regret it. Not at all. You have to move on, don't you, and I think Bad Monday and I had gone about as far as we could together. The fact that my career went into the doldrums afterwards for quite a while was just one of those things. I made a few films which weren't very good, OK. But then I wrote some pretty good songs for quite a few pretty good people.' He reeled off a list of names and titles, some of which I'd vaguely heard of. 'So there you are. Does that answer your question?'

I wrote down what he'd said. 'And the break-up, Mr Monday?'

'Come on, I've already answered that. I told you, McGill and I had irreconcilable musical differences. That was why we broke up.'

'Ah, but –' I reached into my briefcase and, by a stroke of amazing good fortune, immediately found the cutting I was looking for. I pulled it out and laid it carefully on Rick's desk. It was the newspaper item detailing Bad Monday's notorious punch-up. This event was supposed to have taken place late one evening on a West London back street, and by happy coincidence had been witnessed by a local artist, who had sold a sketch of it to a newspaper. The sketch depicted Rick, his face contorted with rage, attempting to drag Will from a Porsche displaying Will's customized numberplate, while a girl looked on in horror. The girl was exceptionally beautiful, and the artist had taken great pains to capture her features (or, more probably, to invent or improve on them): she had a heart-shaped face surrounded by lustrous hair that was loose and wild in the fashion of the day, her eyes were melting and beseeching, and she had the sort of figure film directors write out six-figure cheques for.

'What about this? Surely this wasn't about musical differences?'

'That's a piece of shit.'

'Oh.' I was taken aback. I glanced at the picture again. 'Is it? Are you saying it didn't happen?'

'Yes. Come on. Next question.'

'Oh, well . . .' Reluctantly I slotted the picture back into my briefcase. I didn't quite have the courage to press the point, but I didn't believe him. 'I've heard that you and Will are back on speaking terms and I wondered whether there was any chance of you working together again?'

'Did you?' With something of an effort, he managed a smile. 'Well, you'll just have to wait and see, then, won't you, Chris?'

'Will I? Couldn't you just give me a *hint* – off the record, if you like –'

His phone rang. He ignored it at first, mulling over my question. Then with a bad-tempered sigh he snatched up the receiver.

'Hallo? Oh, hallo, John. Yes, I'm OK, thank you. Knackered, of course, but what do you expect?' He turned his back on me, and perched on the edge of the desk. '. . . Oh. Oh, right . . .'

For a moment, I sat patiently and waited for him to finish, watching his back and glancing idly at the papers he'd left on his desk. On top was a letter from a well-known firm of architects. I began to wonder about this; perhaps Rick was having an extension built, or a swimming pool, or even a recording studio. I got up, dropping my pencil on to the rug, and, when he still didn't turn round, I craned my neck to read the letter.

'Yes, we are definitely going to have to talk about that,' Rick was saying, 'and I'm not going to change my mind.'

21

The letter bore the heading 'Tangley House – Conversion. Plan A'. It all looked too technical to be worth bothering with.

'All right, I'm OK with that . . . Yes, if you want, but I can tell you right now . . .'

Underneath the architect's letter was an appointments diary bound in black leather and half-turned towards me. I could make out the word 'fête' written against today, Sunday. I could also see an entry for Monday – 'Barclays, High Street, 11.00' – but the architect's letter was covering the rest of the week.

'What do you mean? Look, I've told you, forget it. I'm not hungry anyway and that woman will have left something in the fridge. And my bloody manager says he wants to pop in at about eleven, although knowing him he won't show up . . .'

With a sudden, daring, heart-stopping movement, I leaned over and flicked at the architect's letter with my finger. Rick had written the word 'studio' next to Wednesday and Thursday, and against Friday in his neat red capitals he had put 'Will – Old Barn Restaurant 1.00'.

'Well, you just go off and enjoy your recital,' Rick said, tersely. 'Yes, see you tomorrow. Good night.'

I jumped back hastily from the desk and pretended to be looking for my pencil.

'Right,' said Rick sharply. 'Where were we? Is that it? 'Cos I'd really like to call this a wrap. OK?'

'Oh. All right.' I gave up on the pencil and cast a quick glance at my notebook. I was considering the implications of Will and Rick meeting after all this time. Would they attempt to re-form Bad Monday? Could it work? Or would they play safe and opt for the occasional collaboration? I decided not to mention it. 'Um, there is just one question. Sorry – you'll hate it, but I've got to ask.'

'All right. Go ahead.'

'Well, it's about your love life, I'm afraid. Your second marriage ended ten years ago, and I just wondered if there was anybody new in your life at the moment?'

An ironic smile flickered about his lips.

'Sorry. No. There isn't.'

'No?' I took a few steps towards the French windows, which opened on to a paved terrace surrounded by empty stone troughs. From the terrace a path led down through an overgrown rockery to the lawn. You could imagine the troughs filled with houseleeks and alpines, and the rockery blazing with alyssum and aubretia, but at the moment they weren't filled with anything except gravel and yellowed weeds.

'But you've got this lovely house,' I protested, admiring his wide sweep of lawn, which had been roughly cut and was streaked with rain-soaked grass clippings. 'Isn't it a bit big just for you?'

'It's not a problem. My brother and I always fancied this house when we were kids. We said whoever got rich first would buy it.'

'Oh, I see. So it was a lifelong ambition of yours to live here then, was it?' I peered curiously at the disintegrating brick paths meandering round the edge of the lawn past bare borders, and eventually disappearing out of sight beyond untrimmed yew hedges. Further along the terrace, a stack of plastic buckets leaned against a side door, and someone had left a milk-crate at the top of steps leading down to the garden.

'You could say that.'

At that moment, the study door burst open and Sally Beecham and a companion lurched into the room carrying a dozen or so money bags.

'I'm so sorry, Rick,' said Sally. 'But you said you wouldn't mind if we did this in here. We just want to do a rough count, if that's all right?'

'Yes, fine. Chris and I have just finished.' He said this rather pointedly, but he smiled graciously in my direction. 'How's it looking, Sally?'

Sally blushed unnecessarily. 'Oh, marvellous, Rick! It's looking marvellous!'

'Good.' He ushered me towards the door. 'I'll show

Chris out and then I'll be back to give you a hand. Pile it all on the desk.' He winked. I was beginning to be a bit turned off by his winks. 'And don't worry, I'll guard it with my life.'

He showed me out to the porch.

'Would you like to give me a rough idea of what you're going to write about me?' he enquired.

'Er . . .' I hated it when people put me on the spot like this. Especially people like Rick. 'Well, it'll be something about you returning to your roots, you know, moving into this house which you'd always admired – being a part of the community. People will like that. And doing lots of things for young people, of course. Perhaps I could say that you're following in Councillor Monday's footsteps – something like that?'

He thought about this. 'Hmm. I like it. Yes, that's great, Chris. And don't forget to give the new album a plug, will you? I'll get that list of quotes sent round to you in the morning. Will I see you tomorrow?'

'Tomorrow?'

'Yes, at Barclays Bank, for the official counting of the money, and the handover. The Acorn Trust are our charity this year. Haven't you been told about this? It's going to be live on radio. My brother was supposed to be handling publicity.'

'Oh, I expect someone else is doing it. If Three Counties Radio are going to be there, you can be sure we will!' I exclaimed. 'Thank you so much for talking to me.'

'My pleasure,' replied Rick, with another devastating grin.

When I got back to my car, someone had pushed a bundle of ice-cream wrappers under the wiper with a note saying: 'This grass is private property and you may be liable to prosecution for parking on it'. I removed the wrappers and the note, and tossed them on to the back seat along with my notebook. I felt elated. My piece on Rick Monday, local hero, would be our feature of the week: it would be advertised on billboards outside every tobacconist in Tipping. I had done brilliantly; I had even asked a few mildly contentious questions and not panicked when he didn't like them. It didn't matter at all that in the end I hadn't liked Rick Monday quite as much as I'd expected.

2

When I arrived at my desk on Monday morning, there was a note from Mr Heslop propped against my telephone. The note, which was written in angry capitals, said, 'Where are those quotes you promised to get me on the Hatchley Heath Adventure Playground Scheme?' I winced and dropped the note in the wastepaper basket, then turned on my monitor and accessed the *Herald*'s address list of local celebrities. Beside Will McGill's entry was the remark 'Does not speak to local reporters'. Of course, I should have expected this. Will McGill was a fully-fledged celebrity, a member of the successful rock band Modus Operandi; the walls of *his* study – although he was hardly the type to have one – would be positively papered with gold discs. I'd watched him pick his nose on Wogan's sofa and grunt inarticulately at Aspel. He was a bit out of my league, and if I rang him he might lodge a complaint against me with Mr Heslop.

Tentatively, I picked up my phone and dialled his number. This was the first time in my very short career that I'd even been on the verge of something resembling a scoop, and I could always cut him off if he turned nasty.

The phone rang for a few seconds, and then the opening chords of Modus Operandi's most recent hit record exploded into my left ear drum. I held the receiver to one side until it had finished.

'Hi!' began a honeyed female voice with just the faintest South London twang. 'You have reached Will McGill's number, but I'm afraid we're not available at the moment. If you want to leave a message you can do it after the tone. Unless you're

26

from *Time Out*, of course, in which case –' The message ended with a loud raspberry and a lot of giggling, followed by a mechanical beep.

'Ah, hallo,' I began. 'I'm a – a freelance journalist, and I'd like to speak to Mr McGill urgently to confirm a rumour I've picked up on the grapevine that –'

At that moment, the door of Mr Heslop's office burst open with the force of an exploding water heater.

'Chris!'

I put the phone down.

'Chris, get on your bike and get yourself over to Hatchley Heath – now! This is a big one! It's your friend Monday – he's dead!'

'What?'

'Drugs overdose, I imagine. We can only hope the post-mortem results will be through in time for this week's edition. Meantime, find out what he was on, how long he'd been on it – whether he'd ever tried to come off the stuff . . . Do you think you can turn yesterday's interview into some sort of obit?'

This was the first time an interviewee had died on me, and I began to feel a bit queasy. 'But he can't have overdosed,' I protested. 'He wasn't doing drugs any more!'

My phone rang. It was Pete, and at the sound of his voice my stomach did a back-flip.

'Hi. Thank Christ, you're there,' he said, breathlessly. 'I'll be in the *Herald* car park in ten minutes. Meet me there. See you.'

'Yes, all right. I say, have you heard about – Hallo?'

Pete worked for one of the more notorious tabloids. Of course he'd heard about Rick. He was already on his way.

Pete's MGB was in the car park by the time I got down there, its engine racing and its bonnet splattered with dead insects. I jumped in, and he pulled out into the street before I'd got my seat belt done up.

'Arseholes!' he remarked, affably, raising a middle finger in the direction of several motorists who had screeched to a halt behind us and were now hooting angrily. He smiled at me. 'This is a treat, seeing *you* so early in the morning.'

'What do you mean? You already saw me this morning.'

'Oh, come on, two grunts and a "Here are your under-pants" outside the bathroom doesn't count. What have you heard?'

'Nothing. Just that he's dead. Mr Heslop thinks it's a drugs overdose, but I don't believe it.' I felt a bit hurt: I had carefully folded the underpants. 'I really don't believe it!'

Pete leant out of the window and shouted something more than usually unrepeatable at the occupant of the next lane. Then he said, 'Well, I think Bill's probably right for once, whatever you say. And you're going to have to put up with the driving, darling, because if we're not first on the scene I'll never live it down. Especially since you must have been the last person to interview him. Did he say anything quotable as last words?'

I clung grimly to the edge of my seat. When we got to a stretch of clear road, I said, 'Look, I told you yesterday, Rick was fit and well and not on drugs.'

'Oh, and you'd know, would you?' He changed gear ready to overtake. 'Actually, I reckon it's pretty pathetic, waiting till your forties to blow yourself away. If you ask me, all the best rock stars do it while –' We sped round a Volvo, flattened to the back of our seats by G-force '– they're still young. What's the point in hanging round for years looking like a zombie? The only alternative is to become a born-again Christian – or to really hit rock-bottom, if you'll pardon the pun, and end up doing guest appearances on daytime TV,' he added, as an afterthought. He looked rather pleased with this theory; I could see he was working on ways of incorporating it into his piece.

'Cat Stevens became a Muslim,' I remarked, rebelliously.

He gave me a hard stare, and crushed the accelerator to the floor.

When we arrived at Tangley House, there were four police cars and an ambulance in the front drive, and a small

28

crowd of onlookers had begun to gather on the edge of the common.

'I think that's Mike,' said Pete, steering the car on to the grass verge without looking what he was doing and switching off the engine while it was still in gear. He jumped out and ran across the road towards Tangley House. When I'd recovered from the jolt, I followed him.

'Good to see you,' Pete said, pumping Mike's hand. 'Mike, this is Chris – she works for the *Tipping Herald*. Chris, Detective Sergeant Mike Willis.'

'Good to see you, mate!' exclaimed Willis, ignoring me. 'We haven't had a decent piss-up down the Crown since you left the *Herald*!' For some reason I just knew he was the sort of man for whom a good time meant six pints of lager and throwing up behind your neighbour's garage. 'How's the car these days?'

'Fine. How's the bike?'

Willis put the index finger and thumb of his right hand to his mouth and kissed them. 'Superb, mate. Couldn't be better. I'd marry it if it could bring itself into the kitchen and do the washing up. By the way, he's been stabbed,' he added, casually.

Pete did a double-take, and I said, 'Are you sure?' before I could stop myself.

Willis looked at me for the first time. 'He's got a bloody great knife sticking out of him, love. It tends to be a bit of a give-away. The doc's giving him the once-over. His cleaning woman found him about an hour ago, in his study. She couldn't get in through the front, so she trogged round the back and found the French windows open. We think there was a break-in.'

'Anything taken?' Pete asked.

'Don't know. One of that lot on the common says he was keeping the money from the Hatchley Heath fête in the house. She reckons Three Counties Radio gave it a mention. We're trying to get that confirmed, and somebody's gone to collect the brother from Eldon Park School – he's a teacher. And that's about all we know as of this moment. You'll have to wait till the guv'nor's ready to make a statement.'

I had a brief flashback of Sally struggling into Rick's study with the money bags.

'The fête money was in the study. He said he'd guard it with his life!'

Willis rounded on me suspiciously. 'What're you talking about? Where'd you get that from?'

'I was with Rick last night. I interviewed him.'

'Christ, you could've been one of the last people to see him alive! Come on, love, my guv'nor'll want to talk to you.'

Pete and I followed him up the drive, past the police cars with their still-chattering radios.

'It's an awful bloody mess,' said Willis, as we approached the porch. 'I hope you've got a strong stomach, love.'

For the first time, I felt a twinge of alarm. In Tipping, you don't often have to visit scenes of major unpleasantness; in fact, if you keep your head down you can usually avoid them altogether. I'd thought this would just be a matter of standing around outside the house until someone came out and told us what was going on. I like doing that sort of thing. But DS Willis was proposing to take us *into the house*. I glanced nervously into the hall, and then I noticed the front door. It was propped open, as it had been yesterday, only this time it was hanging from one hinge. Someone had propped it in place with a splintered piece of timber that had once formed part of the door frame: you could see the great white gash where it should have fitted in.

It looked violent and awful.

'Jesus Christ – is that how they got in?' asked Pete, getting out his notebook eagerly.

'No. *We* did that,' said Willis. '*They* got in through a door at the back. Made quite a neat little job of it. We had to bash the door in because it was locked on the inside – see –' He indicated an elderly Yale lock with an internal locking handle that was still in place on the front door – 'and we couldn't find a key. We couldn't have everyone traipsing in and out through the back. What you got, Slater?' he

30

added testily, to a young officer who had just run down the stairs.

'There's some very tasty-looking rings, and a watch up there, Sarge!' exclaimed Slater, his face shining with excitement. 'It's a bloody Rolex! It was sitting in one of them poncey little cut-glass dishes on his dressing table. Honest, he's got some stuff up there, Sarge. You want to see it! Guess what, he buys his clothes from –'

'All right, Slater, just get on with it, will you,' snapped Willis. 'You two wait here. I'll have a word.' He left us in the porch. 'Sir ...' I heard him say. 'I've got hold of a reporter who was here last night. She's got some info on the money ... OK, sir.' He turned and nodded to us. 'Right, love, come on in.'

At this, my already unsettled stomach turned to the consistency of wallpaper paste. I thought of protesting, but it didn't seem like the right thing to do, and I always like to do the right thing.

The room was a shambles. Men in blue overalls were all over it, talking in low voices, stepping over fallen furniture, rustling around with polythene bags. The French doors I had peered through curiously last night were now wide open, and outside on the terrace there were more men in overalls. I took two reluctant steps into the room.

'That's far enough,' said Willis.

And at that moment, I spotted Rick Monday's corpse. It wasn't hard really. If you walk into a room with a corpse in it, it's the first thing you look at. He was lying face-down on the sheepskin rug, still dressed in the canary yellow tracksuit, and curled into something resembling the foetal position.

'This is DCI Banks, love,' said Willis.

I didn't look at DCI Banks. I said 'Hallo' politely, but my attention was focused on the corpse. It wasn't really in the foetal position: the arms were scrunched up under the body, and the head was jammed against the thermostat valve on the radiator. A man in white overalls was examining the body. The sheepskin rug had soaked up Rick's blood like a sponge, and there were dark red blobs and splashes on the

31

magnolia-painted radiator and up the whitewashed wall. It looked as if he'd died while attempting to crawl into a corner. And judging by the smell, he had voided his bowels at the moment of death.

'Excuse me,' intruded a voice. 'Are you all right?'

I hadn't expected the smell.

'Yes, I'm all right,' I said. 'I'm fine.' I wasn't, of course.

'Good. Mrs . . . ?'

'Martin.'

'Mrs Martin, if you'll bear with me, there are a couple of points you might be able to help us with. I gather you've been able to provide some information concerning an amount of money that was in the house last night.'

'Yes. The takings from the fête. I don't know how much it was, but there were about a dozen bags of coins and notes on the desk. Rick – I mean, Mr Monday – was going to look after it.'

'Good. Now I'd like you to look at something for me and tell me whether you recognize it.'

DCI Banks was a short, insignificant-looking man in an insignificant-looking blue suit. He held something out towards me in a polythene bag. I looked at it nervously, half expecting it to be something unspeakably gruesome, but it was only an empty money bag.

'It's one of the bags the fête money was in.'

'Good. And this?' He discarded the money bag, which made a faint clinking sound as he dropped it, and held out another polythene packet. I stepped forward over the broken casing of a telephone and a supine standard lamp, and took hold of one corner of the polythene. DCI Banks hung on to his end, and we stood there with it hanging between us. It was a stainless steel knife with a long, narrow blade and an ornamental brass handle, the sort of thing you buy in a moment of sangria-inspired enthusiasm in a Spanish souvenir shop, and then keep at the back of a drawer for the next twenty years. Its blade was encrusted with dried blood.

I let go of it hastily.

'Is it the murder weapon?' asked Pete.

32

'We think so. It was found near the body. What we want to know, Mrs Martin, is whether or not it belonged to Mr Monday. It's been suggested that he might have kept it on his desk for opening letters.'

I tried to visualize the room as it had been yesterday, and couldn't. 'I'm awfully sorry, but I really don't remember seeing it,' I said, apologetically.

DCI Banks looked as though he was accustomed to disappointment. 'All right. Now look, Mrs Martin, it's very important that we establish as quickly as possible what we're dealing with here. I want you to take a good look round the room and tell me if you think anything else is missing.'

I swallowed. I'd just about decided I'd be fine as long as I kept my eyes averted from the corpse and its surroundings – although there was no way I could shut out the smell of it, or the noise the flies were making as they buzzed around the pools of blood – and now he was asking me to take an in-depth look at the place.

I looked at Rick's desktop.

'Well, there were some papers and the phone and things on there – Oh, they're on the floor.'

'Carry on.'

'Take your time, Mrs Martin,' murmured Willis in a patronizing tone, as though talking to a particularly stupid contestant in a TV game show. 'Look all round.'

I glanced warily beyond the desk in the direction of the French windows. Rick and his assailant must have struggled together just inside the room, knocking over a shelving unit, dislodging the items on the desk and smashing the telephone, because the rest of the room, including the recording equipment, appeared to be undamaged. But there was something missing.

'The gold disc!' I exclaimed, flushing with the excitement of the contestant who has just picked the right box. 'There was a gold disc on the wall over there by the door. Look, you can see the hook where it was hanging.'

'Good, good!'

'Excuse me a minute,' interrupted the man in overalls, who

had been kneeling on the floor next to the body. 'But I'd like to turn him over now.'

Willis and Banks immediately lost all interest in me and positioned themselves beside the corpse. DCI Banks said, 'Right, go ahead,' and the man in overalls heaved Rick unceremoniously on to his back. I carefully averted my eyes. DCI Banks, Mike Willis, and the doctor ummed and aahed over Rick, and words such as 'aorta' and 'incision depth' and 'haemorrhage' floated on the air along with the dust motes and the awful stench of Rick's last bowel movement.

The doctor rose to his feet and wiped his brow with a rubber-gloved hand. 'I'd say he's been dead at least twelve hours, possibly more. That puts time of death between, say, nine and midnight last night. I'll need to take a better look at him, of course,' he added, struggling to peel back a surgical glove.

And at that moment I noticed the writing. Or at least, something that very much resembled writing. It was on the wall behind the doctor, a definite vertical stripe – the beginning of a B or a D or an L – with a little tick pushing up from its bottom end. It was completely unlike the random splatters and blobs of gore that surrounded it: in fact, the mark seemed to have been made on top of them. I decided it could have been drawn using two bloodstained fingers held tightly together.

When they'd all stopped nodding and grunting in response to the doctor's pronouncement, I said, 'Someone's started to write something on the wall.'

DCI Banks glanced at me, then leaned forward to study the mark.

'Just looks like blood to me, love,' remarked DS Willis, cocking his head to one side. 'The murderer must have had blood on his hands, and tried to wipe it off.'

'On the *wall*?' I protested.

'I think you'll find, love, that we don't all walk around with J-cloths in our pockets,' smirked Willis.

DCI Banks permitted himself a small, but similar, reaction.

I blushed.

'But it does look like the beginning of a letter! You wouldn't wipe your hands on the wall!' I forced myself to glance briefly at the corpse. 'He could have done it himself, couldn't he? From where he was before you moved him.'

The doctor considered for a moment. 'Yes, I think he could,' he agreed, and then he shrugged. 'In fact, I think it's highly likely he did it when he went down, by accident – you know, a reflex action as he tried to save himself.' He pretended to double up and sink slowly to the floor, reaching out with his right hand and allowing two fingers to slide slowly down the wall. Now, it was so obvious that this manoeuvre would have produced an imprint completely unlike the mark I'd pointed out – the doctor's fingers splayed an inch apart and made two parallel, rather wavy, lines that petered out without showing any tendency to veer upwards – that I didn't even bother to comment on it.

'There you are!' I said. 'Rick tried to write something before he died. It could have been his attacker's name!'

Banks, Willis, and the doctor exchanged glances. DCI Banks leaned forward again and re-examined the mark. He sighed. 'I'll ask forensics to take a look at it,' he remarked.

'I examined a case once,' put in the doctor. 'A woman stabbed to death by her husband. He committed suicide right afterwards – a head in the gas oven job – but before he went he drew the sign of the cross in his wife's blood next to her body. She was very religious, you see.'

There was silence.

'Happen to know if our friend here was religious, love?' enquired Willis.

At that moment, some law of physics – or chemistry or biology – that had previously held its peace decided without warning to manifest itself. Rick Monday's left knee, which had been standing upright since the doctor turned him over, suddenly fell sideways and collapsed with a sharp thump on to the carpet, making us all jump. It was followed a split second later by the contents of his pocket – a bunch of keys and a packet of sugar-free chewing gum – sliding slowly into view and settling themselves comfortably in a tacky-looking pool of blood. Beside the pool of blood, on the edge of the sheepskin rug, was the carefully sharpened blue pencil I'd dropped while I was interviewing Rick yesterday. This was too much. I clutched a hand to my mouth and fled ignominiously from the room.

Pete and Willis followed a few moments later, by which time I'd deposited most of my breakfast in the porch next to the umbrella stand.

'I hope you haven't been sick on anything forensics wanted, love,' remarked Willis, grimly. 'The guv'nor says to thank you for your time. Go on, you can push off now, the both of you.'

'When will we get an update?' asked Pete.

'After the postmortem results. I expect we'll do a press conference. Probably first thing tomorrow. And you owe me a big drink, remember!' He shooed us down the porch steps and out on to the drive, pausing for a moment to stare at the scene beyond the front gate, which now resembled a football crowd straining to get into Wembley. 'Christ, the rest of your gang has turned up. Wouldn't you bloody know it. Oi – you can't go in there!' he added, as a man and a woman emerged from behind the ambulance and tried to push past us into the house. 'It's a crime scene.'

'What do you mean, a crime scene?' The man was heavy-set and perspiring in an overcoat while his companion, a waif-like blonde, wore an incongruous off-the-shoulder little black dress. Well, it wasn't so much off the shoulder, as off just about everything. For several beats, DS Willis and Pete both stared at her with dropped jaws.

'You shouldn't've been allowed past the front gate,' said Willis, when he'd recovered himself. 'I'm going to have to ask you to leave immediately.'

'I'm Ronan Davis, Rick's manager,' said the man, with the irritation of one who has just been dive-bombed by a wasp. 'What's going on? If something's happened to Rick, I want to know what it is.'

'He's dead, sir,' said Pete. 'Could I –'

36

'Shut up. We think he's been murdered,' said Willis. 'Can I ask you when was the last time you saw or spoke to Mr Monday, sir?'

Ronan's eyes rounded. 'But I spoke to him only last night on the phone.'

'What time?'

'Well, I don't know. Early evening . . . sevenish. We were in the process of terminating our contract and I arranged to call in on him on my way back from London. Jesus! That would explain it.'

'It would explain what, sir?'

'Why I couldn't get him later on the mobile, to tell him I was staying over in town with Mireille. I thought there was something wrong with the bloody thing. The operator said his phone was off the hook, but I never believe those pisspots.'

'I see, sir,' said Willis. 'And what time was that?'

'Half-ten, eleven. I don't know. Do you, Mireille? No, she won't know.' He didn't give her a second glance. 'Look, I need to make a few phone calls. This is a real bugger! Have you got a room I could use?'

'I beg your pardon?'

'And I could do with a fax, too, if there's one going spare.'

Willis's eyebrows shot skywards. 'I'm sorry, sir, but your phone calls are going to have to wait. As an intimate associate of Mr Monday you're going to have to answer one or two questions.'

'But I've hardly seen the bugger since –'

'Did Mr Monday have any enemies?'

Ronan clenched his knuckles until they cracked. 'No. No, I don't think so. He wasn't exactly Mother Theresa, but – look, could I just make one call to my associate? It'll take –'

'What about Will McGill?' put in Pete.

'*McGill?*' Ronan gave him a scathing look. 'Now you're into the ancient history department. Come on, give me a break – one phone call is all I ask.'

'Look, sir, we have to take this seriously,' said Willis. 'Was there or was there not animosity between Mr Monday and Mr McGill?'

'Of course there was, but we're talking nearly twenty years ago! It's always the same when a band breaks up, somebody always feels they've had their bollocks kicked in. Look, if you want to know the truth, the whole thing was a publicity stunt – the feud between Will and Rick. Some tabloid editor dreamed it up on a slow news night, and we went along with it because it put a lot of bums on seats.'

'I see.' Willis's pen hovered over his notebook.

I was about to bring up the subject of Rick and Will's public brawl, when Willis said, 'I'm sorry to keep on about this, sir, but at the moment we can't afford to rule out any options. Are you telling me that there was no quarrel at all between Mr Monday and Mr McGill? I'd like to remind you of a specific incident that was widely reported at the time. Are you telling me it was a put-up job for the papers?'

Ronan frowned and shook his head impatiently. 'Oh, come on, Inspector, please! How should I know? You do your best to mollycoddle these kids but they're off at the first opportunity, getting themselves into trouble. It was years ago – what does it matter? *They* told me it didn't happen. *They* said everything was fine. What am I supposed to do – hire nursemaids for them?'

Willis made a note in his book. 'Right,' he said, grimly. 'You can make one call, and then my guv'nor'll want a word. You two, on your bikes!'

Pete would clearly have liked to ask Ronan some more questions, and Ronan was preparing to repeat his demand for a private room for his phone calls, but at that moment Slater appeared, out of breath, from the direction of the road.

'It's the brother, sir! He's just arriving.'

'Good. Stick him in the back of the DCI's car, will you, I'll talk to him there. I don't want him going into the house yet under any circumstances – you got that?'

'Yes, sir!'

'Right, you two – out. And you, sir, stay where you are.'

I watched Slater run back towards the gateway, where two

uniformed officers were assisting a man in a navy jogging outfit to climb under the blue-and-white tape that had been stretched between the gateposts. I looked at him, and very nearly choked. From a distance, he was the image of Rick.

'Thanks, Mike,' said Pete. 'I appreciate this.'

'I hope you do. Come on, clear off.'

I recovered myself hastily, dragging my gaze away from the shocked figure in the tracksuit. 'Couldn't I just go back in and have a quick look round upstairs? Mr Monday wanted to give me a list of the titles on his new album. He said he'd got it somewhere. I'm sure he'd want –'

'*Piss off*!' roared Willis.

We went.

'Nice try,' muttered Pete.

3

Tipping police station's press briefing room had not been designed to accommodate more than half a dozen reporters plus their shopping bags, so the press conference on the Rick Monday murder was held instead in the canteen. I got there late, because that morning in the shower I had made the terrifying discovery that some time since I last looked at them properly my thighs had exploded. Of course, I shouldn't have been surprised because they'd been threatening to do this since my teens, but I was particularly miffed that they'd bided their time until just before my meeting with half of London's media in a short black skirt. And they hadn't *exploded*, either, they'd *imploded*. What was left of them wobbled about limply between knee and groin like deflated hot-air balloons in a light breeze. It was too late to change my outfit, so I borrowed a pair of Julie's black-tinted tights with a high lycra content, and hoped for the best.

Pete had saved me a place at the front, but I didn't feel like vaulting over the several piles of expensive camera equipment that were blocking my approach. Instead, I squeezed in at the back, next to a coffee machine with an 'Out of Order' notice taped over its coin slot. The room was seething with cigarette smoke and gossip about holiday plans, but after a few moments a hush fell and DCI Banks, DS Willis and three uniformed officers filed into the room via a door marked 'Canteen Staff Only'. They arranged themselves in a semi-circle at a large formica-topped table, and Rick's brother, who had followed them in, seated himself at a conspicuous distance from them at the far end of the table.

40

'Ladies and gentlemen,' began DCI Banks, raising his voice above an animated discussion of the Seychelles that was still going on in the front row. 'I'm DCI Banks and I'm here this morning to fill you in on the current situation and if necessary answer a few of your questions.' He was already starting to perspire under a Sky TV spotlight. 'As we suspected yesterday, our investigations have borne out the theory that the motive for Mr Monday's murder was robbery.' He paused, rather hoping, I think, that everyone would leap to their feet with cries of 'OK, fair enough, don't bother us with the details!' and depart for the pub. He loosened his tie uncomfortably. 'I think it might be helpful if I begin by explaining exactly what we're up against in our inquiries.'

An expectant quiet settled on the room, and DCI Banks nodded to a young WPC, who had been waiting in front of the triple-decker sandwich display. She removed the cover from a large easel to reveal a map.

'This is a map which shows Tangley House and its surrounding area.' He picked up a pointer and stabbed it at the easel. 'You can see Hatchley Heath Common – here – and this is Tangley House, and this is Yew Tree Cottage. To give you some idea of scale, Yew Tree Cottage is situated about sixty feet from Tangley House, and there's a yew hedge – here – that divides the two properties and provides a high degree of privacy. On the other side of Tangley House is a field normally used for the grazing of horses. As luck would have it, the occupants of Yew Tree Cottage were out for the evening, and the horses have not made themselves available for interview.' He laughed loudly, his fillings glinting alarmingly in the glare of the spotlights. 'Tangley House is set back from the main Tipping to Hatchley Heath road, although even at night it would be fairly visible to anyone using the road. There's nothing opposite the house except the Common, and this –' He aimed his pointer at a minor road. 'This is Tangley Lane. As you can see, Tangley Lane runs behind Yew Tree Cottage and Tangley House. It winds along through farmland for several miles and ends up –' he stabbed his pointer in the direction of the tea urn – 'at a place called Tangley Lake. It wouldn't have much traffic on it at night.'

'What are the red lines?' demanded one of the reporters suspiciously.

DCI Banks peered at them. 'Er, drains, I think,' he muttered, squinting closer. 'They're drains, aren't they, Joan? Yes, this map was loaned to us by the Water Company. Joan?' Joan turned over the Water Company's map to reveal a greyish-looking chart. 'Now, this is an architect's plan of the ground floor and grounds of Tangley House. You can see the large rear garden of the property, and the two paths down either side of it which converge – here – at this gate leading on to Tangley Lane.'

I leaned forward for a better look. I hadn't noticed a gate at the end of Rick's garden.

'This gate would be out of sight of the ground-floor windows of the house. Apparently there used to be a kitchen garden and greenhouses sited at the end of the garden, and this area of shrubbery was cultivated to screen it off.' He paused for a moment, as though he was a fan of the *Victorian Kitchen Garden* contemplating the garden in its former glory. 'We believe the intruder entered the grounds after dark by this gate. He would have had a good view of the house from the shrubbery, and it must have been quite obvious that Mr Monday was on his own. We think our chappie – there was almost certainly only one person involved – approached the house by this path that leads to the back door of the kitchen. He then broke in by smashing a pane of glass in the kitchen door, and went straight upstairs to the bedrooms. He ransacked Mr Monday's bedroom, which was the only one in use. When he was unable to find the money, he attacked Mr Monday in his study – here.' DCI Banks tapped the plan with his pointer, and while his back was turned several people in the front row leapt up and thrust microphones and cassette recorders in his direction.

'Did Rick put up a fight? Have you had the postmortem report yet?'

'. . . any definite information on the weapon?'

42

'What leads have you got on the killer's identity?'

'Are you expecting to make an early arrest?'

The inspector recoiled slightly. I began to feel rather sorry for him: he was obviously wearing his best saved-for-weddings-and-funerals suit and was not at all comfortable in it. He wiped his face nervously with a bunched-up handkerchief.

'I shall come to all of that eventually, but I want to talk about timing first, because this is where we've made our biggest breakthrough. We know that Mr Monday was still alive at nine forty on Sunday evening because his housekeeper spoke to him on the telephone, and she is absolutely positive about the time of that call. At that time we believe he was in his study, listening to music – in fact his audio equipment was still turned on when we arrived in the morning. We've also established with the help of a British Telecom report that from ten past eleven on Sunday night onwards Mr Monday's phone was "off the hook". Now, in actual fact we know the phone was damaged while Mr Monday was attempting to fight off his attacker, and we're told this would account for the "off the hook" signal. So we're able to say that death occurred between nine forty and eleven ten on Sunday evening. The postmortem report has borne out this theory.'

For a moment, there was complete silence apart from the whisper of pencils across paper and the squeak of a defective cassette recorder.

The inspector looked pleased with himself. 'This is obviously of great help in the investigation, and we'd like to appeal through you for anyone who was in the area of Tangley House around that time to get in touch with us. We're appealing particularly for the driver of a dark blue estate vehicle, possibly an Audi, to come forward. This vehicle was seen parked in Tangley Lane only a few yards from the back gate to Tangley House at about a quarter past ten. And –' he nodded to Joan – 'we also have another vital piece of evidence.'

Joan handed him a large envelope.

'This', he said, reaching into the envelope, 'is a knife almost

43

identical to the one used in the murder.' There was a brief silence as the knife slid from the envelope, followed by the fierce crackle of fifty or so flashes all exploding at once.

The inspector held the knife aloft, as though it were some sort of trophy.

'It's marked "Made in Toledo" and I'm told it's a small-scale replica of the swords used in bullfighting. Unfortunately, we haven't been able to establish whether or not the knife used in the murder belonged to Mr Monday. So –' he turned purposefully towards the television camera – 'if you know anyone who habitually carries a knife like this, or if you've recently had one stolen, we'd very much like to hear from you.'

The buzz of interest continued for several seconds. When it had subsided, he returned the knife to its envelope. 'Now, before I answer questions, I'm going to introduce you to Mr Robert Monday, who would like to say a few words.'

He sat down abruptly, and Rick's brother rose awkwardly to his feet. He was very pale, and there were dark circles under his eyes. He launched immediately into a short, rather rambling speech about his brother, to which I'm afraid nobody paid very much attention. He said Rick had come home from California to start a new life and had instantly been accepted as part of the community – that he (Rick) had been the victim of crime in California and had known what effect crime could have on a neighbourhood – and he thanked everyone in Hatchley Heath for their support and kindness to him since the tragedy. Then he said, 'Of course I'm grateful to the police for everything they've done, but they need help. If you know anything, please, *please* come forward. This man must be caught before there's another tragedy,' and he sat down again suddenly, his head bowed over his hands.

I wrote: '*Robert Monday not happy with police investigation*', and added two question marks.

'Right.' DCI Banks shielded his eyes from the glare of the spotlights. 'Now, ladies and gentlemen, if you've got any questions, and if you will please identify yourselves –'

Immediately, a leather-jacketed man in the front row

jumped to his feet and announced that he was from the *Evening Standard*.

'Inspector, are you hoping to make an early arrest? What did your forensics team come up with?'

'Ah,' DCI Banks looked pleased. 'Well, the lads have pulled out all the stops and I can tell you that –' I watched Robert Monday fiddle uncomfortably with his shirt collar and watch-band – 'although we haven't got any fingerprints – we think our man was wearing gloves – he did leave us a couple of footprints. He seems to have been in such a hurry to get away from the house that he stumbled into a flowerbed. We're having further tests done on the prints.'

'Diana Bryce, *Hudderston Advertiser*,' shouted Diana Bryce, while I struggled to catch up on the bit about footprints. 'Can you tell us if you're linking this burglary with a series of others you've been investigating in the area recently?'

'I beg your pardon? I can't comment on that. We're keeping our minds open at this stage. Next?'

'Ros Parkes, *Daily Telegraph*. Can you give us a full list of items taken during the robbery?'

'Certainly. The cash, which was counted just before the murder, amounted to £5324.77 in used notes and coins. A gold disc awarded to Mr Monday's group for their song "Just for the Money" is also missing, as is a very distinctive bronze statuette of a guitarist in flared trousers. I believe it was an award made to the group by a pop magazine in the early seventies.'

'*Evening Standard* again, sir,' said the *Standard* man. 'Can you tell us what sort of a fight Rick put up against his attacker?'

'Yes. According to the postmortem report, he died as a result of one stab wound to the heart, which caused massive and immediate haemorrhaging. There were also a number of minor abrasions to the backs of his hands and to his face, indicating . . .'

I tried not to think about the massive haemorrhaging. I wrote: 'Cash, disc and very distinctive statuette taken from house.' It was while I was struggling to make my outlines for 'distinctive' and 'statuette' look legible, that an odd thought occurred to me. According to DS Willis's assistant, Slater, Rick's killer had passed up the chance of a Rolex watch and jewellery in the bedroom – presumably because he was only interested in the money. So why had he helped himself to a gold disc and a statuette in the study?

People were scribbling down notes about the postmortem report. I stepped forward from the recess behind the coffee machine.

'Chris Martin, *Tipping Herald* –'

'Inspector! Mick Rogers, the *Sun*!' roared Mick Rogers. 'Can you confirm that you've spoken to Will McGill in connection with the murder, and will you be talking to him again?'

The inspector frowned disapprovingly. 'Yes – and no. Now, if that's all, I'd like to –'

'Oh, come on, Inspector . . .' pleaded the *Sun* man.

'Yes, come on – we've got editors with boots up our backsides!'

DCI Banks held up his hand. 'All right, all right. As you probably know, we did speak to Mr McGill, as a matter of routine. He and his girlfriend apparently spent last weekend in Yorkshire, and at the time of the murder they and the other members of the band were working on some new compositions at an address near Scarborough. We have absolutely no plans to talk to Mr McGill again. Does that answer your question?'

There was a brief murmur of disappointment. I took a deep breath. 'Chris Martin, *Tipping Herald*!'

And then, at the crucial moment, I forgot all about my carefully phrased question concerning the theft of the disc and the statuette. The thing was, Will McGill couldn't possibly have been in Yorkshire last weekend. Not on Sunday afternoon, anyway. He'd been at Tangley House.

'Oh!' I yelped. 'Hang on a minute. You said – Actually I've got two questions. What I –'

'Can we get some close-up shots of the knife?' interrupted one of the photographers.

'Will the WPC pose for us with it?' shouted another.

'Did McGill tell you he visited Rick . . .' I began, but my voice was drowned out by the commotion as a dozen photographers advanced upon the exhibits.

I met Pete in the entrance hall a few minutes later. He gave me an odd look.

'You all right? Why were you so late? I saved a place for you at the front.'

'I know. I'm sorry.' I decided not to mention my thighs or the explosion.

'Well, never mind. Why don't you join us at the Star?' He winked. 'I've always wanted a chance to show you off. Look, I'm double-parked. Gin and tonic all right?'

He blew me a kiss and disappeared into the throng.

I followed him out on to the steps. The car park was alive with the sounds of engines being revved and cries of 'You can come back about two inches more, but watch your left side', and 'God, if it wasn't for that idiot in the Renault I'd've been out of here five minutes ago.' I hadn't minded being shouted down at the press conference – I'd expected it really – but I didn't feel up to being shown off. I started down the steps, pausing to exchange a sympathetic smile with a large woman who was attempting to negotiate the steps encumbered by an even larger box. This was a mistake.

'Excuse me!' she called urgently, snatching at the back of my jacket. 'Are you with the police? They said I could have a car to take me home, but the one that brought me in has gone off shift. I only came in to do my statement.'

'Your statement?'

'Yes – they write it all down and make you sign it, you know. I had to hang around for an hour while they got it typed. Well, I found him, *lying in a pool of blood*. I could've just gone home and left him for someone else to find, couldn't I, when you think about it.'

'Oh! Are you . . . are you . . . ?'

'Mrs Jobson. His housekeeper.' She thrust the box into my arms. It was labelled 'Pure duck-down duvet – special purchase', and I could hardly see over the top of it. 'You

47

don't mind, do you? Only I've got this vein. If you could just help me down these stairs . . .'

'Certainly, I'd be glad to. In fact, let me give you a lift!'

We walked to the car and I forced the duvet box into the back seat.

'I'm with the *Tipping Herald*,' I explained. 'I'm covering Mr Monday's murder for my paper.'

'Oh, how exciting!'

I pulled out on to the High Street.

'Would you mind if I asked you a few questions? Are you up to it? You must have felt awful when you found the body.'

'Oh, my dear. *Poor* Mr Monday! And that lovely rug as well!' exclaimed Mrs Jobson. 'He'd worked so hard, you know. I won't hear a word against him. He was a lovely man – a lovely man!'

She looked a bit tearful, so I let W H Smith and Woolworths slide slowly by in silence, and then I said, 'You'd got to know him quite well, I imagine, so it must all be an awful shock.'

'Oh, yes! I don't know what I'm going to do now. I suppose I'll have to start looking in the post-office window again, won't I?'

I made a mental note to put in my piece that Mrs Jobson was in a state of shock.

She said, 'You know, you can call it what you like, but I swear I *knew* something awful was going to happen to Mr Monday when I put the phone down on him that night. I've always been a bit psychic. I turned to my husband – you can ask him – and I said, "Ron, Ron, I don't like the sound of that one bit!"'

'What do you mean? What didn't you like the sound of?'

'Well, Mr Monday was always such a *nice* man! You get to know people in my business, I can tell you. I'd left my key with him 'cos I had to go away for the weekend, so I phoned to make sure he'd be there to let me in in the morning.' She fanned herself vigorously with a Family Doctor booklet entitled 'You and Your Fibroid'. 'I know it was a bit late to be ringing, but I didn't think he'd mind. I was worried about the

48

cleaning, you see. I do all his shopping and laundry and a bit of cooking, and sometimes I run the Hoover round for him, but I don't do *cleaning* – we get a firm in to do it. Anyway, what with the fête and everything, I thought the house was bound to be in a state, so I asked him if he wanted me to ring the cleaners for him before I came in. And he said, "Oh, do what you bloody like, who cares about the sodding cleaners!" Well, I ask you! And he put the phone down on me!'

'Oh.' I thought about this. 'Well, perhaps he was tired after the fête. Did you tell the police?'

'They weren't interested. All they wanted to know was if I'd seen that knife before. Which I hadn't – Mr Monday never let me in his study, because he'd got all that fancy equipment in there. And he wasn't *just tired*, either. I know people – I'm not stupid!'

At this point the car in front of us pulled over and made a sudden stop without indicating. I braked sharply, and Mrs Jobson's duck-down duvet box hit her smartly on the back of the head.

'Oh!' she gasped. 'Oh dear! *Do* be careful! You're not leaving the proper distance between us and the car in front.'

On balance, I decided it would be best to ignore this. I gritted my teeth and steered round the offending car.

'If you ask me, it was Fate,' remarked Mrs Jobson, while I gave the other driver a hard stare. 'I think sometimes things are set to happen and there isn't anything you can do to stop them. I mean, poor Mr Monday being all alone in the house and that man breaking in. If Mr Bradman hadn't've cancelled their dinner engagement, and if Mr Robert hadn't gone out so he wasn't in when Mr Monday rang him – well, it might all have been different, mightn't it?'

'I suppose so.' We were joining the dual carriageway and I decided the time had come to take charge of the conversation. 'Now, I'd like to ask you a couple of questions about Mr Monday's personal life. It's only for background, so –'

'Mr Robert had *just that minute* gone out jogging when Mr Monday rang him – he missed him by *one minute*. Well, Mr Monday might've been ringing him to ask him to pop round for a drink or something, mightn't he? They were ever so close. The police said that Mr Robert's wife took the call from Mr Monday at half past nine, and *I* rang Mr Monday at twenty to ten, so that makes me the last person ever to speak to him!'

'Yes. I see. So did Mr Monday have many –'

'And Mr Bradman only cancelled their dinner at the last minute because his secretary had got him a ticket to some piano recital or something, otherwise Mr Monday wouldn't've been there, would he? You have to turn left here. Aren't you looking where you're going?'

I turned left just in time, and Mrs Jobson winced gratifyingly as her duvet box lurched about in the back seat.

I launched into this enforced gap in her flow of thought. 'Did Mr Monday give lots of wild parties and have lots and lots of girlfriends? Go on, you can tell me – I won't say where I got it from.'

'Certainly not! I wouldn't have worked for him if there was anything like that going on. Have you been talking to Mr Fletcher?' ·

'Who's Mr Fletcher?'

She gave me a contemptuous glance. 'Oh, go on! If you're a reporter you must know Mr Fletcher. He's famous! He lives at Yew Tree Cottage. He wrote that book, you know, *The History of Hatchley Heath*, or something. You can buy it at the library.'

'Oh.' I had never heard of Mr Fletcher, or his book. 'Didn't he like Mr Monday, then? Why not?'

'Well, I don't know, do I? He used to be on the Hatchley Heath Committee, but he resigned when they let Mr Monday join. I think it was because he doesn't approve of rock music and that sort of thing. He inherited Yew Tree Cottage from his aunt – restored it to its original state. *Mrs* Fletcher's very nice, though. She's a marriage guidance counsellor.'

'Oh. But come on, Rick was very attractive. He must have been seeing someone. I quite fancied him myself!'

She gave me an odd look. 'Yes, dear – well, you're the *age*, aren't you?'

'What?'

50

Mrs Jobson smiled slyly, and declined to explain. 'My Ron said Mr Monday was – what's that word? – celibate.'

'Celibate? Oh.'

'My Ron does crosswords. Anyway, Mr Monday never had any ladyfriends. Well, not if you don't count Tina.'

'Who's Tina?'

'Oh, Tina was ever so sweet. I think she was a fan. She used to call on Mr Monday on Tuesday afternoons and he used to shut her in his study and play his old records to her. She was much too young for him, anyway.'

'How old was she?'

'Well, I don't know, do I? You can't tell these days. She could've been in her twenties, or she could've been sixteen. I don't hold with them autumn/spring relationships – do you? Mr Monday was like an uncle to her!'

We were approaching Hatchley Heath, and I was driving at twenty miles an hour in a sixty mile an hour zone. People were shaking their fists at me as they passed.

'Look, Mrs Jobson,' I began, in desperation. 'You must have known Rick better than anybody. What do *you* think about the murder? Do you think it was robbery, or do you think there was someone who was out to get him?'

'That's a terrible thing to say!' She gave me a shocked look. 'Why would anyone want to kill Mr Monday? I've told you, it was fate, that's all. He was in the wrong place at the wrong time!' She shook her head vigorously, all her various chins wobbling independently of one another. 'They should bring back hanging, that's what they should do! I don't know how you can think such a thing about Mr Monday. Everybody in the village loved him. Is it because of what happened last Christmas?'

'Er, I don't know. What happened last Christmas?'

'Well, the rats, of course! And Mr Monday was so good about it, too. I said to him, "I hope you don't think anyone in the village had anything to do with it." I was really upset, I don't mind telling you, but he said I wasn't to worry. He said it had nothing to do with the village, it was just someone with an old score to settle.'

'What rats? What are you talking about?'

'The rats on his lawn! Big fat black-and-white ones, they were, about twenty of them. Someone poisoned them and left them on Mr Monday's front lawn – on Christmas Eve, too. We had to get the pest-control people in. They said they were bought rats – you know, from a pet shop – not wild ones.'

I was stunned into speechlessness.

'My Susan – she's my eldest – she reckoned it must have been Will McGill, his ex-partner,' went on Mrs Jobson, enthusiastically, 'but Mr Monday laughed when I said that – you know, as if I'd said something stupid. *Stop*!'

She said this with such urgency and authority that I immediately and unquestioningly performed an emergency stop on the soft verge beside the main Tipping to Hatchley Heath road. There was a squeal of brakes and an outburst of hooting from behind.

We were in front of Tangley House.

'Well, weren't you looking? Didn't you know where you were going?' she protested, in an aggrieved tone, fishing for her Family Doctor booklet in the footwell. 'I told you I wanted to go in and get my key, didn't I?' She opened the passenger door.

'No. You didn't. Hang on a minute –'

'I've got to get my key or I won't be able to get in the house,' announced Mrs Jobson, undoing her seat belt. 'Mr Robert will want me to look after the place until he decides what to do with it. I can't let people down. You wait here.'

Before I could stop her, she got out of the car, and waddled off across the road. There was nothing I could do about it, so I got out my notebook and began making notes about the rat incident. It ought to be worth following this up. Then I jotted down Mrs Jobson's remarks concerning the hand of Fate's intervention in Rick's demise. You never could tell exactly what angle was going to look best on a story until you wrote it up. Mr Heslop might like the hand of Fate idea. I wondered whether it would be worth finding out what recital John Bradman had cancelled their dinner engagement for.

And how would Robert Monday feel, knowing that if he hadn't gone for a late evening jog his brother would still be alive?

Mrs Jobson returned a few minutes later and brandished a key at me triumphantly.

'I'm not to go to the house without getting permission from the police first,' she announced, climbing back into the car.

'Good.' I decided to get rid of her as quickly as possible. 'Look, I must be getting back to the office –'

'Oh, this isn't my key!' she interrupted suddenly, halting in mid-manoeuvre with one leg still outside the car. 'It's not the one Mr Monday gave me.'

'What do you mean, it's not your key? I'm due back at the paper, for heaven's sake!'

'Oh, my God!' wailed Mrs Jobson, staring at her key in dismay. 'This isn't my key! *My* key was a sort of old-looking yellowish colour, and it had an "O" on it. Why isn't this my key?'

She climbed out of the car, and I got out too. I snatched the key from her, willing it to be of a yellowish colour and to have an 'O' on it. But it wasn't: it was a silver-coloured key without any lettering on it, and it looked shiny and new.

I wished I was in the Star drinking gin and tonic. 'Look, we'll see if it fits the door,' I suggested, reluctantly.

We approached the constable on duty, and Mrs Jobson explained to him at some length that her key had been hanging on a hook in the kitchen under her Royal Wedding cup, and that he had given her the wrong one. He sighed.

'No, love, that's it – that's the key that was on your hook.'

'But it isn't. Mine was yellow and it had an "O" on it.'

The constable frowned, took the key from her, and tried it in the door.

'There you are, love, works like a dream.' He handed it back to her.

'Oh. So it does. Well . . .'

'Wait a minute.' I took the key from her. I was beginning

to get the oddest feeling. 'If this key isn't yours, then where is yours and what's this one doing in its place?'

'I don't know! I told you, I gave Mr Monday my key on Saturday afternoon, on my way to the station. My Susan had been rushed into hospital with suspected appendicitis and I had to go up to Wolverhampton to see to the baby . . . Well, it wasn't her appendix, but I didn't know that then, so I gave Mr Monday my key in case he needed it for the cleaners before I got back. He hasn't got a spare. He put it on my cup hook, like I said.'

'Who else has a key to the front door, love?' asked the constable, crossly.

She shook her head. 'I don't know. I think Mr Robert's probably got one. But he keeps it at home in case there's some kind of emergency while Mr Monday's on his travels, and Mr Monday was at home all weekend. And Mr Monday had his own key so *he* wouldn't've needed to use mine either, would he? Oh, *why* would someone take my key? I don't want to be blamed for losing it. I've never lost a key in my life – not a client's key!'

The constable patted her on the shoulder. 'Look, love, I expect Mr Monday mislaid his key and borrowed yours and put the wrong one back. I expect he did it when he locked up.' He ushered us off the step. 'Go on, you two, you'd better hop it. I'm not supposed to encourage sightseers.'

Mrs Jobson muttered something incomprehensible, and started down the drive with her shoulders hunched. I took a few steps after her, half convinced by the constable's explanation, but suddenly the pulse in the back of my neck began to throb, the way it always does when my brain is on the verge of getting to grips with something really difficult, like why no matter how carefully you measure it out a packet of lawn fertilizer will never quite cover the area it's supposed to, or what cosines are.

'Hang on,' I said. 'Mr Monday's keys were in his pocket, *on a bunch*. I saw them. He couldn't possibly have accidentally swapped his key for yours. Are you sure he didn't have another spare one?'

'Of course I'm sure! If he'd had a spare I wouldn't have bothered giving him back mine, would I? You can ask Mr Robert, if you don't believe me – or Ted.'

'Who's Ted?'

'Ted Kitchen. He was the one who got the keys cut for Mr Monday. He used to clean the windows at the house till he had his accident. He lives on the Dene Estate with his mum, Ivy. You must know Ivy, everybody knows Ivy – she used to breed red setters. They were always in such *lovely* condition,' she added, managing to convey with a movement of her eyebrows the unspoken rider, *considering they live on a council estate.'*

We were back at the car. I reached for my notebook and wrote: 'Ted Kitchen – Dene Estate'.

'Look, I gave my key to Mr Monday, I didn't lose it,' insisted Mrs Jobson. 'Mrs Beecham and Mr Robert's wife were both there when I gave it to him – they'll tell you!'

I wrote this down, too, in case it was important, and hustled her into the car.

Seconds later, after urging her to phone DCI Banks immediately and report the apparent loss of her key, I dropped Mrs Jobson and her duvet in front of her house. Then I drove back to Tipping as fast as I could. Whenever I thought about the key, the back of my neck tingled with excitement. Despite what teenagers would have you believe, inanimate objects do not move around from one place to another without human intervention. They certainly do not change colour by themselves. If Mrs Jobson's key had transmuted during the course of the weekend from old yellow metal into bright new silver, then some force other than alchemy was responsible. Somebody, at some time over the weekend, must have taken Mrs Jobson's key down from its hook, taken it to a nearby key-cutting shop, and had a brand new copy made of it. Then, probably by accident, they had replaced the *copy* on her hook. Of course, there could have been half a dozen perfectly legitimate reasons for someone to do this, and if Rick hadn't at that moment been occupying a dissection slab in the mortuary, I would probably have taken the trouble to consider them. As it was, only one seemed relevant.

The person who had made the copy of Mrs Jobson's key had done so in order to let himself into Tangley House while Rick was alone. It had been obvious right from the start: Rick hadn't been killed by a common or garden burglar – he had known his killer; after all, he had tried with his dying breath to write that person's name on the wall.

4

Pete sat on the patio, a piece of orange plastic in one hand, and two screws in the other, contemplating our lawnmower, which lay on its back with its grass-encrusted underparts exposed.

'I'm not with you,' he said, trying to fit one of the screws into a washer. 'What's the housekeeper's front-door key got to do with anything? I thought Rick was murdered by someone who broke in through the back door. A burglar. I thought that was what today's press conference was all about.'

I gritted my teeth, because Mr Heslop had reacted in almost exactly the same way, except that he hadn't looked at me with that irritated, long-suffering expression men seem to adopt towards you after you've run their underwear through the washing machine a few times.

'You're not listening,' I protested. 'I've been explaining for the past five minutes – the police theory is wrong. The burglary was a cover-up. Rick *knew* his murderer – he tried to write his name on the wall, for heaven's sake! The murderer must be someone with an obvious motive, someone who knew they might be suspected. Look, a *proper* burglar would have taken Rick's Rolex and his jewellery! A *proper* burglar wouldn't have wasted his time on a gold disc or a stupid statuette. A –'

'OK. I get the gist. Your theory is that the murderer didn't break in through the back door at all and he wasn't after the five thousand pounds. You think he let himself in through the front door with a key he'd had cut, for the express purpose of stabbing Rick. You think he then ransacked the bedroom, broke the glass in the kitchen door, took the money and the rest of it, and legged it across the garden, leaving the police to assume that robbery was the motive. Is that it?'

'Yes.' At last he seemed to be getting it.

He gave me a sideways look, and grinned. 'I'll say one thing for you, you've got a very active imagination.'

'Oh, Pete!'

'Well, explain this then, sweetheart. If your murderer has a key, why was the front door still locked on the inside when the police arrived? Why didn't he leave the house the same way he got in?'

'Ah!' My heart began to pound excitedly. He was attacking my theory and I could still make it stand up. 'Either the Audi in Tangley Lane was his, in which case it's obvious why he went out the back way, or – he panicked. After all, he'd been in the house for quite a while, I should think, and if he went out through the front, someone might see him. There's a main road out there.'

He nodded. 'OK, I get that bit. But what I don't see is why this person would bother to have a copy made of the housekeeper's key. Why didn't he just take the key?'

'But he didn't know it *was* Mrs Jobson's key, did he? He probably thought it was Rick's!'

Pete turned over the mower switch mechanism thoughtfully, and a bit of it fell off and bounced across the patio.

Immediately I forgot all about murderers and motives. The bit that had fallen out of the mower was some sort of spring, and in my experience once springs fall out of things they are never the same again. Even though I knew it was a mistake, I said, 'Do you think you're going to be able to put all that back together?'

'Of course I bloody can! I know exactly how it goes. Just help me find the sodding thing.' He began scrabbling amongst the debris of last year's geraniums. 'And don't change the subject. I heard what you said on the phone the other day to that friend of yours about men not being able to do two things at once. I assure you, we can. Come on,

58

let's polish off this theory. I'm waiting – who are your suspects?'

I heaved the pot of geraniums to one side. 'How about Will McGill? Perhaps he changed his mind about the reunion. He could've –'

'Don't be silly! He was up in Yorkshire with the rest of his band when Rick was murdered. He's got about six witnesses. Why not one of the ex-wives?' He tossed two ring pulls and a clothes peg across the patio, and shrugged dismissively. 'Anyway, there can't have been many people who would have had access to the key. All we need to do . . .'

'Actually, lots of people had access to the key. It was hanging in the kitchen all weekend, and people were in and out of the house the whole time. Apparently, hundreds of fans turned up at the fête because it was advertised on Radio One.'

'I see.' He looked suddenly interested. 'So it could have been some sort of weirdo! I like the sound of that. Except – Oh, shit, I've just thought of something. The fête was on Sunday, wasn't it? Are there any key-cutting shops open on a Sunday?'

Suddenly, my entire theory seemed on the verge of collapsing in on itself like a pair of middle-aged thighs, but then I remembered something else. '*Bangles*! Bangles – the DIY store in Hatchley Heath! Well, it's not Bangles really – it's B. Angles – but everyone calls them Bangles. *They* open on Sundays; all the big DIY stores do and they decided they couldn't afford not to. We did a piece on them last year. They've got one of those Mister Fixit shoe repair and key-cutting franchises, and they're at the top end of the High Street – not more than ten minutes' walk from Tangley House!'

At that moment, Julie emerged from the house.

'What's this, a sit-in? Reliving your lost youth?' she enquired sarcastically.

Pete moved politely out of her way, and she sat down and stretched out her bare legs across the reconstituted York stone paving.

'Oh, God, it makes me want to *puke*!' she exclaimed. 'My

legs are revolting! *Fat*, and *white*, and covered in stubble! God, I hate them! Do you think there's enough strength in this sun for me to get a tan, or skin cancer, or something?'

There was a startled silence.

'Don't be silly. There's nothing wrong with your legs,' I lied. They *were* a bit on the plump side. 'Anyway, how have you been getting on up there with the Geneva Protocol? I would have come up to see you, but –'

'Oh, for Christ's sake, I can't do revision all the time, you know. I'm not a machine. Even convicted murderers are allowed out into the exercise yard occasionally!'

'Yes, that's true,' put in Pete, impassively, 'but then their jailers aren't forever running up and down stairs to bring them cups of soup and slices of chocolate cake, are they, darling? Anyway, you've come down at exactly the right moment because your mother is just putting the finishing touches to a fascinating new theory on the Rick Monday murder.' To my surprise, he sounded as if he meant this. Julie rolled her eyes. 'In fact, all we need is a suspect. Personally I'd put my money on a woman. Someone he's dumped. Now I come to think of it, only a woman would have used a knife like that as a murder weapon.'

She gave a disgusted snort.

'But he wasn't involved with anyone,' I protested, trying to ignore her scowl. 'I got that from Mrs Jobson. She said he only ever had one woman back to the house, and that was a young fan called Tina.'

'And what was so stupid about the knife that only a woman could have used it?' demanded Julie. 'It *worked*, didn't it? The dickhead's dead, isn't he?'

'Hang on,' Pete interrupted. 'What was that you said about a young fan?'

I gave Julie an angry look to show her that the 'dickhead' hadn't escaped me. 'Oh, I don't know!'

'Well, how young was she exactly? Did Rick make a habit of this sort of thing? If you don't know, then I think we ought to find out.' He stood up. 'I wonder if the girl was underage. You get triple word score these days if you can come up with

60

something that's got child abuse in it.' He pulled me to my feet and dusted me down for bits of geranium. 'Let's go and talk to the brother. I promise I'll be the soul of discretion.'

'Now? But what about the mower?'

'Oh, that's *disgusting*!' Julie exclaimed. 'That is really, absolutely, the *sickest* thing I've ever heard!'

'Sod the mower. I'll do it later. Come on – I've got the address in my notebook. We won't phone first, because he'll say no, but I'm sure he'll be interested in your theory about the keys.'

'I don't know how you can live with yourself, thinking things like that!' Julie shouted. 'I don't know how you can sleep at night!'

'Oh, don't you? Well, let me point out that this is exactly the kind of sick and disgusting thing that pays your enormous phone bills, sweetheart. And you never complain about that. Come on, Chris.'

I would have tried to smooth things out with Julie, but she was already back in her room with the door satisfyingly slammed.

By the time we arrived in Hatchley Heath, I had got over my misgivings. Robert Monday was desperate for Rick's killer to be caught, so he was bound to want to discuss my theory. And although it was one of Mr Heslop's unwritten rules that the *Tipping Herald* should never harass victims and/or their relatives, this was different.

We found the house easily enough. Rick Monday's brother lived in a turn-of-the-century farmworker's cottage about half a mile as the crow flies from Tangley House. It backed on to Dene End School's sports field, and was set amid a cottage garden permeated with the scent of wet lavender and broad bean flowers that hummed with bees and butterflies. It couldn't have been much more of a contrast to Tangley House.

Pete rang the front doorbell and bent down to look through the letterflap.

'They're not in!' called a woman's voice, making us both

61

jump. The voice came from beyond the privet hedge that screened off next-door's garden.

'They both went out about half an hour ago,' the voice continued.

'Oh.' Pete tried to peer through the hedge. Through the bottom of it, where the foliage had been thinned by the ravages of time, it was just possible to see two feet clad in sensible leather sandals with lots of buckles, and a half-empty sack of peat-free compost.

'It's *Mr* Monday we're after,' said Pete, to the sandals. 'Do you know where he is? It's rather urgent.'

She craned over the top of the hedge. She was wearing horn-rimmed glasses and a fiercely-tailored tweed jacket. In fact she looked like the sort of woman who, in the War, would have made it her business to go round the village on a bicycle handing out advice on blackout curtains and three thousand ways to use a carrot, but who now had to content herself with forcing the elderly to go off on coach trips, and mustering support for the local bottle bank.

'Are you with the police?' she enquired, imperiously. 'Is it about the murder?'

'Yes,' agreed Pete, only half untruthfully.

'Well, in that case he *might* be at the house. I *could* give you directions, but I'm not really sure if that's where he's gone.'

'Not to worry. We know where Tangley House is.'

'But I don't mean Tangley House. I mean Brook Cottage – his mother's old house.'

'Oh, I see.'

'He's been doing it up and trying to sell it – that's probably where he is. He had to get the builders in in the end. Anyway, if you go back the way you've come, turn right at the church, and carry on for about half a mile, you'll see a sign for Brook Cottage on your left just past the phone box.'

'Thank you. But I wonder, could I ask you one or two extremely quick questions? You see, we're trying to build up a picture of Rick's lifestyle, and we wondered – was he close to his brother, would you say? Did he discuss him with you? Did Rick bring friends round to introduce them to the family, that sort of thing?'

She frowned. 'I don't know what you mean. I'm not in the habit of discussing personal matters with my neighbours. And Rob and Viv are always much too busy for dinner parties and that sort of nonsense. Viv runs an employment agency, and Rob . . . well, you'll know all about Rob and his work for the Trust and the Hatchley Heath Committee, of course. I say, *which* department of the police did you say you were from?'

Pete began an elaborate pretence of looking through his pockets for a warrant card; much too elaborate, in my opinion, to fool Rob Monday's neighbour. 'So, would it be fair to say that Rick might not have felt able to share his most intimate secrets with his brother? About his love life, for instance. Were there any rumours in the village about young girls visiting Tangley House?'

Her eyes bulged angrily behind the horn-rimmed glasses. 'Now, look here, I don't know who you are, but you've got no right to ask questions like that! You should be ashamed of yourselves! What are things coming to in the police these days? In fact, I don't think you are from the police! Just you listen to me –'

She was obviously on to us, so we retreated hastily down the front path and jumped into the car.

When we found Brook Cottage, it was what estate agents are fond of describing as a 'character' cottage: that is to say, a poky little house with a structurally unsound roof, a ramshackle of outbuildings and no mains drainage. Brook Cottage's roof had been completely retiled very recently and presumably at great expense, and its garden had been cleared of several decades' accumulation of brambles and saplings which now formed a great soggy dying mountain in the middle of the front lawn. We picked our way up the potholed drive and knocked at the door. There wasn't a doorbell, and the porch lantern had no bulb in it. Pete lifted the letter flap, peered through it, and reported that the house smelled of damp and new emulsion, and that there didn't seem to be anyone in.

'We'll try Tangley House,' he suggested, 'and if that fails we'll go back and camp at the end of his road until he shows up.'

I thought rather desperately of the ironing at home, and followed him to the car.

We drove back to the main road, and stopped at the junction. Ahead of us the top end of Hatchley Heath Common petered out into a tangle of brambles and discarded bicycle wheels and prams, and I was looking at this and thinking what a good idea of someone's it had been to earmark this particular site for the proposed activity centre, when I suddenly spotted Rob Monday. He was wearing white running shorts and a red vest plastered wetly to his chest, and his face was contorted into an expression of pain.

'That's him!' I exclaimed. 'Quick!'

Pete had just turned into the main road. Without so much as a glance in his rear-view mirror, he swung the car across the road, bumped it over a low bank and accelerated into an innocent-looking patch of long grass. It was at the last instant, and much too late to do anything about it, that I spotted the concealed ditch. I screamed, 'Ditch!' Pete uttered a shocked expletive, and the car suddenly flew through the air independently of our stomachs. There was a nasty grinding noise from the car's newly fitted exhaust system, followed by a final shocked gasp from the engine.

'Jesus Christ!' yelled Pete, leaping out of the car. 'What's the matter with you? Next time, don't say "Ditch", say "Stop"! How am I supposed to know what you mean?'

I tried to protest, but he ran round to the back of the car to inspect the damage (a minor dent to the exhaust manifold). We were poised on the ditch bank, with one wheel spinning helplessly in mid-air. For a few moments Pete stood there muttering unrepeatable things about the countryside, and then he climbed down into the mud and heaved the car back on to level ground. By this time, needless to say, Rob Monday had disappeared from view.

'We could've been stuck in there for bloody hours!' ranted Pete. 'For nothing! It could've cost a fortune!

64

"Ditch", for Christ's sake – who do you think I am, sodding Biggles?'

'But it wasn't really my –'

'Oh, come on, for God's sake – let's not stand round arguing.' He glanced in the direction of the woods. 'He must've gone that way. Let's see if we can find him.'

Pete started off at a sprint across the grass towards the woods, and I followed, still trying to protest my innocence. There were three paths leading on to the Common, all apparently going in more or less the same direction. After a brief moment of indecision, we chose the middle one. Now, I don't know quite how this can have happened, except that Hatchley Heath Common is crisscrossed by paths which dissect one another at regular intervals, but a few minutes later we rounded a bend and found ourselves face to face with Rob Monday.

Pete didn't miss a beat.

'Hi. It's Mr Monday, isn't it? Look, I know you probably don't want to talk to anyone just now and I really wish we didn't have to bother you . . . I'm not going to bullshit you. We're both local journalists. Chris here is on the staff of the *Tipping Herald*.'

Rob's expression began to change. Pete hurried on. 'Our readers are absolutely devastated by Rick's death. We've received literally hundreds of letters. I don't know if you're aware of it, but comparisons are being drawn between your brother's murder, and John Lennon's – who was of course also murdered when he was on the brink of staging a comeback.'

I raised my eyebrows in surprise, but fortunately nobody noticed this.

'Anyway, we'd like to ask you for your reaction to the latest development in the investigation.'

'What development?'

'Aren't the police keeping you informed? Oh dear, I'm sorry. Well, it appears Rick may not have been murdered during the course of a robbery, after all. Apparently his housekeeper, a Mrs . . . a Mrs . . .'

'Jobson,' I put in.

'Mrs Jobson left her front-door key on the premises over the weekend, and someone made a duplicate which they used to let themselves into Tangley House. Through the front door, Mr Monday. The burglary appears to have been merely a cover-up, to fool the police.'

Rob's mouth dropped. He looked wan and ill.

'Actually, that's not *quite* right,' I said. 'What happened was that they had a copy made and accidentally put the *copy* back in the kitchen, and when Mrs Jobson collected her key of course she noticed the difference. *Her* key was an old yellow one with an "O" engraved on it, and this one is brand new.' His astonished expression froze for a second, so I decided he was getting the point. 'I should think Mrs Jobson's key was the original key to the house, wouldn't you? I expect it had a previous owner's initial on it. She says there were only two other keys to the house, and you had one and Rick had the other. Can you confirm that?'

Pete delved into his pocket for his notebook.

Rob remained dumbstruck.

'Mr Monday, obviously what the police are going to be looking into now is your brother's personal life,' said Pete. 'Who had a motive for murdering him? Would there be any jilted ladies, angry husbands, or irate parents lurking in the background – anything like that?'

'*What*?'

He had turned an unpleasant shade of grey. Pete gave him a searching look. 'Mr Monday, I know this must have come as a dreadful shock to you, but everybody in the public eye has enemies.'

Rob was now beginning to get angry. And the angrier he got, the more he resembled Rick.

'I have absolutely nothing to say to you. Of course my brother didn't have enemies. I would like you to get out of my way now, please.'

Pete manoeuvred to block Rob's attempt to sidestep us. 'What about Will McGill?' he demanded. 'You know, whether you like it or not, people are going to start opening cupboards.

Are they going to be deafened by the rattle of falling skeletons, do you think?'

'Look, I don't have to answer any of your questions. I've told you, this is a mistake. The police haven't told me anything about a key. My brother's murder was a random act of violence by a burglar, probably a – a drug addict. Now will you *please* get out of my way.'

'But Mr Monday,' I protested, 'you haven't listened to all the evidence. It's not just the key – there's the writing on the wall, and –' He made a sudden dive to get past me. Quicker than you can say 'osteoporosis' I threw myself bodily into his path.

'Well done,' muttered Pete.

I sprawled in the bracken. Incredibly, Rob apologized, Pete helped me up, and Rob hovered awkwardly while I brushed off twigs.

'You have to listen,' I begged him. 'I know you want to find your brother's killer. Look, Rick tried to get hold of you shortly before he was murdered, so something must have happened between the time you left the fête and the time he phoned you. Why do you think he would have double-locked his front door on the inside even though he was expecting Ronan Davis later? Doesn't that make you think he was –'

'Had it got something to do with a young lady?' interrupted Pete, suddenly. 'Tina, perhaps? Wouldn't I be right in saying your brother made quite a habit of entertaining very young ladies at Tangley House?'

There was a moment of stunned silence, and then, without warning, two women and a black labrador hurtled through the gorse bushes behind us, sweeping us all into a tangled scrum in the middle of the path. The black labrador cannoned into Rob's kneecaps, and one of the women tripped and ended up head-first in a bank of emerging ferns. Chivalrously – or more probably because the woman had good legs, a small bottom and shapely arms – Pete turned his back on Rob and helped her to her feet. While we were all apologizing profusely (and I was wishing that my arms were still young and firm enough to look OK in sleeveless T-shirts when the weather was really too iffy to wear them), Rob Monday bolted off unnoticed across the Common.

'*Damn*!' said Pete, when the women had gone. 'After all that! Oh, well – I know a couple of music journalists. I'll sound them out and see if there were any current rumours about Rick's sex life.'

I shook the last of the twigs from my hair. 'If only he'd let me explain the rest of it to him, I know I could've convinced him. They look almost like twins. He must know lots of things about Rick. They were both in Bad Monday in the beginning, and now they were working together for the Acorn Trust and the village. I'll bet he knows exactly who's got a motive.'

Pete sighed, and tucked his notebook back into his pocket. 'Well, unless I miss my guess, Rob is the sort who'd rather have his testicles wired up to Battersea Power Station than see his brother's honour besmirched. I don't think he'll give anything away. Anyway . . .' He hesitated. 'Look, I'm sorry for what I said back there – you know, about the car. It wasn't your fault. I shouldn't have said what I did. It's just that I spent a fortune last week on that bloody exhaust.'

'I know.'

'Well, I shouldn't have snapped at you, and I'm really sorry.' He bit his lip. 'Sometimes I wonder if it's worth keeping the wretched thing.'

'What? Your car? But you love it!'

'Yes. You're right. I do. But perhaps I ought to grow out of it.'

I stared at him in astonishment.

'Come on,' said Pete, 'let's go home and have another look at that bloody mower.'

5

I went into work early the next morning, because it was Deadline Day. With one eye on the doorway through which Mr Heslop would at any moment appear with a small greasy bag containing two fresh doughnuts, I found a telephone number and dialled it. The number belonged to Sonia, who had been in my class at school. I had run into Sonia several weeks ago in Sainsbury's, and had written down her phone number out of politeness (at school we hadn't liked each other very much). I was way behind on my week's assignments because of the Rick Monday murder, and I needed someone with local knowledge to help me finish my piece on Hatchley Heath's activity centre project. It wasn't that Mr Heslop would have minded my sourcing information from friends – everybody did it – but I didn't want him to know I'd left it till the last minute.

'Sonia? It's Chris, Chris Martin. Christine Bailey – remember? We ran into each other the other week.'

Sonia pretended to be pleased to hear from me.

'Well, I'm sorry to be bothering you so early, but I was wondering if I could ask you to help me with something. I'm supposed to be doing an article on the new activity centre scheme in Hatchley Heath, which is an awful bore, and what with the murder and everything I just haven't had time to get down to it. The thing is, *you* live in Hatchley Heath, and I was wondering whether you could give me a few phone numbers of people I could ring for quotes.'

There was silence.

'Gosh,' said Sonia. 'So you really *do* work for the *Tipping Herald*.'

69

I thought this over, and didn't much care for her tone.

'Exactly what sort of people do you want to talk to?' asked Sonia.

'Oh, anybody with an opinion on the scheme, really. I don't know if you've heard about it – have you?' I got out my street map of Hatchley Heath and tried to explain to her without using my hands where it was to be sited. 'As I say, the whole thing's a pain in the neck, but there's a public meeting coming up next week and we're trying to get a bit of a debate going. As if anybody cares! It's an Acorn Trust scheme. Local children can use it, but it's mainly for children bussed in from deprived areas, apparently, so it would be nice if I could talk to some of the local mums whose children would benefit from it. And if there are any old busybodies you can think of who might feel like opposing it – well, perhaps you could give me their numbers, too.'

Sonia was silent again for another long moment, then she said, 'I see. I'll tell you what, why don't I ring round a few people I know and see what they say?'

I was taken aback by this unexpected generosity.

'Oh, no, I couldn't ask you to do that! Heavens, no! And besides, I really need this by lunchtime. I've already done an introductory bit explaining what the scheme's all about, but I need some opinions from people who won't mind me using their names.'

'Oh, that's all right! I can get it to you by lunchtime. I'll start phoning right away and I'll type it all out nicely – and then I'll get one of the girls from Jack's office to pop round and collect it and she can fax it through to you. How about that?'

'Oh, but really, I couldn't –'

'Nonsense!' exclaimed Sonia. 'It'll be a hoot. I've only got my poetry group this morning and this sounds like much more fun!'

I thanked her profusely, gave her our fax number, and promised to fix up a lunch at the very earliest opportunity. I felt a warm glow of something or other: it's nice to be pleasantly surprised by people once in a while. Even if I had to spend half an hour editing Sonia's quotes down to usable length, she had got me off the hook.

I spent the rest of the morning adding the finishing touches to my interview with Rick, and trying to get hold of someone at Tipping police station for an update on the murder investigation. The Press Office kept insisting that there had been 'no new developments'. I phoned Will McGill's number several times in the hope of getting him to confirm that he and Rick had been considering a reunion, but his answerphone seemed to be permanently switched on, and when I tried his record company they hung up at the sound of the words, 'I'm from the *Tipping Herald'*. Immediately after this, I had a brief argument with Mr Heslop, who insisted that my interview with Rick should be twinned with coverage of the Hatchley Heath fête and printed on our centre pages, and that coverage of his murder should be confined to a report on the front page. I tried to persuade him that Rick's final interview was much too important to be linked with a write-up on the fête, and that in the circumstances nobody would be interested in the result of the 'Guess the Weight of the Cake' competition anyway. I suggested instead that we devote the centre-page spread to a sort of 'countdown to murder' account of the afternoon, but he was adamant. He said he had only recently been bought lunch by members of Tipping's Christian Society, whom he'd promised that the *Herald's* centre pages would remain an oasis for 'good news' stories. 'Murder countdowns' were completely out of the question, no matter who the victim was.

By mid-afternoon I was not in the best of moods. I rang Tipping police station for the umpteenth time and asked to be put through to DS Willis. The switchboard operator performed his usual routine of asking me who I was and referring me to the Press Office, but this time I'd had enough. I disconnected the call, redialled, and informed the operator in breathless tones that I was a learner driver and I'd got to speak to Mr Willis urgently to explain about the terrible accident I'd just had with his Harley Davidson.

He came to the phone immediately.

'Chris Martin, *Tipping Herald*,' I said. 'Look – don't hang up. Please! I've got a deadline in two hours and I need an update on the Rick Monday murder.'

There was a long silence.

'I suppose you think that's bloody funny. Right, now piss off!'

'But we need an –'

'I heard you. You don't need an update because there haven't been any new developments. So –'

'What do you mean? Of course there have been developments. Look, I'll buy you a drink,' I suggested.

There was another long, resentful silence.

'All right, Mrs Martin, if you want an update I'll give you one,' he said, noisily rustling papers. 'This is it. According to forensics, they've found fibres at the murder scene which they're trying to match up against fibres found at an earlier crime scene by our colleagues at Hudderston. There. How's that? Exciting, isn't it?'

I thought about this. It wasn't at all what I'd been expecting to hear. 'But that means you're linking Rick's murder to one of the other burglaries. You still think the motive was robbery. What about –'

'Well, I think we've established the motive was robbery, haven't we?' interrupted Willis. 'Haven't you been paying attention? Tut, tut! And let's get this straight, we're not linking the burglaries at this stage, we're *checking* for a link. All right?'

'But the key – the housekeeper's missing key . . . Oh!' An awful thought occurred to me. 'Didn't Mrs Jobson get in touch with you?'

He gave a snort of laughter. 'Oh, that. Yes, of course, that was you, wasn't it? You got that silly old bat all fired up with excitement and we ended up wasting a whole morning sorting her out!'

'Oh.' I was taken aback. 'You mean, she's found her key after all?'

'Of course she hasn't found it. She never lost it. Apparently one of her former employers used to engrave people's initials

72

on their keys, so Mrs Jobson – aided and abetted by you, as I understand it – managed to convince herself that there ought to have been an "O" engraved on her Tangley House key. She also seemed to think that Tangley House keys were made of a gold-coloured metal, so we checked the one in Rick's pocket and the one his brother's got, and – what do you know? – they're both a nice bright silver! Pretty much like the one you recently had on your twenty-first birthday cake, I imagine, love.'

'But that wasn't what she said,' I protested. 'She didn't say *all* the Tangley House keys were yellow, only the one *she* used to have!'

He muttered something under his breath. 'Look, love, I haven't got time for this. In future I'd like it very much if you'd stay away from my witnesses. I don't need you to make up their statements for them. We do that very well here ourselves,' he added, recklessly.

'And do me another favour, will you?' he went on, his tone becoming even chillier. 'Forget about that bloody drink.' And he slammed down his receiver.

For a moment, I listened in disbelief to the hum of the dialling signal. How could the police completely ignore Mrs Jobson's evidence just because it didn't fit in with their theory?

'Problems?' enquired Mr Heslop, placing a hand on my shoulder. 'I do hope not. I was hoping to get away early tonight.'

'It's ridiculous!' I exclaimed. 'You remember me telling you about the missing key? It's a vital piece of evidence, and the police aren't going to do anything about it!'

'Ah . . .'

'Just because Mrs Jobson's in her fifties and she's a woman and a housekeeper, they think she doesn't know what she's talking about! If it was a *man* and he was a company director or a brain surgeon –'

'Yes, yes. Is this your report on the murder? Is it finished?'

'Well, I'm going to follow it up myself!' I said, jumping

up and scrabbling in the bottom drawer of my desk for my handbag.

'Have you mentioned the key in your report? Ah, yes. Let's see, we'll just move it out of here – and put it down there.' He fiddled ineffectually with the mouse, finally moving my paragraph explaining the significance of the swapped keys to the bottom of the screen. 'That way, if you turn out to be right, we can say we were on to it first, and if you don't, nobody will remember.'

'Look, I'm going to talk to the handyman who had the original keys cut, and then I'm going to Bangles to get a description of the person who copied Mrs Jobson's key. Don't do anything – hold the front page till I get back!'

'Are you mad? I warn you, I'm not holding the front page beyond five o'clock. And you'd better be sure of your facts.' He skimmed through my piece as I collected up my things. 'Hmm. Well, it seems OK. And by the way, that canvassing you did on the activity centre story worked out very well.'

'Oh. Yes.' I had almost forgotten Sonia's contribution. I searched frantically for my car keys.

'Not quite the outcome we'd expected, of course, but it'll certainly raise a few blood pressures.'

'Will it? What do you mean?'

'What do you mean, what do I mean? You put the bloody thing together, didn't you? All that stuff about an imminent crime wave and people having to lock their doors against an influx of hooligans if the centre goes ahead – pretty inflammatory stuff.'

'Ah.' I had no idea what he was talking about, because I hadn't actually *read* the quotes. I'd just checked they weren't too long and that they all had people's names and addresses attached to them. Still, if Mr Heslop was pleased, that was all that mattered.

'Well, off you go then,' he said. 'Remember – five o'clock, and only if you're absolutely sure of your facts, and –'

'Don't worry, I won't let you down! *Keep the front page open*!'

*   *   *

74

By the time I got to Hatchley Heath it was already half past four, thanks to a snarl-up in the one-way system, so I decided to call first on Bangles. B. Angles & Sons Limited – 'Hardware, Ironmongery, Everything for the DIY Enthusiast, Plus See Our Extensive Range of Gardening Equipment' – occupies a prime site at 3 High Street, Hatchley Heath, and is one of those stores where assistants (most of them members of the Angles family) are always on hand to peer at you suspiciously from behind every counter display. I ignored them and marched through Kitchenware, detoured the 'Wonder Duster' display, and strode purposefully towards 'Paint and Wallpaper'. Mister Fixit's lurid yellow kiosk had been sited at the rear of the ground floor, presumably on the principle that its customers wouldn't be able to make it out of the store without being tempted to impulse-buy a couple of plastic plates or a five-litre can of trade white emulsion. When I reached it, its massive, whirring, rattling machinery was in the process of coughing and grinding its way to a halt.

'We're closing, love,' announced the assistant in charge, with a satisfied smirk. 'I haven't had a tea break.'

'That's all right,' I said. 'I only want you to answer a few quick questions. I'm a reporter for the *Tipping Herald*, and I'm trying to find out whether someone came in here last Sunday afternoon to have a copy made of a yellow-coloured house key with an "O" engraved on it.'

At this, the assistant, who had been chewing gum to some frantic, relentless rhythm audible only to him, stopped chewing in mid-stroke and let his chin fall on to his chest.

'Huh?'

I had rehearsed my question several times during the journey and it had sounded perfectly clear, but I apologized and started again. 'I'm a reporter for the *Tipping Herald*, I'm enquiring about a key you copied for a customer, and I was hoping you could describe the customer to me.'

'Right.' His smirk was back again. 'I'll get my uncle.'

He backed off in the direction of Bathroom Fittings, to return a few moments later accompanied by a middle-aged man in old brown overalls. This man wore a badge pinned to his breast pocket announcing him to be Kevin Angles, and he had the same thin, sandy hair as the assistant.

'That's her,' said the assistant, pointing at me with a ballpoint pen.

'Thank you, Tony. Can I help you, madam?'

'Yes, hallo, I'm a reporter for the *Tipping Herald* and I was wondering if you could give me any information on someone who had a key cut in here last Sunday.'

'See?' muttered Tony, grinning.

I felt a little prickle of embarrassment and, to my dismay, realized I was starting to blush.

'I see,' said Kevin, squaring his shoulders in the shabby overalls. 'Well, Mrs . . . Mrs . . . ?'

'Martin.' I smiled hopefully.

'Mrs Martin. So, you're a reporter, are you?'

'Yes, that's right.' The twinge of embarrassment turning to one of pride. 'I work for the *Tipping Herald*, and I am in rather a hurry.'

'An *investigative* reporter, are you? You use your powers of analysis and deduction to put together facts and come up with reasoned conclusions?'

'Er, yes.'

'OK. So glancing over your shoulder for a moment –' he nodded in the direction of the by now silent machinery in the kiosk '– and using your powers of deduction and analysis, what would you say *that* was?'

I frowned. 'It's a shoe-repair and key-cutting machine, isn't it?'

'Yes! Oh, well done! It is indeed!' Kevin and Tony exchanged mocking grins, and then Kevin took a step forward and stabbed at my arm with a grease-stained finger. 'And now let me tell *you* something. We use that machinery seven days a week, three hundred and sixty-two days a year, to repair shoes and cut keys. We do a bloody good job; sometimes we even do it with our eyes closed – although if you quote me on that, I'll sue. But we never, ever, fingerprint our customers or ask them to supply photographs or chest X-rays.'

'Oh, no. But –'

'No, *you* listen. Last year I wasted a whole afternoon of my time on you people. I showed your girl all over my store. I gave her a Moulinex hand blender at trade price. And what did I get for it? Two paragraphs on page six under the Women's Institute Keep-Fit weekend! You didn't even use the photo I gave you.'

I knew I was still blushing, and I wished I wasn't. 'But Mr Angles, please, it's very important. This is a murder investigation! This could be a vital clue! My editor is holding the front page! I just want to talk to the person who was on duty in the kiosk on Sunday. Was it Tony? Did he cut any house keys that afternoon? Do you –'

'No, Mrs Martin,' interrupted Kevin, 'I'm not having you wasting my staff's time. I'm just not having it – and your editor can hold what he likes. For your information, our Mister Fixit kiosk was open all day on Sunday – as it is every Sunday – for the convenience of our customers. You can print that on any page you like. And now I'd like you to leave, please. I'm running a business here.'

He took another step towards me, and I began to retreat through Paint and Wallpaper.

'But Mr Angles, it would only take *two minutes*. I could interview the person at their home.'

He frogmarched me round the 'Wonder Duster' stand.

'Well, could you ask them yourself for me, please? Just ask them if they remember anyone coming in to have a copy made of a yellow house key with an "O" engraved on it – and if they do, could you get them to ring me?'

We were halfway through Kitchenware, and I thrust my card into his outstretched hand.

'Please, get them to ring me on their own time,' I said.

Kevin and Tony Angles escorted me across their 'Welcome to our Store' doormat and positioned themselves strategically in the doorway with their arms folded. 'Good afternoon, Mrs Martin,' said Kevin. 'Do have a nice day.'

I reversed out across his frontage, still protesting, and backed into a small group of curious onlookers.

'Are you all right, love?' enquired a woman. 'We all do it, you know. I walked out of Marks and Sparks a couple of years ago with a pair of size sixteen trousers over my arm!'

'Don't worry,' said a voice from the back. 'I'll go in and vouch for you, shall I?'

It was Sally Beecham. She was wearing a navy linen suit and a lot of unflattering make-up.

'I'll tell them who you are, shall I?' she suggested.

'No! Don't do that.' We retreated out of sight of the Angles family into Boots the Chemist.

'Are you all right?'

'Yes, I'm fine. Look, Mrs Beecham, you were at Tangley House over the weekend; do *you* remember Mrs Jobson calling in on Saturday and giving Rick her key?'

'Do I what?' Her eyes glazed over oddly. 'Do you know, I've been *so* depressed – I simply don't know what to do with myself. It's such a dreadful, dreadful thing. Rick was so wonderful, wasn't he? I had to force myself to dress up and come out today.'

'I see. Look, this is important. I need to know whether you can remember what colour Mrs Jobson's key was.'

'But I do feel a bit better now I'm out. Sorry, what did you say? Is Mrs Jobson the rather large lady who was fussing on about the kitchen floor? I'm afraid I don't remember anything about a key. We were terribly busy, you know.'

I sighed. It was now a quarter to five, but the time no longer mattered. I wasn't going to get my scoop. I glanced at my notes. 'Do you know someone called Ted Kitchen? I think he lives on the Dene Estate and he's some sort of handyman.'

'No. Sorry.'

'Never mind. Thanks for your help, anyway.'

Sally forced a smile and headed into Boots. She was well on her way to the Max Factor counter when I remembered something.

'Hang on!' I ran into the shop after her. 'There's one other thing you could help me with. Do you remember you told me you saw Rick with Will McGill at the fête? Because

78

Will apparently told the police he was away in Yorkshire all weekend.'

'Did he?' She reached for an eyelash curler. 'Oh, well, I definitely saw him. I ran into him by the porch. He was peering in through the front window.'

'You're sure it was him?'

'Oh, yes, positive. I told you, I used to be a fan of Bad Monday. I went to quite a few of their concerts and I met them all backstage once. I nearly said to him, "If you're looking for Rick he'll be on the podium in a few minutes" – but he turned away when he saw me, and walked off.'

'I see.' I thought this over. 'So you didn't actually see him and Rick together? Rick might not even have known he was there?'

'Well . . .' Sally held up a kohl pencil and drew a line with it across the back of her hand. 'He must have, mustn't he? I should think he invited him, wouldn't you?'

'I don't know. Maybe he didn't. Maybe . . .' I couldn't work out what might have happened. 'Mrs Beecham, you are *sure* it was McGill, are you? His face isn't all that . . . distinctive, is it?'

She smiled. 'Oh, it wasn't just his *face*,' she said. 'Although I did get a good look at him. It was this –' she retrieved the kohl pencil from the stand, pulled up her left sleeve, and slowly and deliberately wrote something across the knuckles of her left hand.

'It was the tattoo,' she said, thrusting her half-clenched fist towards me. 'I remembered it, from when I met him before. Well, look at it. It's quite unusual, isn't it? I should think he did it himself or something, wouldn't you? D, E, A, and then TH, squeezed together on the knuckle of the little finger. *Death.*'

6

There were two Kitchens listed in the phone book for Hatchley Heath; one of them, a Mrs I., lived on the Dene Estate, and the other was a Lt. Col G.H. (retired). I decided Mrs I. would have to do, and found the house with the aid of a street map. It turned out to be in one of the more respectable parts of the Dene Estate; that is to say, its neighbours' front gardens had flowers in them, which is unusual for the Dene Estate, where old fridges and cars propped up on bricks are the more usual form of ornamentation. Several of the houses, including the Kitchens', had obviously been purchased under the Council's 'right-to-buy' scheme, because their standard Council-issue front doors had been replaced by standard Texas-issue Carolina-style ones, and some people had even tacked on porches.

A large woman in her seventies opened the door. She was wearing a crisp blue overall, and her hair was of a suspicious-looking dark auburn colour.

I asked her if I could speak to Mr Ted Kitchen.

'He's my son. What do you want him for?' she demanded in a proprietorial tone, as though I had enquired about borrowing her hover mower.

'It won't take a minute. I'm from the *Tipping Herald*.'

'The *Tipping Herald*? What would a newspaper want to talk to my Ted for?'

I didn't want to have to explain the whole thing to Mrs Kitchen, so I adopted a pleading tone. 'Couldn't I just come in for a minute?' Her hall smelled of boiled cabbage. 'I won't interrupt your tea.'

She looked suspicious, but she led me into her front room, where I dithered awkwardly in front of the gas fire, waiting for guidance.

She turned off *Blue Peter*.

'Sit down, then!' she snapped, tapping a very uncomfortable-looking settee with her walking stick. 'He'll be back in a minute – he's gone to fetch me a bit of lettuce from his allotment. What d'you want him for?'

'It's about some work he once did for Rick Monday. I'm covering the murder.' I sat down gingerly on the edge of the settee.

'*Covering* it? What's that mean? I don't read the papers. Waste of time.'

'Oh.'

'If you ask me what *I* think, I think he had it coming, that young hooligan, that's what I think!'

'Oh!' I was shocked.

Mrs Kitchen looked smug. 'People these days don't remember anything longer than a week. That's the trouble with the modern world. *These days*, people can get away with anything. Look at that Cecil Parkinson!'

Unaccountably, she shot a fierce glance in the direction of a glass display cabinet next to the gas fire. I followed her gaze, half-expecting to see Cecil Parkinson's likeness leering out at me from among the china ornaments.

'You should've been here when your precious Rick Monday was in that group and they had that record in the hit parade,' she went on. 'People didn't think so much of him then, I can tell you. You should've seen the types that used to hang around this village. Drug addicts and criminals. And *girls* – oh, yes, lots of girls – and none of 'em any better than they ought to be. What's that they call themselves? Guppies? Eh? Guppies?'

I was baffled. 'Guppies? I think you mean grou –'

'You can call 'em what you like, my dear! In my day they wouldn't've dared flaunt themselves in a village like Hatchley Heath! There are places for those sorts of women!' At the sound of her excited tones, a turquoise budgerigar in a cage by the window began chirping animatedly. 'Yes, I could've told you he'd come to a bad end. He was always in trouble when he was a kiddie. Fighting. Damaging school property. I should know. I did the dinners at his school.'

'Oh, really.'

'Yes. That brother of his used to stick up for him all the time. And his dad. Well, that's no way to carry on, is it? Boys need a firm hand from the start or they get themselves into trouble.' For a moment, her gaze rested on my knees, which were crossed and exposed, and a frown of disapproval creased her forehead. 'They used to say he put one boy in hospital – lost his temper and pushed the lad's head through a window. Well, it comes as no surprise to me. Nasty temper he had.'

Suddenly the turquoise budgerigar broke into an ecstasy of joyful song, and began bouncing up and down on his perch and banging his head against his mirror. Mrs Kitchen muttered something, heaved herself out of her armchair, picked up a heavy green cloth, and lumbered forward menacingly. For a horrible moment I thought the cloth was destined for my knees, and that I was going to have to pretend I didn't mind it, but instead she threw it over the budgerigar. The bird immediately stopped singing, and with a couple of disgruntled clicks, fell silent.

'Yes, boys need a proper firm hand, that's what they need,' she went on. 'They should never have stopped the National Service, that's what I say. It never did my Ted any harm – made a man of him, I can tell you!'

And at that moment, the man who had been made by National Service appeared as if by magic in the hall. I don't mind admitting, I was very relieved to see him.

'Ted!' barked Mrs Kitchen. 'You get yourself in here. This lady's come to talk to you about that job you did at Tangley House. I told you that you should never've worked for him! Don't blame me if you get into trouble. Where you been all this time?'

Ted was slight and stooped, and he sidled into the room without touching anything or making a sound, staring at me with his mouth open. He was in his early fifties, and he looked like the sort of person who might spend a lot of time scouring through magazines sent to him in plain brown wrappers. He also looked extremely worried. 'What d'you want to know about Tangley House for?' he demanded. 'I don't know nothing about it. I haven't been there since January, honest I haven't.'

Mrs Kitchen snorted and left the room.

I smiled reassuringly. 'Look, I'm from the *Tipping Herald*, and I've been told that you did a few odd jobs for Mr Monday, including getting his house keys cut for him. Well, I've got a theory he wasn't murdered by a burglar. I think someone may have stolen a key from his house and let themselves in with it.'

His mouth dropped open.

'So, I was wondering if you could tell me how many keys you cut for Mr Monday.'

'Oh.'

'And if possible what colour the original key was.'

'Oh.' He looked down at his feet, which were clad in brown woollen socks that looked unpleasantly damp. 'Oh, well, I don't know really. I got two keys done for Mr Monday the first day I worked for him. Picked them up in Bangles when I went down to buy some washers to fix up a leaky tap he had in his bathroom.'

'Good!' I was encouraged. 'Now, are you quite *sure* it was only *two* keys?'

'Think so. He said they only gave him the one key when he bought the house, and he needed two more – one for the housekeeper, and one for his brother. He said he wouldn't bother having any more made, because he was having a lot of work done on the house – a new front door and windows and so on. 'Course, he never did,' added Ted.

'No.' I was even more encouraged. 'Now this is very important. The original key Rick gave you to have copied – can you remember what colour it was?'

'Don't know what you mean, missus. It was just metal.'

'Yes, but what *sort* of metal? Did it look like silver – or brass? – or gold?'

'Yes.'

I tried to hide my annoyance. '*Which*? Come on, was it a sort of yellow colour or a sort of grey colour?'

'Yes, yes, that's it – a yellow colour.'

'Really? Are you sure?'

'Yes. Said so, didn't I?'

I jumped to my feet excitedly. 'And can you remember anything else about it? Was there anything written on it?'

'Nah, don't think so. Don't think there was anything written on it.'

'Not a letter or a number or something?'

'Nah, don't think so.'

'Oh.' I was disappointed, but it didn't really matter if he couldn't remember the engraving. I looked at my watch. 'Mr Kitchen, I'd like you to come with me now to Tipping police station.'

'What?' He was obviously shocked. 'Oh, no, missus, I couldn't do that! I couldn't go talking to the police. Anyway, I've got to be at work in half an hour.'

'But, Mr Kitchen, this is important! This is a vital clue in a murder enquiry. I'm sure your employers will –'

'Oh, no, I'm not going to the police. I told you – it was months ago. I don't remember nothing about them keys.'

'But you just said you did!' I could scarcely believe my ears. 'You told me . . .'

'I was only trying to be helpful, wasn't I. I like being helpful, but I don't want to go getting into trouble. I've got me mum to think of, haven't I?'

'But why would you get into trouble? All you have to do is make a statement –'

'No, I've got to be having my tea,' interrupted Ted, vehemently, edging towards the door. 'I wouldn't mind telling you about the work I did for Mr Monday, though, if you want to come round in the morning. The house was in a right state, I can tell you. You want to hear about that?'

'No. What I want is for you to –'

'I put up some shelves for him and nailed down the

84

floorboards in his bedroom. Mr Monday was all right – he always gave me cash and he didn't breathe down my neck or ask me what screws I was using, know what I mean? If you want to come round one night when I'm not working, I'll tell you all about the stuff I did for him.'

I decided to give up. It was hopeless. Between them, for their own very different reasons, Kevin Angles and Ted Kitchen had left me in limbo with my key theory. I could go no further with it. I was furious.

'Thank you, but I'm not interested. I'm sorry to have bothered you.' I let myself out through the front door without saying goodbye to Mrs Kitchen.

Ted followed me down the path. 'Paid me thirty quid, he did, just for making a couple of shelves from some old wood I had knocking around in me shed and a half-dozen brackets from B & Q. You don't want to listen to me mum – he was a good bloke. I could tell you all about the work I done for him, and . . .' he hesitated. 'I could tell you something else, an' all.'

'I don't want to hear about shelves and brackets, thank you.' I got into the car.

He grabbed hold of the door so I couldn't shut it.

'No, missus – it's about him, and something that happened to him.'

'What?'

'Well . . .' he hesitated again. 'It's about his daughter, isn't it?'

'His what?'

'His daughter. Tina.'

It had been a bad day.

'What do you mean, "his daughter"? He didn't have a daughter.'

'Well, that's what he thought, wasn't it! Turned up on him out of the blue, she did – just showed up on his doorstep. There I was, nailing down a gripper-rod where his stair-carpet had come up, and there's this knock at the door. He gave me twenty quid and a bottle of whisky and sent me home. He was right pleased with himself.'

I studied him suspiciously. 'Is this true? And he told you her name was Tina?'

'Yes. And he told me to keep it to meself. He said if I was short of a few bob he'd find me a few more bits to do, like. Well, it's all the same to me. I work nights, see, since I had me accident and stopped me window-cleaning round. I'm a night watchman. It's all I can do now. My GP's put me down for a disability allowance.'

'I see. Can you give me this girl's full name and address?'

'No, 'course I can't. All I know is she was off to Australia with her parents – you know, the ones that adopted her – and she wanted to meet her dad before she went. And her mum as well, I expect. You going to give me a few quid for this?'

Unwisely, he let go of the car door.

'No,' I said sharply, and drove off.

Next morning I decided to get it over with first thing, and to confess to Mr Heslop that I'd drawn a blank with Bangles.

'I did get the handyman to confirm that there were only three keys to the house, and he said he *thought* the original key might have been yellow, but he won't go to the police,' I explained. 'He also told me that Tina – the girl Mrs Jobson saw Rick with – was Rick's daughter, not his lover. So I think from now on we're going to have to concentrate on finding suspects. I'm going to have another try at getting hold of Will McGill this morning, and of course by next week something new is bound to turn up, so –'

It was at this point that I realized that Mr Heslop had neither smiled nor spoken since I entered his office. He didn't smile now. He leaned forward and picked up a sheet of paper from his desk. 'Can I ask what the letters S O C C O mean to you?' he enquired.

Of course I knew the answer to this one. 'It's something to do with the police. It means their "scene of crime officers", doesn't it? You know, the ones responsible for gathering all the evidence and everything.' I had picked this up from *The Bill*.

He handed me the sheet of paper. It was headed 'From the

Members of SOCCo (the Save Our Common Committee, a committee of Hatchley Heath residents formed to fight the threat posed to our Common)', and addressed to the Editor, and it began: 'The purpose of this letter is to inform local people who love the environment and our village of the threat posed by . . .' I wasn't very interested in it.

'I don't know whether you're aware of it, but there's been a bit of a problem in our post department,' said Mr Heslop.

'No, I didn't know.'

'Of course, you wouldn't. You reporters think our entire weekly output is down to you. You have no idea what goes on behind the scenes. Anyway, that's beside the point. This letter was addressed to the editor and should have gone into our Letters page yesterday, but instead it's been sitting at the bottom of a sack in the post department. Well, have another look at it. I'd like an explanation – of this.' He stabbed at the bottom line of the letter. 'Look at the names of the committee members. Would you like to tell me why it is that all these names – with the exception of one – belong to people *you* canvassed for opinions on the activity centre?'

For a moment, I was struck dumb by the unlikeliness of such a coincidence. I snatched the letter and studied the list of names. I didn't recognize any of them, of course, except for the first one: it was Sonia Staples.

Slowly, the truth behind this incredible 'coincidence' began to dawn on me. Sonia, who had told me that, yes, she thought she might have heard something about the activity centre, and that, oh, it would be such fun to canvass a few opinions on my behalf, was the chairperson of the 'Save our Common Committee'. Far from having just about heard of the proposal, she had been actively stirring up opposition to it. For the first time, I took a proper look at her address. *Sonia lived almost opposite the proposed site.*

The blush started at the base of my neck, and spread upwards and outwards until it overlapped itself and my face glowed incandescently like a ripe tomato. I tried to explain the whole thing as nonchalantly as I could, as though it was just a minor slip-up. Then I said defensively: 'Anyway, haven't these people got a right to air their views?'

'Of course they have – if we say who they are. *Not* if we represent them as a "random sample of residents". For God's sake! Fiona and her gang over at the *Hudderston Advertiser* will have a field day if they find out about this!'

I gritted my teeth. Sonia could kiss goodbye to lunch.

'And you needn't think this is going to get you off covering the public meeting next Monday, either!' went on Mr Heslop, grimly. 'Because however little work you've done on the story it's a sight more than anyone else has. No – you'll go and you'll give it your best shot, and what's more, you'll write a second piece, this time extolling the virtues of Acorn Trust Adventure Centres! Good God, I've already got two so-called reporters at home with sick children and one on maternity leave . . . What is this – a newspaper or a kindergarten?'

'I'm sorry, Mr Heslop,' I mumbled, and with head down, went obediently back to my desk, still blushing. I felt pretty bad about the two reporters at home with sick children: I'd let them down; Mr Heslop would be in a bad mood for a week and would take it out on them. I didn't really think my mistake would have any further repercussions, though. The Hatchley Heath interviews had been printed as part of our 'Around and About' section, which came between 'What's on' and 'Situations Vacant'. Nobody ever read it.

After my hot flush had subsided, I got myself a coffee and scanned briefly through Will McGill's biographical notes. There wasn't a lot, just a list of song titles, chart placements and record sales, plus a brief outline of the major events in his life. His story went like this: children's home, probation, Bad Monday, Modus, superstardom; married once, two children. He was apparently never to be seen in fashionable nightclubs and restaurants, rarely gave interviews, and was believed to have salted away a small fortune in carefully selected business ventures. He kept himself to himself, and photographers and reporters who got too close tended to end up suing for damage either to their equipment or their anatomy (Will's record company always settled out of court).

And today was the day – according to Rick's diary – when

he was to have met Will for lunch at the Old Barn Restaurant. I dialled Will's number, and, to my surprise, was answered almost immediately by a woman's voice. I searched feverishly through the biography, according to which Will was currently 'separated from his wife and childhood sweetheart Aimee, the mother of his two children, and living with air hostess Jackie at his mansion near Hudderston'. But the notes were probably months out of date. I decided to take a chance.

'Jackie? Hi, I'm Chris. Look, sorry to bother you – this is my fault. I'm supposed to be meeting Will today, but I need to have a quick word with him. Could you put him on?'

'Sorry, I can't. He's not here.'

'Oh, isn't he?' I must have got *her* name right at least. 'But I was supposed to be interviewing him after the meeting. The agency arranged it.'

'Did they? What agency? What meeting?'

'You know, the meeting with Rick this lunchtime.'

'Rick who?' demanded Jackie, blankly.

'Rick Monday, of course! I mean, I realize that –'

'What the hell are you talking about? You mean the Rick Monday that got murdered last weekend?'

'Yes.'

'You must be mad! Which agency did you say you were from?'

'Er, it's a promotions agency. You know, Star Promotions,' I added, in desperation.

She laughed. She might have been laughing at my unimaginative choice of name, but she wasn't. She said, 'Your agency have got their wires crossed then, love. Will's at a recording session today. It was arranged weeks ago. He's not supposed to be meeting anyone. Not you – and certainly not Rick.' She sounded very definite.

I wasn't going to be put off. 'They were meeting at one o'clock today at the Old Barn Restaurant,' I said. 'And I was supposed to be interviewing them afterwards to get the story. Anyway, do you think I could pop round later to talk to Will?'

There was a long silence.

'I don't believe you,' she said. 'Who told you about this?'

'Rick.'

'*Rick* did? Rubbish! I don't believe a word of it!'

'Why not? They were on speaking terms again, weren't they?'

Suddenly, her manner changed. 'Hang on,' she demanded, stridently. 'This is a trick, isn't it? I know what you're up to! You know Will's not allowed to talk about Rick, so you're trying to get *me* to give you a quote! I know your game! Well, I'm not going to, so –'

'No, this is the truth! They *were* meeting today! Who says Will's not allowed to talk about Rick?'

She reeled off a string of names, including that of Will's record company and a promotions agency.

I jotted down some of the names on my pad. 'Perhaps Will didn't tell you about the meeting,' I suggested. 'Perhaps he didn't want you to know – or perhaps he just didn't want the record company to know. I was told they arranged it when they spoke last Sunday at the fête at Tangley House.'

There was another long silence.

'You're making this up,' said Jackie. Suddenly, in the background, what sounded like several dozen very large and very angry dogs began barking in unison. Jackie ignored them and shouted into the phone. 'It's nonsense. Who's been telling you this?'

'I told you – it was Rick.'

'No! Will wouldn't do something like that without telling me. And anyway,' she added, while I considered my response, 'he couldn't have, could he, because he was with me last Sunday, all day and all night, so I'd know if he'd spoken to Rick, wouldn't I?' The barking was reaching a crescendo. 'Oh shit! There's somebody at the gate. Hang on! *Who is it? The pool man? Oh, all right, I'm just pressing the thingy!*' There was a loud bleep from an entryphone. Jackie picked up the phone again. 'I haven't got time to talk to you,' she said, abruptly. 'The men are here about the pool. I don't know what your game is, but you don't fool me. I'm telling you, me and Will drove up to Yorkshire last Sunday after lunch and we didn't come back till Tuesday. Will wouldn't waste his time going to stupid garden fêtes, he's too busy. He's been working on the new album for weeks – you can ask anyone. And he wouldn't waste his time making lunch dates with that creep Rick Monday, either. And get this: everybody in the band – plus Jerry and Mark the technician – has made a statement that Will was with them the whole evening that Rick was murdered!'

'Oh.' I was taken aback. I glanced at the notes I'd made during the press conference. I'd written: 'Will and girlfriend in Yorkshire all weekend'. 'But I thought you told the police you spent the *whole* weekend in Yorkshire, not just part of the Sunday –'

Jackie banged down her phone.

When I looked up, Mr Heslop had come out of his office and was standing over me.

'I've got something else for you,' he announced grimly, pushing a piece of paper towards me. 'Here, take it. Three Counties Radio have had one of these, and so apparently have most of the nationals. Ours was held up in the post room. And before you start getting too excited about it, I've already faxed a copy of it to CID and they don't want to know.'

He handed me a wonky photocopy of a typed letter, headed 'To the Editor'.

Warily I took it and read it. It said:

Dear Sir or Madame,

I read all the things you wrote about Rick Monday today, and I want you to know that you don't know anything. You think he was a saint and a martir but thats because you don't know the truth about him. He wasnt a person that helped children and did things for people. He was a murderer. He deserved to be killed in an abattoir or with poison that would burn his insides to pieces and not come out if they pumped his stomach. I wanted him to die feeling so much pain he would of screamed and begged me to stop. I wished to God for it, but its too late now.

I hope you will put this letter in so people will know what

he was like. I have suffered enough without going through it all again so I can't tell you any more.
Thank you.
ANONYMOUSE

I tried to suppress a squeal of excitement. Eagerly I turned the letter over and looked at the envelope stapled to the back of it. It was postmarked 'Taunton, Somerset', and bore the *Tipping Herald*'s full address, including our post code. It had been mailed at 3.15 p.m. on the Tuesday after the murder, the day when all the nationals had printed their first reports of Rick's demise.

'But Mr Heslop!' I exclaimed. 'This could be from the murderer! Do you think we should be handling it?'

'Oh, for God's sake, I already told you; there are letters like this all over the place. The police have seen several of them and they're not interested.'

'Why not?' I studied the typing: it wasn't up to much – uneven spacing and lots of messy attempts at corrections. It had probably been done on an old portable, the sort of thing people who couldn't really type kept tucked away in their attics for writing complaint letters to the Gas Board. And even though it was a photocopy, you could see that some of the keystrokes had been hit with such force they'd cut holes in the paper.

'Because it's a crank letter. It's got crank letter written all over it. It's accusing Rick Monday of being a murderer, which is patently absurd.'

I bit my tongue and decided not to argue.

'Now, will you please put it away,' he went on, 'and do what I pay you for. Which, in case you've forgotten, is reporting real, genuine news stories that have actually happened and may affect local people's lives – not inventing knife-wielding psychopaths for your own weird gratification.'

'Certainly, Mr Heslop,' I agreed, tersely, and I put the letter inside a plastic insert and tossed it carelessly into my bottom drawer.

7

The following Monday, when I arrived at the Hatchley Heath Arts Centre in time for the public meeting to discuss the activity centre, I was surprised to find the car park almost full. The last public meeting I had attended had been in Tipping, and had been called to consider the closure of a local riding school to make way for a link road. Only six residents and their au pairs had bothered to turn up. A notice on the door said 'Public Meeting to discuss future of Hatchley Heath Common'. Slightly alarmed, I walked through the entrance hall following signs for the Lecture Room, past a glass cabinet containing a display of Hatchley Heath Arts and Crafts (six baskets of dried flowers and two black-and-white photos of a pair of trainers). A man at the Lecture Room door wearing a green rosette gave me a leaflet headed 'Hatchley Heath Common – don't forget our wildlife have rights too', and ushered me inside. The room was full to bursting point. People were spilling out into the coffee shop, and perching on tables at the side of the hall. Most of them were clutching copies of the 'Wildlife' handout and some of them were armed ostentatiously with notepads.

I began to get the nastiest feeling.

A woman with a Hatchley Heath Society badge pinned to her Arts Centre T-shirt offered me a seat next to her in the ticket attendant's booth. She told me her name was Jane, and asked me if I needed to plug anything in, but before I could explain that my most high-tech asset was a ballpoint pen, Rob Monday and John Bradman – whom I recognized from his occasional appearances in the columns of the *Tipping*

Herald and on regional news bulletins – climbed on to the platform.

'That's John Bradman,' Jane pointed out helpfully, looking over my shoulder to make sure I wrote it down. 'The other one's Robert Monday – and that's Councillor Hobday,' she added, as another man joined them on the platform.

The patter of applause quickly grew to a clamour as people began to recognize John Bradman, who was well known for his support for 'green' issues and therefore extremely popular. Everyone knew that his firm, Bradman Homes, had been building housing estates innocent of threatened hardwoods long before anyone else had known or cared that hardwoods were threatened. A Bradman home would cost you more than an ordinary common or garden home, but living in one entitled you to congratulate yourself every time you slammed your front door for not having just slammed one of the vanished bits of a rainforest. Of course, most Hatchley Heath people owned homes bulging with teak and mahogany and other politically incorrect substances, but they all wanted to show they got the point.

I wrote down: 'Packed hall gives speakers enthusiastic welcome. Villagers keen to learn more about adventure centre project.'

'Huh!' muttered my companion, sharply. 'A lot you know!'

'What do you mean?'

'Ssh! They're about to start. It was that article in the paper!'

'What do you mean? Which article?' My scalp began to prickle.

'I don't know. The shop had sold out of papers by Friday lunchtime. Something about the centre ruining the village and causing a crime wave. A week ago nobody had even heard of the centre.'

'Really?' Now I began to feel sick.

'Yes. Nobody would have bothered about the wretched thing if it hadn't been for that article. Oh, apart from a few selfish people who live near the site. And Clifford, of course. There he is, look, sitting behind Mrs Monday.'

She pointed towards an attractive blonde woman in a red dress, but while I was trying to work out who she meant and if I cared, John Bradman rose to his feet, and a hush fell over the room.

'Ladies and gentlemen, thank you for coming,' said Bradman. 'I am very happy to be here tonight, and to have the opportunity to . . .'

He launched into a long discourse on the aims of the Acorn Trust, most of which I managed to get down in shorthand, even though he delivered it in the sort of hesitant monotone that sets people's minds to wandering and makes them remember urgent tickles at the back of their throats. He seemed a bit grim, not at all the Prince Casually Charming who normally appeared on television in a nice sweater and interspersed his comments on environmental issues with lots of reassuringly diffident 'you knows', as if to say: 'Hey, I don't really understand this either, but you can take it from me it's right.' He just read from a pre-prepared speech and kept his charisma to himself.

Afterwards, it was Rob Monday's turn. I eagerly wrote down his comments verbatim in preparation for the positive piece I'd been ordered to write on the activity centre, and as a matter of fact he just about had me convinced that the centre would be a Good Thing. But there was an ominous silence as he sat down. Councillor Hobday rose to his feet.

And that was when all hell broke loose. A dozen people at the back leapt up and shouted angrily at the councillor; one woman accused him of spearheading a campaign to destroy common land, and a second woman – whose voice I instantly recognized as belonging to Sonia Staples – demanded to know how the councillor would feel about having coachloads of hooligans delivered daily to within a few feet of his front doorstep. The councillor tried to counter some of these accusations by putting the case for the integration of unfortunate children from 'adjoining areas', but this only made things worse, because some people seemed to think that the whole of the EC constituted an adjoining area, and that contingents of knife-wielding Mafiosi children were about to descend on Hatchley Heath.

After about an hour, Councillor Hobday declared the meeting over. He said that both the Hatchley Heath Society and the Parish Council would meet again to reconsider the scheme and would take note of local people's feelings. Amid the cynical laughter that followed this remark, people began to disperse.

I immediately made a beeline for the platform. If I could catch hold of Rob Monday while his guard was down, I might be able to persuade him to give me a comment on the anonymous letter.

I got as far as the platform before the blonde woman in the red dress intercepted me.

'Can I help you?' she enquired, her icy tone suggesting that her intentions lay in the opposite direction.

'Yes. It's Mrs Monday, isn't it? Could I have a quick word with your husband?'

At this point I realized that Mrs Monday looked thoroughly fed up. She had tawny, expensively highlighted hair and a mid-thirtyish, lithe, toned body. Her thighs, which were somewhat over-exposed by the skimpy dress, showed no signs of exploding either inwards or outwards, and she was clearly not in her element in a village hall – even if it had been tarted up and called an Arts Centre.

'Why?'

'Because we've received a letter at the *Herald* that could be from Rick's murderer. I thought your husband might like a chance to comment on it before we print the letter.'

She looked shocked. 'Why haven't we been told about this before?'

'Well, I'm telling you now, Mrs Monday.' I felt a rush of blood to my head as I said this; it was so – cool.

'All right. Wait a minute. I'll get my husband.'

She leapt athletically on to the platform, took Rob to one side, and explained it to him. I watched the frown spread across his face. He came to the edge of the platform and looked down at me.

'What's in this letter?' he asked, grimly.

Of course, I didn't want to tell him just like that.

96

'I don't think we can talk about it here,' I said. 'There are some . . . allegations in it you might like a chance to refute.'

'What allegations?' I didn't answer, so he said, 'All right. Do you know where I live? I'll meet you there in half an hour.'

I could hardly believe my luck, so I thanked him profusely and retreated hastily to the car park.

The Mondays' living room looked as if it hadn't been hoovered since Christmas: books and newspapers adorned every chair arm, and the remains of a ready-meal clung to its microwaveable container on the coffee table. For the first time in quite a while I allowed myself to feel slightly superior.

Rob cleared spaces for us on two armchairs, and I handed him the letter in its plastic cover. 'This is a copy, of course,' I lied, just in case.

He read the letter, slowly, twice, and I watched his face while he was doing it. He didn't move a muscle.

Then he handed it back to me.

'This is rubbish,' he said. 'You're not going to print it, are you? It's obviously been written by some weirdo with nothing better to do.'

I was disappointed, but I tried not to show it.

'I can't agree with you there. For a start, this was posted in Taunton. Does that mean that the person who wrote it lives in Taunton? In which case, how do they know about the *Tipping Herald* and Three Counties Radio? Or was it written by a local person who then travelled a hundred miles to post it?'

Rob gritted his teeth. 'How should I know? Look, my brother was famous. Being famous means you attract hate mail. I'm sure if you worked for a bigger paper you'd know that,' he added. And he didn't say it sarcastically; in fact, he said it quite kindly.

'As a matter of fact,' he went on, 'I've got some other letters I can show you.' He got up and crossed the room to an untidy desk in the corner, and, after a short search, produced a large buff envelope. He tipped its contents out on to the coffee table next to the ready-meal.

I leaned forward and selected a flimsy folded sheet from the pile. He hadn't kept the envelopes. The letter was dated November 1977 and handwritten in neat capital letters. It said:

> *I heard one of your songs on the radio this morning, and the DJ said it was ever so sad about Bad Monday and that you are a loss to our country. It made me so angry I wanted to ring him up and tell him the truth. I rang the number but they never put me through so I got a razor and cut out a bit of my wrist with it.*
>
> *One of these days when you think I've forgotten you, when you think you're safe, you're going to hear a footstep behind you and it'll be me. I'm never going to forget you. I'm going to make you feel what I feel – and it will be the last thing you feel.*

When I'd finished reading it I felt a bit sick. I stared at Rob in amazement.

'You don't think this letter is serious? It's awful! Have you told the police? Are they all like this?' I spread the letters out across the table, counting them. There were more than a dozen, some handwritten in capitals, some typed. I didn't really want to read any more of them.

'Yes, I told the police. They said since we got them some years ago, and bearing in mind the circumstances of the murder, there wasn't really much point in their looking into them. Apart from the one you got at the paper – even assuming it's from the same person – we haven't heard from her since 1987. I don't know why I kept them really.'

I was flabbergasted. 'You said you hadn't heard from *her*. Does that mean you know who she is?'

'No! It doesn't.'

I didn't believe him. 'Oh, come on, you do, don't you? Was it some girl Rick went out with and then dumped?'

'No, of course it wasn't!' He volunteered this rather too

hastily, in my opinion. 'I'm telling you, I don't know who they're from.' He studied one of his fingernails thoughtfully. 'Well, there was this girl – I suppose you'd call her a groupie. She used to hang around at Bad Monday's gigs in the early days while I was still playing with the group. All I remember is that when the first couple of letters arrived, Rick said he thought they were from her. He thought she was a bit unhinged.'

'What was her name?'

He stared out of the window at a perfectly formed red rose that was swaying against the glass. 'I think it was Jo or Josie, but I don't know anything else about her. I wish you'd forget about it. My brother's dead, and nothing will bring him back. There's no sense in reopening old wounds.'

I decided he was probably telling the truth. 'Perhaps Will McGill might remember something more about her,' I suggested.

'No, I shouldn't think so.' He gripped the arms of his chair tightly, as though to steady himself. 'Mrs Martin, please – try to understand. I am perfectly satisfied that the police are doing all they can to find the man who killed my brother. I've never believed in hanging, or flogging, or any of those sorts of things, and as badly as I feel about the murder I'm not going to change my beliefs now.' The toe of his left foot, which was crossed over his right, began to jerk up and down in a nervous, uneven rhythm. 'Even if they catch him, which I hope they will, and he's behind bars paying his debt to society, it won't change anything, will it? Look, I'm sure you mean to help, but you're not. I want to hang on to the fact of my brother's life – do you understand? – not his death.' Rob was smaller and thinner and less intimidating than Rick, and his voice was softer, too. I quite liked him. He'd stopped short of admitting he'd rather his brother's murderer went free than that various unpalatable truths came out, but I was sure this was the gist of it. He was clinging to the robbery theory rather than face up to something worse.

'Mr Monday, I do appreciate your feelings, I *really* do, but the fact is, whoever wrote these letters appears to have hated your brother enough to do something about it. What about the rats?'

'What rats?'

'You know what rats I mean.' He was actually blushing. 'Supposing the same person who wrote those letters came here last Christmas and delivered the rats – as a warning?'

Rob got up and went to the window, apparently to study his garden, which was gradually disappearing into the dusk.

'And what about Will McGill?' I went on. 'All right, I know he's got an alibi and Bad Monday broke up years ago, but did he come here on the day of the murder? Were he and Rick planning a reunion?'

'Wait a minute, wait a minute. Where on earth are you getting all this from?' I didn't answer. 'Look. Please. If I put you straight on a few things, will you promise not to quote me?'

I nodded. 'All right.'

'Well, for a start, the thing with the rats had nothing to do with the murder. If you must know, I think it was down to Clifford Fletcher.'

'*Clifford Fletcher*? You mean the Clifford Fletcher who lives next door to Tangley House and writes books and used to be on the Hatchley Heath committee?'

'Yes. It was shortly after he resigned from the committee. I could be wrong, of course, but Rick and I both thought so at the time. You see, a couple of years ago I had an argument with Fletcher about using place names that were historically connected with the village for new streets and so forth. I thought it was a good idea, but Clifford didn't approve. And during the discussion he mentioned Tangley House – this was a long time before Rick came back on the scene. He said it was built on the site of the old rat-catcher's cottage, and how would the present occupants like it if we insisted on calling it *Rat* House?'

'Oh.' I thought this over.

'Clifford's a traditionalist. I'm afraid in a small community like this, things can get very personal, as much as one tries not to let them.'

To Rob's alarm, I made frantic notes in my book. He lunged forward but stopped short of grabbing my pen.

'For God's sake, you can't print this! I've told you, it was simply a bad and stupid joke. If you print this I'll . . .'

'I won't, *honestly*. It's just background.' I put the pad away. 'You said you'd tell me about Will McGill. I won't use anything you don't want me to.'

'But there's nothing to say about McGill.'

'Yes, there is. They were supposed to be having lunch together yesterday. Didn't you know?'

He looked genuinely baffled. 'I don't know what you're talking about.'

'I saw it – in Rick's diary.'

He shook his head. 'No, he would've told me. I don't think they've spoken for years.'

'Then how do you explain the picture in the paper?'

'What picture? Oh, you mean at the concert? Rick was quite pleased with that – getting his picture on a front page again. But it was purely a photo-opportunity, I'm afraid. It didn't mean anything.'

'Are you saying they still hated each other then?'

'*No!*' He leaned forward urgently. 'I am definitely not saying that. The whole feud thing was just a publicity stunt, and after the break-up things got blown out of all proportion. It's always the same in the music business. Look at the Beatles, look at Take That, look at –'

'But this was different! McGill made a threat against Rick's life! And they had that fight, Rick tried to *strangle* Will –'

Suddenly Rob leapt angrily to his feet, upsetting the coffee table and sending letters and newspapers cascading to the floor.

'No! I absolutely will not go over and over all that! Would you like to leave, or am I going to have to call the police?'

I was a bit shaken by his reaction, but I tried not to show it. I seemed to remember that Rick had responded in much the same way when I showed him the newspaper cutting.

Rob began to pick up the letters and put them back on the table.

'I'm sorry, Mr Monday,' I said. 'I'll go.'

We crossed the hall together without speaking. He hesitated with his hand on the door-latch.

'Mrs Martin, I do assure you that the police are on the right track, so all this is a waste of time. They've been able to piece together everything that happened that evening and they've explained it all to me. Apparently Rick's ex-manager, Ronan, rang – while you were there, I believe – and was abusive because he'd found out on the grapevine that Rick wasn't renewing their contract. He threatened to call round some time between ten and eleven to have things out, and *that's* why Rick tried so desperately to get hold of me.'

'But that's ridiculous! That isn't what happened at all!' I could still remember the contemptuous expression on Rick's face as he put the phone down on Ronan. 'If that's what the police think, they're wrong! Rick wasn't worried about seeing Ronan – surely you know that. Something else must have happened.'

Rob closed his eyes and shook his head. 'According to the police, what happened is this: my brother spent the evening in his study listening to music. He was probably working on some ideas for the new album. He would have locked his front door on the inside as a precaution – as you or I would if we had a large sum of money in the house. And also, as I told the police, because while he was living in California someone broke into the place he was renting and carried off a lot of very expensive recording equipment through the front door while he was asleep upstairs . . .'

'But he was expecting Ronan, and he had the money with him – in the study!'

Rob gave me one of his tired looks, the sort of look teachers reserve for pupils they've given up on. 'Mrs Martin, I know the police don't always get things right, but I think they have this time. And as for the other thing – the point you raised about Mrs Jobson and her key – well, perhaps you don't know Mrs Jobson very well. I believe she is now on some form of hormone medication . . .'

'Oh, I see!' I was furious. 'So it's all down to lack of

oestrogen, is it? Is that what you think?' I decided it was hopeless. 'I'm sorry. Thank you for seeing me, Mr Monday.' I stepped out on to the path. 'Could I just ask you one final question? Can I ask whether you've been in touch with Tina since the murder?'

He was in the process of extending his hand for me to shake. He let go of the door and it flew backwards, catching him a nasty blow on the elbow.

'His daughter,' I added, although I was sure he knew exactly who I was talking about. 'I wondered if you were keeping in touch.'

'I don't – I don't – I'm sorry, I don't know what you're talking about,' he lied, blushing and retreating over his threshold. 'I'm going to have to go now. Good night.'

He went in and closed the door. Actually, at that moment I felt more than a bit sorry for him, because he was one of nature's apologizers, and I knew what that was like. It meant for ever being compelled to excuse the shortcomings of one's relatives and friends, while fighting the urge to tell the truth: 'Yes, I'm afraid my husband/brother/daughter is an absolute shit who doesn't give a toss about anyone and I'm terribly sorry I haven't able to moderate his/her behaviour . . .' He had almost won the battle not to apologize this evening, but in the end I'd tripped him up.

When I got back to the Mini, a black BMW was pulling up behind it with Viv Monday in the passenger seat and John Bradman at the wheel. They both looked at me and exchanged glances, then Viv got out of the car and walked past me with a crooked little smile.

'Excuse me,' John Bradman called. 'Are you from the *Herald*? Could you spare me a few minutes?'

I tossed my bag into the Mini and walked over to the BMW. I leant towards the open window, keeping a respectful distance from his paintwork.

'I believe there was an article last week in your paper about the activity centre.'

'Um, yes.' Alarm bells started to go off in my head. 'But it wasn't an article. It was a series of interviews with local people – we're doing another piece this week on the centre itself.'

'I see.' He tapped his fingers on the steering wheel. 'So whose idea was it to do these particular interviews?'

'My editor. Well . . .' Oh, God. 'He told me to do some interviews, and I . . . you know, went out and interviewed a few people.'

'At random?'

'Yes. I . . . er . . . of course I do know a few people in Hatchley Heath.'

He got out of his car. 'I see. I suppose you would. Thank you, Mrs Martin.'

He had finished with me. I didn't care for being so easily dismissed, even though I was beginning to get a very bad feeling about this whole thing.

'Actually I'd like to ask *you* a question,' I said. 'How do you feel, knowing that if you hadn't cancelled your dinner with Rick he might still be alive?'

There was a short silence. Bradman's eyebrows, which contained grey flecks, bunched into a frown. It struck me that he was rather nice-looking, and I began to lose my nerve. 'What I mean . . . what I mean is that if you hadn't, you know, called off the dinner, then Rick wouldn't have been at home when whoever it was let themselves in and . . .'

'That's a bit of a wild suggestion.' He aimed his remote-control locking device at the BMW, which bleeped back at him obediently and flashed its lights. 'Is that the sort of question this editor of yours sends you out to ask?' He managed a smile.

I blushed. 'Why *did* you cancel the dinner? Is it on your conscience?'

'On my . . . ? For your information, this so-called dinner engagement you keep on about was nothing more than a casual arrangement between Rick and me to have a meal together after the fête was over. I cancelled it because, unknown to me, my secretary had got me a ticket for a piano recital at the Wigmore Hall on the same evening.'

'Oh.'

104

'I used to play the piano myself. I'm a keen follower of certain pianists.'

'Oh.'

'There are one or two I never miss an opportunity to hear. Good evening, Mrs Martin.'

I watched him walk up Rob's front path. I think I was a bit surprised by John Bradman, but I didn't waste time thinking about him – or about the consequences of tonight's public meeting. While Rob hadn't been looking, while he'd been gazing out of his window and trying to dream up new ways of deterring me from investigating his brother's personal life, I'd slipped the letter from the unhinged groupie into my jacket pocket. And it was still there now.

8

When I got home, Pete was in the kitchen, stirring something on top of the cooker. The house smelled of curry and washing powder.

'Where've you been? I did the sheets for you. Julie's gone out with Gavin – she said you said it was OK. Are you hungry? I made this.' He pointed proudly to a luridly red sauce spluttering fitfully in the saucepan.

I didn't have the heart to tell him it reminded me of the last time I saw Rick. Monday.

'Pete, you'll never guess what's happened! I've managed to get hold of a letter written to Rick in the seventies by this deranged groupie who used to follow the group! I got it from Rick's brother. It's exactly the same as one we got at the *Herald* this morning! You probably got one, too.'

'Christ, what have you been up to?' he replied, jauntily. 'Climbing through windows in that little short skirt of yours? I do hope not.'

'What do you mean? What's wrong with my skirt?'

'Nothing. It's fine.'

'Is it my legs, then?'

'No – what's up with you? I just meant . . .'

I glowered at him and pushed the letter into his hand. 'Read this. Go on, I want to see what you think.'

Obediently, he stopped juggling with rice and plates and read the letter. When he'd finished, before he could say anything, I handed him the one Mr Heslop had given me.

'Whoever wrote these was pretty serious, don't you think?

And probably slightly deranged. I think my next move should be to interview Will McGill. He may remember her.'

'I wouldn't do that if I were you.' He handed me back the letters, plus several grains of rice and a tomatoey fingerprint. 'If you want to know what *I* think, I think these were written by some empty-headed checkout girl with nothing better to do. Listen, I've been waiting for you to come home. There's something I want to ask you.'

'What do you mean?' I was outraged. How could he attribute my best piece of evidence so far to a checkout girl – and what was wrong with checkout girls, anyway?

'I'll tell you in a minute. Come on, come and sit at the table.'

The table had tulips and wine on it. I looked at the tulips, but I didn't take them in.

'What do you mean?' I repeated, aggressively.

'I'll *tell* you in a minute, sweetheart! Sit down. I tried to get roses, but that bastard at the petrol station didn't have any. Wait –' He pulled out my chair for me. 'There. Sit down. OK? Chris, I've got something to tell you –'

'What do you mean, the letters were written by a "bored checkout girl with nothing better to do"? Are you saying you don't think we should take them seriously? How can you say that? You can't have read them properly.' Angrily, I pushed the tulips to one side, spilling their water on to the table cloth. 'You could at least take the trouble to *read* them properly. You don't know the trouble I went through to get this one.' I hadn't of course gone to very much trouble at all, but he wasn't to know that. I took a gulp of chilled white wine. 'Listen, when someone's been getting hate mail, and they've had dead rats deposited on their front lawn, plus strange girls turning up out of the blue and claiming to be their daughter – don't you think it's just a *little* bit much to expect people to believe they've fallen down dead with an ornamental dagger in their heart *by accident*?' The wine tasted expensive. I took another gulp. 'Well, not exactly by accident, but you know what I mean.'

'Yes, I do. But then I would, wouldn't I?' He put the tulips

107

back in place and patiently rearranged them. 'Because I love you and I hang like a damp sock on your every word.'

'Good. You can read the letters again, then. And there's something else.' The wine was making me feel a bit better. I leant forward and clasped his hand desperately. 'Pete, I think I'm going to be in big trouble over this write-up I did on the activity centre proposal. I'm really worried about what Mr Heslop's going to say. You remember, I told you –'

Pete shook his hand free from my grasp and, with an impatient snort, clamped it over my mouth.

'Shut up. Just shut up for a minute! I don't want to hear another bloody word about dead people or the *Tipping* sodding *Herald* or your latest deadline for this week's planning committee report! Can't you ever give it a rest? I have had it up to here with your job!' And for a moment, I had an awful sense of déjà vu. I had had this conversation before with someone else. Several times, in fact. I wished he hadn't said it. 'Look, I am trying to talk to you about us. I've been trying to talk to you about us for weeks, but you never let me. There's always the mowing or the ironing or that bloody Gavin loafing about the place eating hamburgers. So tonight I've done the ironing and the cooking and the mowing, and you can sit there and bloody well listen.'

I stared at him in amazement.

'I think we should get married,' said Pete. 'And as soon as possible. Do you agree? I wanted to be sure you'd agree before I asked you, because I don't want you to turn me down, but in the end I couldn't read your signals and I decided to take the bull by the horns and just do it.'

'Oh!' I tried to laugh. 'How romantic.'

He didn't laugh. 'I thought you wanted it.'

'Of course I did.'

He took my hand and kissed it. 'But you don't now?'

'I didn't say that. All I meant was that back then, when *I* wanted to, *you* didn't.'

We stared at each other for a moment.

'OK. All right, I'm sorry I was an arsehole. I know saying it doesn't make it right, but at least give me a chance to make amends. Listen, Chris, I know this fantastic little hotel in Montmartre – we'll get married and we'll have a weekend in Paris, just the two of us.'

In the hall, the phone began to ring.

'I can get on to the register office tomorrow. They're bound to have a cancellation. We could do it next weekend. Isn't there some sort of special licence you can get –'

'Hang on, I don't want to get married because someone else has changed their minds! I don't want us to rush into this.'

'What do you mean? Christ, this isn't rushing. Look, I want to take care of you properly. I'm trying to do the right thing. You're always complaining about how irresponsible I am.'

'No, I'm not! I've never said any such thing.'

'Haven't you? Well, you've thought it, then. I've felt it oozing out of you when I've come home late on a Friday night without giving you an alibi. Oh, come on, we love each other – it's as simple as that. Isn't it?'

'Yes, but . . .' I gesticulated towards the phone. Pete ignored both it and my gesticulations.

'But what? Don't you realize, darling, that if anything were to happen to me tomorrow, the way things are at the moment, I would leave you with precisely nothing, probably not even my half of this house!'

'But nothing is going to happen to you!'

'You wouldn't even get a slice of my pension!'

I had never heard him refer to his pension before. I don't know why, but I was touched.

'Oh, Pete! Don't you think we should answer the phone?'

'No, they'll ring on the mobile if it's important. Look, either you want to marry me or you don't.' The phone stopped ringing. 'Which is it?'

My hands were beginning to shake. I put down my wine glass. 'I want to marry you – very much – but we have to do it properly. We have to talk it out with the children first. It's only fair. Julie's in the middle of exams.'

In the kitchen, the mobile started to warble.

'I see.' He hesitated, then leant forward and kissed me. 'Thank you. Thank you for saying yes.'

'That's all right.' I got up quickly. I felt odd – light-headed and jittery. 'I'm getting the phone,' I said, and I made a dash for the kitchen.

Pete's mobile was on the ironing board, next to the washing powder.

'Ah, have I reached Mrs Martin?' enquired a voice.

'Yes, this is me.'

'Well, this is Tipping police, Mrs Martin. There's nothing for you to worry about, but we've got your daughter here, and we'd like you to come down and collect her as soon as possible.'

'*What*?'

'As soon as you can, please.'

'But *why*? What's happened?'

'It's just routine, madam. The sergeant will explain it when you get here. There won't be any charges.'

'*Charges*?'

'What's up?' called Pete.

'It's a routine bust, that's all, madam.'

'Right. I'll be there as soon as I can.'

'What's up?' called Pete, again.

His daughter was a straight 'A' student whose hobby was helping out at the church crèche; I didn't want to tell him what was up. 'Nothing,' I muttered. 'A bit of a mix-up, that's all.' And I made a bolt for the door.

I drove to Tipping police station in ten minutes flat, parked on the yellow lines outside the front entrance, and jumped out of the car without locking it. On the stairs I bumped into Gavin and Gavin's father. They both looked at me, looked away, and Gavin's father said, 'How're you doing, then, all right? Bit of a game, this, in' it?' in a perfectly normal conversational tone of voice as though we had just collided with one another in the stamp queue at the post office. And then of course the whole thing became clear to me. This was all down to Gavin. Gavin lived with his father and brother in a run-down council flat; he ate saveloys; he liked Dralon furnishings and programmes with Bruce Forsythe in them. There wasn't a council estate

110

anywhere that didn't have one of his cousins living on it, and most of his cousins had histories that sounded like extracts from the Offences Against the Person Act. I should have put my foot down about Gavin a long time ago.

The sergeant on duty at the desk said he'd have Julie brought up as soon as someone was free, and went back to filling in a form.

'Now, look, I've had enough of this!' I shouted, banging my fist on the desk angrily. 'I know my rights! My daughter is sixteen and you can't keep her here! I insist on being allowed to see her *at once*! Do you hear me?' I was glad I was still wearing my jacket with the big shoulder pads.

'I hear you all right. We're keeping your daughter here for her own protection, madam. We are perfectly entitled to do that. She was found drinking in the Admiral Napier.'

I thought about this. At first, it didn't make much sense, but after a while, it did, and after a little while longer, I began to feel relieved.

The sergeant stooped over his form again. 'There you are,' he remarked, without looking up. 'Nothing to worry about, was there? After all, it's not drugs or joyriding or anything that'd embarrass you with the neighbours, is it? A couple of minutes from now you'll be able to take her home and tear her off a strip for keeping you up late when you've got to be in the office tomorrow.' He glanced up, a sarcastic smile lifting the corners of his lips. 'Not worth the shouting and the desk-thumping really, was it? In fact it'll stand you in good stead for a couple of dinner parties – "The night I collected little Julia from the police station." I think we've got another Julia down there tonight, as it happens, and a couple of Rebeccas and an Abigail, so I suppose we'll be getting the carpenter in tomorrow morning after all that desk-thumping.'

I didn't like his tone, and was very nearly worked-up enough to say so, but at that moment the door next to the counter opened. I thought it would be Julie, but it wasn't: it was DS Willis.

'Oh, it's you,' he remarked, rudely. 'What are *you* doing here? Isn't it past your bedtime?'

111

I ignored him and sat down on the bench under the anti-Rabies posters.

Willis produced a cigarette and lit it. He stared at me for a moment, as though making his mind up about something, and then he said, 'Have you heard about our breakthrough?'

'No. What breakthrough?'

'In the Monday case. We've got a witness.'

'Have you? What witness?'

He looked pleased. 'You remember the Audi that was parked in Tangley Lane? Well, there was a couple in it the whole time, apparently. They saw the bloke that did it.'

I felt too numb to react with more than a little tingle of surprise. 'Really?' I remarked, politely.

'Yes . . . What's up with you?' He scowled. 'This bloke practically fell over the bonnet of the Audi – he was covered in blood and carrying a heavy bag. We've got a description. Do you want it, or what?'

I tore my gaze away from the door, and found an old shopping list I could write on at the bottom of my pocket.

'Get this down,' said Willis. 'He was about five foot eight, small-built, clean-shaven, and he was wearing a dark-coloured sweater and a grey woollen bobble-type hat. They didn't get a proper look at his face because it was raining and the car was all steamed up on the inside, but they think he was middle-aged.'

I considered this for a moment: a middle-aged man in a woolly hat. Somehow it didn't sound like the sort of person I'd had in mind as a murder suspect.

The door opened, and two WPCs appeared, laughing.

'This couple didn't report it before because they didn't want their husbands and wives finding out where they were. We should've chucked the book at them,' Willis remarked grimly. 'Pair of wankers. Their story is, they thought it was mud he was covered in, not blood. They said they thought he was some old dosser who'd fallen over. It was only when they heard about the murder and no one else came forward that they decided to get it off their consciences.'

112

'I see. So does that mean they didn't actually see the man come out of the house?'

'No, of course they didn't see him come out of the house! I told you, they were parked in the lane. He slipped and fell on their car at approximately twenty-five past ten, then ran off towards the main road like a bat out of hell. He must've come out of the back of Tangley House. There's nothing else up there.'

'Oh.' I thought about the letters and Rick's unhinged groupie. 'Are they absolutely sure it was a man?'

He blew smoke over my head in a noxious cloud. 'Why? What did you have in mind? A transvestite alien?'

I decided not to dignify this with an answer.

'By the way,' Willis went on, 'the forensics reports we were waiting for have come through. Apparently the footprints in the garden were size seven – just about right for the guy our witnesses described, don't you think? And this is the other big news –' he drew enthusiastically on the cigarette – 'we sent some fibres recovered from the scene for analysis, and they've turned out to be very similar to ones we found at a burglary two months ago in Hudderston.'

'Oh. *Oh.*' I did a mental double-take. How was this possible? 'Are you sure?'

He narrowed his eyes. 'What do you mean – *am I sure*? What kind of a question is that? You take the biscuit, you do, really!' Angrily he stubbed out the cigarette. 'There I go, giving you the benefit of the doubt . . . I said the fibres were *similar*. I didn't say they were the same. We're having more tests done, OK? If we decide the burglaries are linked, someone'll let you know. I'll make bloody sure it isn't me.'

And he walked off, grumpily, into the night, leaving me alone on my plastic bench to wait for Julie. I was sure he was wrong. The fibres at Tangley House would turn out to be quite different from the ones left at the earlier burglary. It was very unscientific to get excited about things that were similar.

A few moments later a young policewoman bundled Julie through the door – rather unnecessarily roughly, I thought, but I bit my tongue and said nothing. If the object of the exercise was to put Julie off spending time in police stations, then so be it. When we got to the car I told her that I had never in my life been so humiliated, and that she had let me down badly and had better have a very good explanation for her behaviour. Of course, we both knew that I had been more humiliated than this on an almost daily basis, and that there is really only one explanation for going into a pub and drinking lager, but I think we felt better because I had said it.

The following morning I wrote up my account of the public meeting at Hatchley Heath Arts Centre and put it in Mr Heslop's in-tray. I had a lot of trouble getting it just right. It started with some attendance statistics, quoted large sections of John Bradman's speech verbatim, and then went on to record in the final paragraph that a few residents had expressed minor concerns about the scheme. Mr Heslop read it and seemed relieved, but then he hadn't been at the meeting.

After lunch, with a pounding headache brought on by the events of last evening, I drove over to Hudderston. Will McGill lived on the outskirts of the town, beyond the golf course and the crematorium, in a mock-Tudor mansion of the type much sneered at by writers on style in upmarket newspapers. It was set in a lush landscape liberally dotted with mock-Tudor mansions and large, ranch-style bungalows with lodges for live-in chauffeurs. I parked opposite the wrought-iron gates of Will's home, next to a sign announcing 'Blue Lagoon Pools – another dream becomes a reality', and stared at the house for a moment or two, trying to work up a good sneer at its naffness – but actually I couldn't. In fact, after studying its sweeping drive and nicely timbered symmetry, I decided I quite liked it, and that if in another life I came back as a millionaire I would probably buy one very similar. I put on my sunglasses and got out of the car. And that was when I started to have second thoughts. Will McGill was on the verge of being a bona fide superstar. Modus was almost a national institution. True, his face was unmemorable – thin

114

lips, thinning hair, small eyes set too close together – and when he appeared on television or in the newspapers, which wasn't very often, people were inclined to say: 'Isn't that Thingy from Thing?' or 'Isn't that the man from Dyno-Rod who unblocked our drains?' But he was still a major celebrity, and Mr Heslop considered it very bad form for his reporters to pester celebrities.

Also, I wasn't sure the Rick Monday story was worth the risk of ending up in Casualty.

There was a small plaque attached to the gate which read WARNING: GUARD DOGS ALWAYS ON PATROL, and on the gate post was an intercom. I stared at it for a moment, wondering what to do. I could simply go away and forget the whole thing, or I could announce myself over the intercom and hope for the best. But if I announced myself, whoever answered it would simply tell me to clear off. And there was another thing – *the gate wasn't shut.* I took a deep breath. If I walked up the drive and banged on the front door, somebody would have to answer it. And in the drive was a red Porsche with the initials WMG. Will McGill was almost certainly at home.

With my pulse rate going into its spin cycle, I strode briskly up the drive and hammered boldly on the front door. There was a bell, so I pressed that as well. And before I could think better of it and retreat to the car, the front door opened and on the doorstep stood four Dobermans the size of small horses.

I froze, staring at the assembled ranks of teeth.

A blonde had accompanied the dogs. 'Yes?' she enquired.

I said the first thing that came into my head. 'Er, it's Blue Lagoon Pools, madam, about your pool.'

'Oh, but the pool's been done! What do you want?'

'Well, I'm . . . I'm Customer Relations. I have to do a follow-up with clients whenever there have been problems.' I wished I was dead.

She looked me up and down with mild interest, as though I was an unusual specimen in a rather boring zoo. 'Customer Relations? Well, you shouldn't've come without an appointment then, should you? That's not very customer-related, is it? Still, I don't mind letting you in to have a look if you want.

I s'pect I've spoken to you on the phone. Will likes everything to be just right, and he was on my back night and day about it, so if I was rude to you, I'm sorry.'

She winked. My stomach gave a nasty heave, but I managed to smile back.

'Lovely day, i'n'it?' she remarked. 'Come and have a look at it. It's turned out really nice in the end – just like the picture I sent you. I'm really pleased with it. Will's pleased, too. Matter of fact, I got him in for a dip this morning. Come on.'

She whistled to the dogs, and I followed her along a narrow path through aromatic shrubbery to the rear of the house. She was in her late thirties, with fluffy ash blonde hair and deeply tanned skin. As she walked, she made clucking noises to the dogs and issued friendly warnings about minding the cracks in the paving the gardener hadn't fixed. I liked her, and this made it worse.

The pool was situated in a vast conservatory attached to the back of the house. It was overshadowed by potted palms, and surrounded by Roman-style mosaic tiling. White wrought-iron tables were set at intervals around it, and the wall of the house had been painted with a mural depicting a shimmering swathe of tropical beach. Somehow, even if Jackie hadn't told me, I'd've known it was her idea.

She gestured vaguely towards the pool.

'Well, I expect you know what's what,' she said. 'You go ahead and do your stuff.'

Naturally, I had no idea at all what was what, or what my stuff was, so I gave her an agonized smile, and pretended to peer knowledgeably into the water.

She watched me for a bit, and then, to my intense relief, got bored.

'Well, I'll go and see what his nibs is up to,' she said. 'I'll ask him if he can spare you a minute.'

'Oh, that would be kind!'

When she'd gone, I allowed myself a minor panic. I spotted a large square brass grille just beneath the surface of the water, and decided it looked like the sort of thing pool engineers might shake their heads over and say, 'There's your

116

problem, mate,' so I got down on my knees and pretended to inspect it. I thought I ought to look as if I were testing it for a correct fit, so I reached down into the water and gave it a hearty tug. To my horror, it made a muffled rasping noise and began detaching itself from the side. Several brass screws rippled through my fingers and drifted slowly towards the bottom of the pool.

When I looked up, Jackie, Will and the dogs were standing a few feet behind me. I recognized Will instantly, of course, even though he didn't look anything like his stage persona. His skin was golden and perfect – not a trace of sweat or grime, scarcely even a wrinkle, and his hair was clean and bleached, every strand glowing with health and conditioning.

'Ah.' I hoped fervently that they hadn't seen what I'd done to their grille thing. I stood up, wiped my hand on my skirt, and offered it to Will. 'Mr McGill. How nice to meet you.'

He ignored my hand.

'This is just a courtesy visit, Mr McGill, to make sure you're happy with everything. You know, the pool and the filtration unit and everything.' Oh God. 'Anyway, it was really good of you to see me without an appointment. I do appreciate it. Especially under the circumstances.'

He was wearing a pair of spotless white jeans and a sleeveless T-shirt that revealed well-honed biceps, and he had no flesh on his middle-aged stomach. In fact, he was surprisingly and unsettlingly good-looking.

'What circumstances?' he asked.

'Rick Monday being murdered and everything.'

'And what's that got to do with me?'

'I don't know. I just thought . . .'

'You thought wrong then, didn't you? So what's all this about then? Do you want to know what I think? I think your firm is crap, if you'll pardon the expression. I think I want my money back.'

For a moment, I had no idea what he was talking about. 'Oh, you mean the pool.'

'Yes, of course I mean the pool! After what we've been through with you people – *three months* it's taken to get this sorted – I've got a good mind to get on to your boss and tell him I want the bloody thing taken out! By Friday,' he added, with a crooked smile.

There was an awful silence. Suddenly, I knew I couldn't go on with this.

'Look, Mr McGill, I'm really sorry – I don't know how to tell you this. I'm not from the pool people, I'm from the *Tipping Herald*.'

Jackie drew in her breath sharply.

'You're from where?' He laughed suddenly. He looked really nice when he laughed. 'The *Tipping Herald*? What's that? Something to do with the waste disposal industry?'

'Oh, Will, it's the local paper!' Jackie seized hold of his arm and clung to it.

'I know that, you stupid bitch.' He pulled her off his arm with a flick of the wrist, as if she were a piece of Velcro that had got stuck in the wrong place. She looked hurt and I felt sorry for her. 'Get rid of her, will you.'

'Get out!' shrieked Jackie, with exaggerated enthusiasm. 'If you don't want to end up in the pool – get out!'

I stopped feeling sorry for her, and retreated a few steps. My skirt was 'dry-clean' only. I said, 'All right, I only wanted a comment, but if you won't give me one I'll say that if Rick hadn't died, you and he would be announcing your reunion plans any day now, and you're very sorry about what's happened.' I turned on my heel and made for the door.

'Wait a minute. What did you say?'

I opened the conservatory door. 'I said, you don't have to comment if you don't want to. I've already got my story.'

'No – wait.' He advanced on me, smelling of aloe vera and Gucci for Men. When he put his hand on my shoulder, it felt as soft as silk. It was his left hand, and I caught a quick glimpse of lettering tattooed across the knuckles. 'What story are you talking about?'

'About the reunion of Bad Monday, of course.'

He frowned. I had a mental flash of him leaping about

on stage, his guitar clasped to his groin, his features taut with effort.

'I don't know what you're talking about, but you'd better get this straight, because if I see anything in any paper about a reunion between me and Rick, I'll know where it came from and I'll sue you till you've got your kidneys in hock. Understand?' He let go of my shoulder abruptly. 'There has never, ever been the slightest chance of me and Rick working together again. Not on Bad Monday – not on anything. Who are you? Are you really from the *Tipping Herald*?'

I ignored this. 'But I happen to know you were supposed to be meeting Rick last Friday for lunch in the Old Barn Restaurant,' I protested.

'No. I don't have lunch, and I've never heard of the Old Barn Restaurant.'

'Yes, you have,' interrupted Jackie. 'Don't you remember? Mum went there and had the saddle of lamb and wouldn't pay the bill, and you –'

'Shut up!' He turned his back on her. 'I suppose you're a big fan of Rick's, are you?'

'No, not really.' Actually, apart from admiring Rick's physical attributes, I had never been into his sort of music, being more of an Abba fan. Fortunately, he didn't give me the chance to mention this.

'Good, because he was a no-talent lump of snail-shit who couldn't write a decent song if he slept with a grand piano up his arse for a week,' Will remarked, with sudden feeling.

I was shocked. 'Oh, was he?'

'Yes, he was.'

'Willie, *don't*!' hissed Jackie, gesticulating wildly.

'Shut up! And get me a beer, will you. And while you're at it, make sure that Filipino tart has cleaned the fridge out properly.'

'A beer? Are you sure? But I thought you said this was your no-sugar week.'

'Oh, stuff that!' Jackie departed, followed by the dogs, and Will watched her attempts to run in her spike-heeled sandals with amusement. Then he said, 'Who put you up to this? You

119

think you're pretty smart, don't you? Well, it's not exactly a secret what I thought of Rick, so it isn't going to earn you any brownie points if you put what I just said on your front page. Who sent you?'

'Nobody! I saw the appointment in his diary. It said "Will – Old Barn Restaurant".' I was beginning to wonder if later, when I'd finished all my questions, I'd dare to ask him for his autograph.

'I see. Well, it must've been some other Will then. He ripped me off once, and that was enough. What would you call someone who stuck their hand in a lump of dogshit and came up with a five-pound note?'

He'd got me there. 'Er, unhygienic?'

'Jesus! I'd call it lucky. That was him: lucky all his life. He was born in the right place, at the right time, and his face fitted. He never had to break out in a sweat for anything unless he wanted to – do you know what I'm talking about?' He looked me up and down contemptuously. 'No, of course you don't. Well, I'll tell you something anyway. When I met Rick he was poncing around with that prat of a brother of his playing folk-rock at art colleges. He pulled the birds in all right, but that was all he could do – he was nothing more than a pretty face. He'd never've been anything if it hadn't been for me. Name one song he's written since we broke up.'

I thought for a moment. 'Well, there's "Reaching out for No one", of course, and –'

He scowled angrily. 'There's nothing. You want to come in and look at *my* gold discs, do you?'

'Oh, yes, please!' I could scarcely believe my luck.

'Don't be stupid! Listen, I've got a trout farm in Sussex and a villa in Spain. I've got two Porsches and an Aston and sixteen gold albums.'

'Have you?'

'Yes. I could *buy* your paper if I wanted. I might do it, one day.'

Jackie emerged from the house, carrying a bottle of Guinness and a glass.

120

'I see. So is that why the group broke up then, because you didn't think Rick was good enough for you?'

Will took the bottle and glass from Jackie without looking at her. 'You know bloody well why the group broke up.'

'No, I don't.'

He held up the glass to the light and studied it minutely.

'Don't you know anything about the music business? Does your editor think I'm stupid or something? Jackie, take this back.' He thrust the glass at her. 'The bitch hasn't wiped it properly – I've told her before to use the glass cloth and nothing else.'

'Oh, but Willie, she's doing the fridge!'

'That's what I pay her for, isn't it? And put the radio on while you're in there so we don't have to listen to that racket!' he added, indicating the sparrows chirping merrily on the conservatory roof. Clearly, he was not a nature-lover. He took a swig from the bottle and studied me through narrowed eyes. 'You know, I feel sorry for you. You got the short straw, didn't you? OK – you want to know why Bad Monday broke up? It was because Rick decided he didn't want to play at being a rock star any more – he wanted to play at being a film star. Someone – probably that pus-head Ronan – told him he could do it and he believed them. But he forgot two things. The first was that Bad Monday was *my* group, not his – so it wasn't down to him to say when it broke up or when it didn't. And the second –' he grinned maliciously – 'was that he couldn't act.'

'I see.' I couldn't argue with the last bit. 'But surely that wasn't the reason you had the fight with him, was it?'

The bottle hesitated on its way to his lips. 'What fight?'

'You know – the one that got in the papers.'

He grinned again. 'Oh, that.' He took a long swig from the bottle. 'Why don't you ask Rob about that? Now, go on, clear off – before I get Jackie to set her dogs on you.'

A loudspeaker in the roof crackled suddenly into life, and the conservatory began to throb to the strains of Elton John's 'Our Song'.

'I *did* ask Rob, but he won't tell me.'

121

'Oh, what a shame. You're buggered then, aren't you? Come on, I don't do charity, I want you out of here – I've got things to do.'

'All right.' I opened the door to the garden and extended my hand to him. He shook it reluctantly. 'Er, Mr McGill, I don't know if you're interested, but the police have just issued a description of the person they're looking for in connection with the murder,' I remarked, trying to glance down at his feet without making it obvious.

'I assure you, I'm not.'

His feet were at least size eleven. He was too tall, in any case, to match the police description and he had an alibi, but it was worth the look. 'You see, the thing is I've got my own theory. Do you remember Rick going out with a girl called Jo?'

He frowned. *'Who?'*

'Jo. Jo or Josie. It was right back at the beginning of the group, before you were famous.' I inched reluctantly towards the door. 'I think Rick may have dumped her or something.'

'What are you talking about? Of course I remember Jo. She didn't go out with Rick – she went out with me.'

'Oh.' I was taken aback. Elton John lapsed into silence, and the voice of a Capital Radio disc jockey went into spasms over some traffic hold-up on the M25.

'Jo Randall, that's who you mean, is it? Tall girl, student nurse – bit soft in the head.' He glanced towards Jackie, who had just returned carrying a fresh glass. 'Good legs,' he remarked, with a spiteful grin.

Jackie, whose legs resembled rake-handles, blushed.

Baffled by this, I said, 'Well, would you happen to have her address?'

'Don't be silly. She was a student nurse from the hospital. Me and Rick had dozens of 'em chasing after us when we had that place together in Notting Hill. We –'

At that moment, before I'd had a chance to write anything down or work out whether I could risk asking him any more questions, several things happened almost simultaneously.

122

First, from the loudspeaker in the roof issued the familiar and haunting sequence of guitar chords that introduces 'Reaching out for No one'. I recognized it instantly, so did Jackie – and so did Will. I saw his eyes flicker. Temporarily, he was beside himself with anger. He whirled the Guinness bottle back over his shoulder and hurled it up into the roof of the conservatory. He was probably aiming at the loudspeaker, but he missed. The bottle hit the glass with a resounding crack, ricocheted off, and bounced on to a roof-strut, where it smashed spectacularly, showering down on to the tiled floor amid hissing cascades of beige-coloured foam.

Naturally, I was stunned. In my house, when people don't like something on the radio, they turn it off at the switch.

'*Reaching out for no one,*' sang Rick, '*touching in the dark. Waiting for your hand on mine, your . . .*'

Jackie made a run for the house.

'*. . . hold upon my heart . . .*'

'I'll get Maria!' shrieked Jackie. 'I'll get the Vax! I'll turn it off!'

At the mention of the Vax, I immediately came to my senses and decided the moment had come to leave. I began fumbling with the door handle, but Will caught me by the wrist and held me back.

'Hang on a minute. You like that crap, don't you? I could tell.' Unbelievably, his expression was as calm as a millpond on a summer's day. 'You think it's his best ever, don't you? Come on, I want to know.'

'Well, yes, I do actually.'

'I see.' The music stopped. 'Why?'

'Er . . .' I couldn't think of a single reason for liking 'Reaching out for No one'; how can you describe what you like about a particular piece of music? 'Reaching out for No one' was melodic, sad, catchy, disturbing – I didn't know anyone who didn't like it.

'Oh, forget it!' he snapped. 'What do you know? Who gives a toss about the music, anyway? It's all about making money, isn't it? Do you know his bloody record company are bringing out all our old Bad Monday stuff on CD as a tribute to him?

As a tribute to him!' He was still holding my wrist. '*My* songs, that *I* wrote. And I won't get a penny out of them, because I sold out all my rights in them, didn't I. To him, years ago – for peanuts – when all I wanted was to be shot of him. He's dead, and he's still screwing me!'

I tried to make sympathetic noises, but the blood was draining out of my hand.

'You understand? He's dead and he's still bloody screwing me. Every penny will go to his bloody estate. That poncey brother of his, his sodding parents, his ex-wives . . . I don't know. Every penny *my* songs earn will go to them. How do you think I feel about that?'

'Oh . . .' I didn't care how he felt about it: somewhere at the back of my mind, one half-formed idea began to connect with another.

'His *estate*,' I repeated. 'His beneficiaries. His *Will* . . .'

'Hang on. You don't get it, do you? You're standing there nodding, but you don't know what the hell I'm talking about. You think I've had a great life. You think, why's this guy whingeing about a few thousand quid down the drain? That's what you think, isn't it? And you think I ought to put the red carpet down for you and snap to attention because you think I *owe* people like you. Well, let me tell you something – most of my life has been shit. I don't owe you a thing – not you or the recording industry or anyone. Have you got *any* idea what I'm talking about?' I hadn't, but I said yes so he'd let go of my arm. He laughed. 'OK then, forget it. Who gives a toss what you think.' He let go of my arm, and I stumbled out gratefully into the garden.

'Thank you, Mr McGill,' I mumbled. Behind Will, Jackie and the maid had appeared with mops and the Vax. I made a bolt for the exit.

'Why don't you go home and listen to the music?' shouted Will. 'That's what it's for, sweetheart – all you have to do is bloody well listen!'

9

I drove straight home, wrote WILL in capital letters on a blank sheet of paper, and propped the paper up against the kettle while I made some tea. Of course, Rick was bound to have written a Will: most people made Wills when they passed thirty-five and spotted their first wrinkle. I had made one long ago. But Rick was hardly Onassis; could his Will really have provided someone with a motive for killing him?

I went into the living room and found an old Modus record. According to the sleeve, Will McGill had written five of the tracks on the album, and, if the helpfully printed lyrics were anything to go by, it was all pretty angry stuff about alienation, pain and driving cars too fast on the wrong side of roads – just the sort of things teenagers like to go to sleep thinking about. The record was probably Pete's. I put it on the turntable and dropped the needle on to it in the middle of a track called 'Silver Spoon'. Immediately there was a blast of tortured guitar strings accompanied by the lyric: 'You took my world and you broke it in two. You broke my heart now I'm gonna screw you!' It did something awful to my eardrums and I turned it off. I might have once liked it, but you grow out of these things. 'Silver Spoon' had been written shortly after the break-up of Bad Monday, when Will had first joined Modus: '. . . your pretty face, your perfect smile. You left no creases in my bed, just lies . . .' Maybe it had been written with Rick in mind. One thing was certain, though, the Old Barn Restaurant entry in Rick's diary had had nothing to do with Will McGill. Will had probably been dying to visit Tangley House to gloat over Rick's deficiencies in the swimming pool and Porsche departments, and the fête had provided the perfect opportunity. Afterwards he'd got Jackie to cover up for him, to avoid the embarrassment of admitting it, and Jackie had made a bad job of it. He still had a huge chip on his shoulder about Rick, but that was as far as it went, and anyway, his alibi was unshakeable. I was glad I'd got the reunion thing sorted out.

I took my tea to the dining room and opened up *Yellow Pages* on the table. To my horror, the Solicitors' entry continued for eleven and a half pages, and included the ominous suggestion that you should: '*See also under* Legal Services'. I wasn't sure if this was worth it. Eventually Rick's Will would be made public anyway. I half-closed the book with my thumb still in the middle of it. The Will *would* be made public, but there'd be no way of knowing whether he had been planning on changing it or whether it mattered. I was angry with myself for caring, but I reopened the book and decided to give it my best shot.

After a few moments of careful deliberation, I decided to start with Hatchley Heath solicitors, then move on to Tipping, and finally, if it came to it, to Hudderston. Of course, if Rick had used a flashy London show-business solicitor I was wasting my time. I found a pencil and marked the list with crosses for Hatchley Heath and Ts for Tipping, and pinned my hopes on Hatchley Heath.

By the time I'd finished making my list, it was already a quarter to five. I carried the phone into the dining room and dialled the number of Alexander, Trewin & Potter, High Street, Hatchley Heath. Their receptionist said she'd be glad to put me through to their Wills Department. Had I got my Will in store with them already, or did I require advice about making one? I said that in fact my enquiry was regarding a Will they were executing for someone who had recently died. She greeted this news impassively, and put me through to a man called Atkins who asked how he could help.

'I'm really sorry to bother you,' I said, 'but I believe I may be a beneficiary of a Will you're executing. I've only just heard that the person has died, and I thought I should ring you and let you have my new address in case you've been trying to contact me.'

'I see,' said Atkins. 'May I have the name of the deceased person in question?'

'Eric Arthur Monday,' I replied, crisply, pleased with my efficiency in having looked it up.

'I'll just keep you a moment,' said Atkins, and dropped me on his desk. For several interminable minutes the phone emitted the sort of claustrophobic silence that lingers in a room lined by fireproof steel cabinets stuffed to their rims with yellowing documents. When Atkins returned he sounded rather less friendly: he said he had been unable to locate a Will for anyone of the name I'd given him, and that he was afraid I might have made a – I'm afraid I hung up at this point, and moved on to Anthony Bell, 'All Matters Handled Personally'.

I'd got all the way down to the Hatchley Heath Rs, when Julie came home. I had scored six definite 'no's, three 'I can't give you any information regarding Wills we may or may not hold's, which I classed as probable 'no's, and one recorded message asking me to ring back the following day. I didn't think I was doing very well.

Julie slumped on the sofa arm and listened open-mouthed to my tired little speech about being the beneficiary of someone who had recently died. I had made up my mind to leave her in no doubt how upset I was by her behaviour the previous evening, so I turned my back on her.

'What's going on?' she asked, when Richardson, Clough and Richardson had hung up on me. 'Are we going to be rich?'

'No,' I said, frostily. 'I'm trying to find out if Rick Monday had made a Will, and was planning on changing it or something, but unfortunately I don't know who his solicitor was.'

'Couldn't you just say you're a reporter? Surely they'd tell you then?'

I gave her a hard stare, in case she was sending me up.

She sighed, and left the room.

127

I'd finished the last of the Hatchley Heath Ys, and was just wondering whether to bother starting on Tipping's As, when Julie reappeared carrying a tray laden with tea in a proper pot and hot buttered toast.

'I couldn't find any jam,' she said, 'so I brought you some Marmite.'

I know it's an odd thing to say, but at that moment I think I liked her better than I had for a very long time. She was rearranging the toast in neat overlapping layers.

I didn't know what to say, so I just smiled, and dialled the number of Amery, Heathcott & Co., West Street, Tipping. Perhaps Julie and I had drifted apart, and it had been both our faults, and last night had given us the shock we both deserved. I gave her another smile, and then the receptionist put me through to a woman called Mrs Mossop.

Mrs Mossop listened to my little speech and said, 'Fine. Could I have your name and address then, please?'

For a moment, I was too taken aback to say anything. 'I'm sorry?'

'Well, if you're one of Mr Monday's beneficiaries we'll be wanting to notify you in due course. I don't think a date's been set yet for the reading. Mr Amery would know, of course, but he's with a client at the moment.'

'Oh. Ah.' My eyes met Julie's. 'I'm afraid the problem is that I'm on the move rather a lot. I was wondering if you could tell me who Mr Monday's beneficiaries are so I can see if I'm one of them?'

Her tone turned frosty. 'I couldn't possibly do that,' she said. 'Are you a relative?'

I reached desperately for the tea. 'Well, no, but I think Mr Monday made an appointment with you people shortly before he died and I was wondering if you knew whether he'd planned to –'

'I'm going to have to stop you there,' she interrupted, in tones that were by now arctic. 'Do you wish to leave your name and address or not?'

It was no good. I'd got as far as I was going to get with Mrs Mossop. 'I'll ring back,' I said, and replaced the receiver.

'Bloody hell!' enthused Julie. 'That was exciting!'

'No, it wasn't. They wouldn't tell me anything.' I drew a ring round the Amery, Heathcott & Co. entry in *Yellow Pages*.

She peered over my shoulder. 'Well, you can't win 'em all. Have some toast.'

At that moment Pete's key turned in the front-door lock. He looked at the tea tray in surprise.

'What's all this?' he enquired. 'Is it someone's birthday?'

Julie leapt up. 'Do you want some then? Here – have my chair, I'll go and get you a cup!' And she dashed off to the kitchen, pausing only to smooth out her cushions.

When she'd gone, Pete stared after her for a moment, and brushed a hand lightly over her seat before sitting on it, as though suspecting something sharp or unpleasant might be concealed there. 'What's happened – did she come back from school via Damascus?' he remarked, unkindly. 'And what's with the phone book?'

I told him.

'Good God,' he said. 'Well, that's A for effort.' He looked impressed. 'You know, you might be on to something. After this girl Tina turned up, perhaps Rick decided to cut Rob out of his Will and to leave everything to her instead. What about the house? Didn't you say both Rick and Rob fancied Tangley House, and that they'd made some sort of pact that whoever got rich first would buy it?'

I thought about this. I couldn't imagine that Rob would give two organically produced figs for either Rick's money or his house.

Pete helped himself to toast. 'Listen to this: impoverished teacher, jealous of successful younger brother who he'd always secretly hoped would die early from a drugs overdose, suddenly discovers that not only is his brother now a health freak who rarely pollutes his body with anything stronger than orange juice, but he's on the point of changing his Will in favour of someone else.' He took a bite of toast. 'Did you know Rob used to play bass guitar with Bad Monday when they first started? He's supposed to have given up to pursue his teaching career, but maybe he was just no bloody good. And he hasn't got an alibi. He's supposed to have been out jogging – in all that rain.'

At that moment Julie returned with the tea. 'Oh, a bit of rain wouldn't put off a sports freak,' she remarked. 'Dad used to go to cricket practice every Monday night without fail, even when it was chucking it down!'

Of course, Pete and I both knew that her father had not in fact been a sports freak at all; his Monday nights had been reserved for a rather more strenuous activity. I had never forgiven myself for faithfully washing and ironing his cricket things every Tuesday morning when they hadn't needed it.

'I expect you're right,' I said. 'And Rob wouldn't have needed to copy Mrs Jobson's key, because he had one of his own.' All the same, I decided that next time I saw Rob I'd be sure to find out what size his feet were.

'OK, then.' Pete sounded slightly miffed. 'If you don't like my theory, you're stuffed, aren't you? Who else is there to suspect?'

I wrote down 'Rob – feet?' in my notebook. 'Actually, I've still got two more suspects. There's Clifford Fletcher, for a start. According to Rob, he hated Rick enough to dump those dead rats on him, and he lived next door, so he could have popped over any time for the key, and –'

'Oh, come on, even in Hatchley Heath people don't stab each other over disputes about where the public toilets are to be sited!'

'But we don't know that that's why they hated each other, do we? Maybe there was something else. I think I'll go and talk to the Fletchers and find out. Anyway, they aren't my favourite suspects. *Jo* is. Her name was Jo Randall and she was a student nurse at a hospital in West London. She used to go out with Will when he and Rick were sharing a flat together in Notting Hill.'

To my surprise, Pete got out his notebook. He scribbled: 'Randall, Joanne or Josephine, possible Somerset connection.'

'I know someone on the *Hammersmith Echo* who owes me

a favour,' he remarked. 'I'll see if he'll do it. It might be worth giving Fanconi's syndrome a try.'

'What's that?' asked Julie.

'I don't know what it is exactly. I think it's some sort of inherited genetic defect. You tell people you're trying to trace someone who might be a carrier, and before you know it, they've dashed down to their archive department like bats out of hell.'

There was a short silence. 'Cool,' remarked Julie, impressed. 'More tea, anyone?'

Pete and I exchanged surprised glances, lifted our cups and let Julie pour tea into them. And after we'd drunk the tea, and had another round of toast, the conversation lapsed into comfortable silence, and we all thought our own thoughts.

Just for once, for half an hour, we were a proper family group.

It was raining the following evening as I drove over to Hatchley Heath. Not serious rain, more a grey drizzle that clung to the air miserably like an old nylon shirt. I knocked on the front door of Yew Tree Cottage and waited. According to the biographical notes on the dust jacket of 'Hatchley Heath Through the Ages', Clifford Fletcher was manager of a local branch of Barclays, so he ought to be at home by now, having his tea.

The front door was opened by a smartly dressed boy of about Julie's age who smelled vaguely of TCP.

'My parents are about to have dinner,' he said. 'Can I ask whether they're expecting you? If it's about photographs of our house taken from a helicopter, or the Bible, I'm afraid they won't be interested. We're Catholics, you see,' he added with earnest politeness.

For a moment, I wondered sadly whether Julie could be persuaded to fall for someone like this.

'I'm from the *Tipping Herald*,' I said. 'I'd just like a quick word with your mum and dad about . . . you know, what happened next door. Were you here that night, by any chance?'

'No. I was away at camp. And I don't think my parents will want to talk to you about that either. They were out, too.'

'Well, could you ask them please?'

A few moments later, Clifford Fletcher came to the door, and I immediately dropped my gaze to his feet in an effort to assess his shoe size, but he was wearing ancient, very worn carpet slippers and it was hard to tell.

'Yes?' he enquired.

'Look, I'm sorry to disturb you. My name's Chris Martin and I've been working on the Rick Monday murder. I was wondering if you could spare me a few minutes to talk about it.'

He shook his head. 'I'm sorry. We have absolutely nothing to say about the murder.' He moved as if to shut the door.

'Oh, but this isn't only about the murder. What I'm really trying to do is a sort of profile on Rick's work for the Hatchley Heath Society which we can publish in the future when the murder is solved – as a tribute. I thought as a member of the Society and his neighbour you might like to contribute to it.'

At that moment a woman appeared behind Clifford Fletcher. She had dark hair drawn tightly back into a pleat and fine, high cheekbones, and was probably in her mid to late thirties. I had the vague feeling I'd seen her somewhere before, but I dismissed this feeling without a second thought. When you reach a certain age, *déjà vu* becomes a more or less permanent affliction.

There was silence.

'I think you've been misinformed,' said Clifford, finally. 'I am not a member of the Society committee.'

I feigned surprise. 'Oh, but I thought you were one of its leading lights!'

They exchanged glances. Clifford was quite a lot older than his wife, definitely mid-fifties at least. He had silver hair, gold-rimmed glasses, and a slight stoop. He looked like a bank manager of the old school, the ones who very much prefer to say no.

'I'm sorry,' he said. 'I don't mean to be rude, but I really don't think we have anything to say to you.'

132

'Why not?' There was no point beating about the bush. 'Is it true you resigned from the Society because of Rick?'

Clifford blinked. He took several seconds to formulate his answer, then he said carefully, 'I left the Hatchley Heath Society because Marianne and I both care passionately about the village and its future, and we no longer felt able to support the aims of the Society. I really don't think it's helpful to bring personalities into it.' He moved again to shut the door, then added: 'This village has survived for centuries. It's in the Domesday Book. Its configuration of church, manor house and high street is almost unique for this part of the country. It has survived wars, plagues and all manner of political interference, but I'm not sure it can survive efforts to turn it into a miniature version of Croydon. Do you get my point?'

Of course I got his point. Everyone gets the point about Croydon. 'Don't you think perhaps you've got a rather old-fashioned view of village life? I'm sure lots of people would like to see more facilities here. Not everyone lives in a house as lovely as yours, Mr Fletcher – some people would really benefit from better local facilities for their children. Were you born here?'

'No. And if you're implying that we're incomers who view the village through rose-coloured glasses, let me tell you that nothing could be further from the truth. My wife was born here and spent her childhood here, and I inherited this house from my great-aunt eighteen years ago and have lived here ever since. I met my wife through her late father who was Chairman of the Hatchley Heath Society in the seventies.' He glanced at Marianne, who gave him an odd look in return; not quite a frown, almost a wince. 'We have as much right to our views on the future of the village as anyone.'

'All I meant was –'

'I think we know what you meant,' interrupted Marianne, angrily. She was wearing a brown skirt and sweater that looked like rejects from Oxfam. 'We know what you meant, and we are not going to answer any more of your questions. My husband has told you why he resigned from the committee, and he has also told you that he has nothing to

133

say on the subject of Mr Monday.' She glanced instinctively in the direction of Tangley House, which was just visible through gaps in the yew hedge. 'You may find it hard to understand that anyone could take a strong stand over a matter of principle – in fact, yes, I imagine you would – but there it is.'

I stepped back from the porch. I didn't like her tone. 'All right, Mrs Fletcher. Would you like to explain to me what your principles had to do with the dead rat incident? Everybody knows it was you and your husband who did it! Who else would know that Tangley House used to be the site of the local rat-catcher's cottage?'

There was a shocked silence.

'That's it,' muttered Clifford. 'Goodbye, Mrs Martin.'

He slammed the door whole-heartedly. For several seconds, I stared at it in dismay. Bits of ancient dust and grit began to trickle down from the roof of the porch and the house martins skimmed agitatedly across the garden. Somehow I hadn't managed to get to the part where I said I understood how they felt and that I simply wanted to hear their side of the story.

I walked slowly back to the Mini, got out my notebook and rested it on the car roof. I was about to jot down a few notes about the Fletchers when my attention was distracted by a movement on the far side of the road. There was someone in the trees on the edge of the Common. I peered into the gloom, and caught a glimpse of him silhouetted against a patch of sky at the end of the path. He was about five foot eight inches tall and wizened-looking, and he wore a dark jumper with a matching woollen hat pulled down low over his ears. Across his right shoulder a large rucksack mottled with army camouflage sagged emptily.

I dropped my pencil. He'd disappeared, swallowed up by the trees and the drizzle. But I didn't need another look. It was the man who had been in Tangley Lane on the night of the murder. He was almost exactly as the witnesses had described him, and he was at that very moment walking briskly away from me across the Common.

134

10

I jumped across the ditch that separated the Common from the road, and clambered on to the path. I was too excited to stop and work out what I was going to do. The man in the woolly hat and jumper matched the police description to a T, and I'd found him. Not for more than a fleeting second did it cross my mind that following a suspected murderer into a patch of woods might not be a very good idea. I was just hoping I wouldn't get involved in an embarrassing scene on the main path in front of old ladies walking their Yorkshire terriers.

But he didn't stay on the main path. He detoured off along a narrow track that meandered through the undergrowth towards the thickest part of the wood, his hat bobbing up and down as he weaved between clumps of bramble. Without stopping to consider the alternatives, I followed. I had to run merely to keep up. Then, quite suddenly, just as I was beginning to consider calling out something along the lines of, 'Excuse me, I've been following you to ask you about a murder . . .' he stopped, looked this way and that, and disappeared behind a large oak tree at the side of the path. My stomach did a somersault. This was my chance. I could catch up by taking a detour through the undergrowth. I vaulted a clump of nettles, dived through some whippy oak saplings – and leapt out at him triumphantly from behind the blackberries.

To my horror, there stood Ted Kitchen, having a pee against the oak tree.

'Oh!' I exclaimed. 'Ted!'

At first, I was baffled. How could I have made such a stupid mistake? Then I realized I hadn't made a mistake at all. If ever there was a person born for skulking about in woods and darkened lanes and giving people cause to suspect him of things, it was Ted Kitchen.

My heart sank.

'The police want to talk to you,' I announced. He was wearing a heavy navy jumper with matching hat, obviously knitted with tender loving care from the finest bulk-buy double-knitting wool by his mother. She probably turned them out by the score and made him wear them all year round. 'What were you doing in Tangley Lane on the night of the murder? Why haven't you told anyone? You could've told *me* when I came to ask you about the keys!' I added angrily, glancing down in horror at my torn tights.

Ted had been hastily doing up his trousers.

'No, no – not me, missus,' he muttered, reddening and backing off. 'I don't know what you're talking about.'

I couldn't believe I'd ruined a pair of tights for nothing, and I didn't care if I offended him. 'Oh, yes you do! There was a couple in an Audi parked in Tangley Lane – they described you exactly! If you don't want to get into serious trouble you'd better come to the police station with me *now*.'

He gave me a horrified glance, pulled his hat down over his ears, and stumbled back on to the path. I had to run to keep up.

'I'm telling you, missus, there's no point me getting involved with the police, 'cos there's nothing I can tell them! It was *dark*, I was minding me own business. If I'd seen anything, I'd have come forward.'

'Would you? Are you sure? You were spying on that couple in the Audi, weren't you?'

Ted almost fell down a rabbit hole. 'I never! Look, you've got to believe me, missus, I wasn't doing anyone no harm and I didn't see nothing. There was no one there except for them two in the car. That's the truth! I told you – I liked Mr Monday. If I'd've seen the person that killed him I'd say so! I'd do it for the reward, wouldn't I?'

136

Well, that at least sounded truthful.

'All right, but if you don't come with me now,' I began, menacingly, 'I'll go back to my car and ring the police from the phone box in the High Street. You'll find them waiting for you when you get home!'

At this he pulled up sharply in his tracks. He was out of breath, his face purple, the stubble round his thin lips beaded with rain or perspiration. 'No, you don't want to do that,' he protested, adopting a wheedling tone. 'Look, I told you about that girl, didn't I? You wouldn't turn me in – you can't! Matter of fact, I've been a bit of a silly bugger, haven't I?'

I stopped too, and kept my distance. I didn't like him much.

'In what way?'

He shook his head. He was beginning to look desperate. 'I can't tell you. It's me mum, isn't it?'

'What about your mum?'

'It'd be a shock for her. I've been lying to her, see. About me job.'

'What do you mean?'

'Well, I told you, I had this night-watchman's job at Anderson's.' He shifted uncomfortably from foot to foot, glancing up at me from under his hat. 'And they made me redundant, didn't they? They closed down – just after Christmas.'

'So?' The drizzle was clinging to my hair and dripping slowly down my neck.

'Well, I didn't tell Mum, did I? I couldn't – not at Christmas. I pretended I was still doing me shifts, didn't I, four nights a week.'

'Oh. I see.'

He stared at me desperately. 'But then I had to go on with it, didn't I, 'cos I couldn't get meself another job – and I can't tell her now. It's a right bugger, but I have to keep it up for me mum's sake. I used to go up the old factory and sneak in under the wire, but then they turned the power off so you can't even plug in an 'eater. I don't do no harm, missus. I

137

kip in me car most nights, but me legs get cold. I was injured in Cyprus, you know, doing me National Service.'

I tried to look sympathetic. 'I see. How awful.'

'The bloody Army discharged me 'cos I was unfit, and I didn't get no compensation, and then I couldn't get a proper job 'cos I didn't have no apprenticeship . . .'

'But you won't be able to stay out of the investigation.'

'. . . So I did this and that, and then I had me window-cleaning round but I come off this defective ladder, and –'

'Mr Kitchen, *please*!' I interrupted, sharply, as a large cold drip trickled suddenly down my spine. 'I'm trying to understand your problems, but you're a witness and you have to go to the police!'

He gave me an odd look, then turned and began walking on again. After a few moments, he said:

'OK, missus, I suppose you're right. I'm sorry about what happened to Mr Monday. I'd like to help the police if I could, honest I would . . .'

'Oh, good!'

'. . . so I'll go home right now and explain things to me mum. You're right. It's what I've got to do. I'll go into the station in the morning.'

The path had emerged at the roadside, about a hundred yards on from Yew Tree Cottage.

'You've got to let me square things with me mum,' he said, before I could protest. 'She's an old woman. How'd you feel about it if she had an 'eart attack and it was down to you?'

'Oh, but I'm sure she wouldn't!'

'How d'you know? How's she going to feel if they keep me down the station doing paperwork and stuff and she doesn't know where I am? They might not believe me – they might send someone round the house to talk to her. You don't know much about the police, do you, missus? They get hold of someone like me, they're going to be asking questions.'

Well, of course, he had a point there. I thought for a moment. I really didn't want to drive to Tipping police station with Ted in the car. He hadn't shaved properly and he didn't use deodorant. Also, he wasn't going to advance the police investigation much further, so it wouldn't make any difference whether he went to the station now or in the morning.

I was hungry, and I could feel a very nice shepherd's pie coming on.

'All right,' I agreed. 'I suppose it won't make any difference. But first thing in the morning, mind – and I want you to ring me afterwards and let me know what happens. Here's my card.'

'Thank you,' said Ted, eagerly, snatching my card and putting it in his pocket. 'I reckon you've saved my life. Thank you. You won't regret this – I'll tell 'em it was you put me on to them.'

The following morning, when I still hadn't heard anything either from Ted, or Tipping police, I rang Wayne and arranged to meet him for lunch at the Red Lion. I hadn't really expected to hear from Ted, and Mike Willis was hardly likely to put in a thank-you call either. I told Wayne I'd got some new evidence in the Rick Monday murder case I wanted him to look at (the letter I'd purloined from Rob), and he promised to fill me in on all the latest titbits of information emerging from Tipping CID.

I arrived shortly before noon, and there was no sign of Wayne in the bar, which was almost empty, so I ordered a slimline tonic and a menu and sat down to wait. I was beginning to feel a bit twitchy, because I'd rather expected Tipping police station's Press Office to have been on the phone by midday at the latest with a request that we withdraw Ted Kitchen's description from our late editions. I'd got a horrible feeling I was going to end up in trouble for something, and I had just decided to change my mind and ask for a gin to go with the tonic, when the door to the cloakrooms opened to admit a smartly dressed blonde I immediately recognized as Viv Monday. She seemed to waft across the room on a cloud of expensive perfume.

She looked at me and frowned. 'I know you. Are you in the club?' she demanded.

139

'Sorry?'

'The Luncheon Club.' She retrieved a gin and tonic that had been waiting for her on the bar, and muttered something about professional women and lunch and the advantages of being able to bounce ideas off one another. Then she said, with a frown, 'Oh, no, I know who you are. You're that woman from the newspaper.'

'Yes. Chris Martin. You arranged for me to speak to your husband the other day.'

'Hmm. So I did.' She contemplated her drink for a moment, and I prepared myself for a rebuff, but when she looked up she was smiling. 'You know, you really ought to consider joining our club. We could do with an insider at the *Tipping Herald* – someone of your sort,' she added, in what was obviously intended to be a pointed manner. 'We arrange gourmet luncheons at one of the local restaurants on the first Tuesday in every month. What do you think?'

'Oh.' I didn't know what her point was, but I decided I ought to be flattered. Mr Heslop would never agree to it anyway. 'I'd like to very much, but I'll have to ask my editor.'

'Fine,' said Viv. 'Excellent. And remember – looking out for one another's interests, that's what it's all about.' She gave me another pointed look. 'Everyone else does it. Why shouldn't we?'

'Right. Absolutely.' I had no idea what she was talking about, so I smiled effusively. 'Mrs Monday, I hope you won't mind my asking this – but would you happen to know anything about your brother-in-law's Will? Do you know when it's being read?'

'Rick's Will? Heavens, no! Who cares anyway? He'll be leaving everything to some charity or other, won't he?'

'Oh, will he?'

'I imagine so. That's what the Mondays usually do, isn't it? Haven't you heard about the Stan Monday bequests to Hatchley Heath – the Memorial Hall and the Monday Scholarships? That's what the Mondays do best, you know – leave things to people with all kinds of strings attached to them.'

'I see.' I began to wonder how many gin and tonics she'd had.

'I suppose you think it's a picnic being married to an altruist like Rob. I suppose you looked at him the other night and you thought, "What a nice chap, so kind and caring – how wonderful it must be to come home to someone like that after a hard day's struggle with the bank manager."' She swallowed her gin and tonic. 'Well, a lot you know. What I get when I come home are ghastly tales about revolting children with learning disabilities whose appalling mothers have been beaten up by their boyfriends. Serve 'em right is what I say.' She leaned forward confidentially. 'Do you know, I've been married twice, but really I wish I hadn't bothered. You'd be better off getting yourself a new secretary or a dishwasher. They'd be so much more useful in the long run, wouldn't they?' She allowed herself a short peal of laughter. 'Must go. Appointment with a client.'

'Wait – about the Will: do you know if Rick was thinking of changing it?'

'How would I know? Listen, let me give you a piece of advice.'

I leaned forward eagerly. 'What's that?'

'Don't eat here,' she hissed, and made for the exit.

In the doorway, she collided with Wayne.

'Nice set of pins on that one,' he remarked, appreciatively, as she sauntered off to the car park in her tight little black skirt.

We ordered drinks and food and carried our drinks out to the garden, which had an uninterrupted view over cabbage fields to the bypass. I was beginning to get a bad feeling about this place. There had been hardly anything on the menu that didn't either have chips with it or come in a basket, and the tables and chairs were made of a particularly nasty plastic. In fact, I was just wondering whether I ought to apologize to Wayne for having suggested it, when he leaned back in his chair, surveyed the other diners at their wet plastic tables, admired the distant view of the green and yellow BP station on the bypass, and smiled affectionately at the sparrows gathering on the high-voltage power lines soaring above us.

'Ah, this is the life,' he remarked. 'Sun, blue skies and a beautiful woman buying me lunch. If there's anything else a man could ask for, I don't know what it is.'

'Oh, good.'

'So go on then, what's this exciting information in the Rick Monday murder case you can't talk to Tipping about?'

I produced the letters from the deranged groupie and thrust them towards him. I couldn't wait for him to finish reading them. I watched his brow furrow thoughtfully as he pored over the letter that had been written to the *Herald*. He picked up the second letter. 'You can probably get latent fingerprints off them,' I suggested, 'and the glue on the envelopes might have saliva in it. You could do genetic testing.'

Wayne suddenly put down both letters, even though he couldn't possibly have finished reading the second one. 'Glue off the envelopes – Christ! You've been watching too much television.'

'Why? What do you mean?'

'Well, in the first place, we don't send anything away for genetic testing unless we're pretty sure of getting a result – it costs too much. And in the second place, even if there was enough saliva mixed with the glue to warrant running a test – which I'm not sure there would be – and even if you're going to tell me you know the address and telephone number of the writer, I'm 95 per cent certain he or she had nothing to do with the murder. OK, the letters look pretty nasty on the face of it, but it's like suicide notes, isn't it? If you write it down, you're not serious about doing it.' He pushed the letters back across the table towards me. 'My guess is these were written by some miserable, lonely old biddy without a life. Probably she offered herself to your friend Rick once a long time ago and he rejected her. You know the type – some dim-witted, bored . . .'

'Supermarket checkout operator?' I suggested, angrily.

'Yes. That's it. That's it exactly.'

I was furious, but just at that moment, our food arrived.

The beef stroganoff we had ordered turned out not to be beef stroganoff at all, but a sort of tomatoey stew mottled with curdled cream and reheated on a bed of rice. I was plucking up the courage to complain about it, when Wayne said, 'This looks good! Let's tuck in, shall we?' and picked up his fork and began mixing the sauce into the rice. 'Mmm, this is great. Tell you what, I'll bet you're a good cook, aren't you? I'll bet your friend what's-his-name rushes home from work every night to see what you've got on the go for him, doesn't he?' He took a large mouthful of the stew, and continued, between bites, 'My wife does everything in the microwave. She's got me so conditioned to the bleeps the bloody thing makes that every time our computer in the office starts up I look for the brown sauce. By the way . . .' he paused to extract a piece of gristle from between his teeth, 'how is everything these days between you and what's-his-name? Pete, isn't it?'

'Yes. As a matter of fact, we're getting married.'

Wayne dropped his fork.

'Really? Are you having me on or something?'

'No. Why should I be?'

'Well, why would you want to do a stupid thing like that? Have you gone nuts? You've got everything! What do you want to chuck it all away for?'

I was taken aback. 'I don't think I *am* chucking anything away.'

'Don't you? Oh, come on! Think about it. You're where everyone else would like to be. You've got your kids and your husband off your back. You can go anywhere, do anything – be anybody you like. Don't you know how many people would give their right arm to be in your position?' He reached for his drink. 'If you want to know the truth, I really admire you.'

I was stunned. No one had ever said they admired me before. 'What do you mean?'

Wayne blushed slightly. He opened his mouth, raised his glass, and poured a quarter pint of lager down his throat. He looked embarrassed and slightly annoyed. 'Oh, come on, what do you think I mean? I mean, I wish I'd got some of your guts. I wish I'd got the courage to do what you've done. I wish I could see some way out of the hole I've dug myself into. I wish . . . Well, never mind. My wife pisses me off, if you must know. So does the job, so does every bloody thing.'

There was an uncomfortable silence, during which something strange and alarming happened to the cruets on the table, Wayne's shirt, the beef stroganoff and the sparrows on the overhead cables. They all jumped up, nodded their heads to me, and then sat down again as if to a round of applause. I knew that in some subtle way neither they nor anything else would ever look the same again. I began to feel a tiny bit queasy. I had never seen myself as a role model for anyone's rebellion, and I didn't like it.

Wayne resumed eating.

'You didn't finish telling me why you're so certain Rick wasn't murdered by the writer of these letters,' I prompted, after a moment or two.

'Oh, neither I did.' He looked relieved. 'Right. Well, strictly off the record, I know it wasn't your little friend with the typewriter, because I know who did do it.'

'Really?'

He grinned. 'Don't get excited. I don't mean we've found his autograph at the crime scene, but as good as. This guy's a real pro. It's definitely the same man who's been responsible for all the other burglaries over the last six months.'

'Oh.' I frowned.

'We're still pretty sure he's local, but we don't think he's part of the usual villain fraternity, because none of the stuff he's nicked is turning up where we'd expect it to. He may not even have any previous convictions. We think he's probably been at it for years, but for some reason he stepped up his activities last Christmas.'

I thought about this for a moment.

Wayne tucked into his lunch. 'Anyway, after the murder we reinvestigated about three hundred burglaries, hoping to find a link. We went over literally hundreds of statements and reinterviewed dozens of witnesses. You see, there are always people who fall over themselves to tell you about odd-looking

144

guys they saw hanging around prior to the event, wearing this or that outfit, or driving a particular car. Most of the time, you just make notes and file them away. Well, you couldn't go out and arrest every middle-aged man carrying a large bag and wearing a woolly hat on the strength of a couple of witnesses' statements, could you?'

I frowned again. 'What do you mean? The man in the woolly hat had nothing to do with the murder or the burglaries.'

Wayne frowned, too. 'What do *you* mean? He's our prime suspect.'

I laughed. 'But he can't be! He just happened to be in the lane that night.'

There was a long silence.

'Let's go back a bit, shall we,' said Wayne, a slight edge to his voice. 'I'm telling you that the man with the woolly hat and the bag is our prime suspect because he's been described by at least a dozen witnesses over the past few months – and you're saying he didn't do it. Does that mean you know who he is?'

Slowly, my stomach did a three-point turn.

'Look, I think there must be some sort of misunderstanding, actually. *I* meant the man the couple in the Audi saw – the one with the woolly hat and the bag who fell on their car. *He* can't have had anything to do with the murder or any of the other burglaries.'

'What are you talking about? Of course he did. I don't know why you have a problem with this. Look, we've got enough on this guy to put him away for years for burglary – never mind the murder. If we can get into his wardrobe, I'll bet we find a nice selection of woolly sweaters to match up to our fibre collection. The lab reports came back this morning. All the fibres are from something called double-knitting wool.'

'What?'

'Double-knitting wool. Apparently it's what old ladies use to make hideous jumpers with.'

For a moment, I thought I was going to faint. In fact, I

rather wished I could. How could I have been so gullible? *Ted Kitchen*. His shifty eyes, his refusal to talk to the police about the keys, his attempts to extract money from me for stories about Rick, his feet in the damp brown socks slithering about on the pavement . . .

I'd followed him into the woods and threatened to report him to the police. If I hadn't backed off, I might at this very moment be lying on the Common with my throat cut, bleeding into the undergrowth. If I wasn't so gullible, I'd be dead.

'What's up?' demanded Wayne.

'The man you're looking for – I do know who he is. He lost his job last Christmas. In fact, he's lost lots of jobs. He used to be a window cleaner, he's got tons of local knowledge . . .' It was all horribly obvious now I thought about it. 'And it's his mother who does the knitting. His name's Ted Kitchen.'

Wayne's mouth fell open, revealing an overcooked mushroom. I leaned forward urgently.

'Your burglar. The murderer! He lives on the Dene Estate!'

There was an agonized silence, then Wayne seized his fork and began shovelling food into his mouth indiscriminately.

'What number?' he demanded.

'Number?'

'On the Dene Estate.'

'It's number 73 I think. Listen –'

'Good. You not eating that?' He snatched my plate. 'This is great, you don't know what you're missing!'

'Well, I know, but . . .'

'The calories, right? Listen, you're a marvel and I love you. I've got to go.' He leapt to his feet.

'But Wayne, wait, I think I may have –' What did he mean about the calories? 'Please, wait –' He kissed me on the head, hugged me, and vaulted athletically over the fence to the car park.

I raced after him the long way, via the gate, but by the time I reached the car park he'd already started up his engine and whirled the Escort carelessly out of its space in that macho way men have, as though they and the car are all of a piece.

146

I waved my arms frantically. 'Wayne, I didn't tell you all of it! Please wait! The thing is – I've tipped him off!' I shouted, desperately.

But I don't think he heard.

11

Pete put down the phone.

'No news, I'm afraid. They're still searching his allotment shed – it's a regular Aladdin's cave, apparently – but no one's seen him since Thursday.'

Sun streamed in through the kitchen window, and glinted off next door's mower as it went through its Saturday morning paces. I hoped Pete wouldn't notice how miserable I felt.

'They've found the cash from Tangley House, but there's no sign of the gold disc or the statuette. Look, I've got to go or I'll miss my flight. I wish I didn't have to, but I do. Come here a minute.'

Obediently I abandoned the washing-up and kissed him.

'Will you please ring me this evening?' I begged.

'Of course I will. Are you OK?'

I kept thinking about standing in the woods with Ted Kitchen. 'Of course I am.'

'Good. You've got to put it behind you, you know. It's like getting back into a car after you've had an accident.'

'I've never had an accident. Not a bad one.'

'No, that's because you don't take risks. Keep it up.' He picked up his overnight bag. 'Oh, I almost forgot – I got you this.' He delved into his pocket and produced a piece of paper. It was part of a computer printout. 'I don't know if you'll still want it – it's the address we got for Jo Randall. Or rather, it's a next-of-kin address. She worked at St Charles's hospital in Ladbroke Grove for about a year back in the seventies and then she disappeared without leaving a forwarding address. I don't think anybody bothered to look for her – her attendance record at the hospital was pretty appalling.'

'Thank you.' I crumpled the paper into my pocket. 'I do love you.'

'Good. I'll be back tomorrow. You're not crying, are you?'

'Of course I'm not! I'm much too busy to cry.'

When he'd gone, I went upstairs to tidy the bathroom and to feel sorry for myself in front of the mirror, but I got no further than the landing because there, lying beside the linen basket, was a plain buff envelope inscribed with the word 'Mum' in Julie's handwriting. It looked as if it might have been propped up on the linen basket and fallen off. What on earth was Julie doing, writing notes to me and sealing them up in plain buff envelopes? I threw open the door of her room, and peered through the gloom at an untidy mound in the centre of her bed. The mound wasn't moving. Suddenly fearing the worst – i.e. a heap of pillows under the duvet and Julie gone for ever – I made a grab at the covers, whereupon the untidy mound moaned, said 'Get off!' and farted vigorously.

When I'd got over the shock, I took the envelope downstairs and stared at it. I felt sick. If Julie had something to say that she couldn't bring herself to tell me to my face, it could only be one thing. A whole panorama of agonized discussions with Keith and arguments with the Child Support Agency opened up before me. Almost shaking with foreboding, I ran my finger under the lip of the envelope and tugged at its contents. To my amazement a thick stack of word-processed A4 pages came reluctantly into view. They looked official. I spread the pages out on the coffee table and stared at them. They were photocopies of documents belonging to a firm of solicitors called Amery, Heathcott & Co., High Street, Tipping.

'*Dear Rick,*' began the first letter, which was addressed to Mr E. Monday at Tangley House, Hatchley Heath.

Dear Rick? I did a double-take.

Dear Rick,

It was good to hear from you yesterday, and to learn of your very ambitious plans for the future! I have already taken one or two steps on your behalf, and thought I should put you in the picture straight away.

Firstly, your Will. Attached is a draft which I believe should meet your requirements. You will see that provision has been included for Miss Tina Warrington to receive a pecuniary legacy in the sum of £10,000 free of tax, and that Miss Warrington, as you requested, is also to receive your 'collection of memorabilia connected with your career with the group Bad Monday'. I feel I should point out that this is dangerously loose wording, and I would urge you to compile a complete list of items for inclusion with the final version.

I have, as you requested, made provision for Rob to receive the sum of £15,000, and for the residue of your real and personal estate to be bequeathed to the Acorn Trust.

Excitedly, I glanced at the top of the letter; it was dated ten days before Rick's death.

As regards your plans for Tangley House, of course I bow to John Bradman's superior knowledge of these things, but frankly I do not believe that getting planning permission for the venture you describe is going to be the 'piece of cake' you seem to assume. As we discussed, I have instructed a colleague who is more expert in this field than I, to initiate enquiries on your behalf. He has already confirmed the fact that some years ago the Planning Committee did grant permission for the Sherman Language School without a qualm. However, I have to say that in my opinion a project which is concerned with the reform of young male offenders will be quite a different kettle of fish, and I would urge you to avoid any further financial outlay until the position is clearer.

It is my experience that people who are as committed to a cause as John Bradman obviously is, sometimes permit themselves to be blinded by their own enthusiasm,

underestimating the difficulties that may present and, if you
will excuse the colloquialism, 'carrying on regardless'!

Look forward to seeing you for lunch next week. Unless
I hear from you to the contrary, I shall prepare your new
Will in accordance with the attached draft, and bring it
along with me for signature.

Best regards

The letter was signed Henry Amery, Junior.

I re-read it immediately, twice. The letter seemed to confirm that my interpretation of the word 'Will' in Rick's diary had been correct, but this hardly mattered. If Rick had been intending to convert Tangley House into some sort of refuge for young criminals, it would have been the story of the decade as far as Hatchley Heath was concerned – it would have made the activity centre row look like a storm in a teacup. What were the chances that the project would still go ahead, and would Mr Heslop let me follow it up?

Eagerly, I riffled through the rest of the papers. They seemed to constitute Henry Amery Junior's entire file on Rick. He had acted as his solicitor for the best part of twenty years, corresponding with other solicitors about contracts and copyright, and handling the purchase and subsequent sale of a flat in Notting Hill. He had also acted for Rick when he'd purchased Tangley House. And, back in 1979, he'd drawn up a previous Will. There was a bad photocopy of the draft of this document, with alterations scrawled all over it. As far as I could see Rick had bequeathed the bulk of his assets to Shelter, with a lump sum of £3,000 going to Rob, and a similar amount to his mother.

Julie yawned in the doorway.

'Well? What do you think? Am I Mata Hari or am I Mata Hari?' she remarked, sleepily.

I was a bit surprised she'd even heard of Mata Hari, but then I remembered Trivial Pursuit. I didn't know what to say. 'How on earth did you get these? Good God, these are a solicitor's confidential documents!' I gasped, as the full reality of what Julie had presented me with dawned.

151

'I know. But you needn't worry. I haven't been shinning up drainpipes in a balaclava. I got what's-his-name to get them for me – you know, that funny-looking boy up the road that Pete says fancies me, the one he got to fix the mower. His mum works at Amery Heathcott and he works there in the evenings doing the filing.'

I hadn't known Pete had got someone else to fix the mower; I'd thought he'd done it himself. I frowned. I still didn't know what to say. Julie had incited someone else into the commission of an illegal act, and this seemed almost worse than shinning up drainpipes. Eventually I said, 'Good heavens!'

'Well, I thought you needed a bit of help. I thought it would be nice if *I* helped *you* for a change.'

'I see.' If Amery Heathcott found out about this, they might prosecute. They would certainly sack what's-his-name and his mother. But at the moment I didn't feel like spoiling Julie's day by pointing this out. 'Thank you. Um . . . I don't know what to say.'

'That's all right. Don't mention it!' She stabbed a button on the hifi, and began jigging about to the tail-end of an advertising jingle. 'There you are, you see; even if I fail all my GCSE's I'll still be able to get a job at MI5!'

I decided a tactical withdrawal to the kitchen would be a good idea, so I thanked her again, scooped up the bundle of Amery Heathcott papers, and offered to cook her bacon and scrambled eggs. In the kitchen, I stuffed the papers out of sight behind the bread bin. Just having them in the house probably constituted a serious offence, then there'd be conspiracy, incitement, concealment – and God knew what else. I tried ramming the bread bin back against the wall as far as it would go, but you could still see the corner of the envelope, and a trail of mouldy crumbs led out from beneath the bin. I'd have to say it was all my idea. Better still, after Julie had gone upstairs with her breakfast, I'd take the papers out on to the patio and burn them, and then, even if what's-his-name suddenly took it into his head to confess to someone, there wouldn't be any evidence.

In the living room, the radio began blaring out a news item concerning the police hunt for Ted Kitchen. I gazed out of the window and listened as I whipped up the eggs. Checks were to be made at all ports along the south coast, and they were trying to trace Ted's car, an old brown Ford, which had last been seen heading towards Hudderston and, presumably, the Channel. I frowned. This was silly. Ted couldn't be making for the Continent. He hadn't even gone to his allotment shed to collect the proceeds of the robbery at Tangley House, and he probably didn't have a passport. I couldn't imagine him on one of the Costas. They gave out his registration number, and I watched a blackbird take off from our fence and soar carelessly towards the skyline. If only I hadn't gone to work at the *Herald* I would almost certainly at this very moment be at my old sink watching blackbirds take off from my old fence – and Julie would be in her lovely room with the fitted desk and wardrobe Keith had made for her. She would never, for one instant, have contemplated charming the neighbours or their children into committing illegal acts for her. I watched the blackbird fly off over the roofs of the houses in Wodeland Avenue, past the serrated outline of the Magnum Print Works, and disappear in a scrawl of rooftops beyond the glass tower attached to the Stag House office block. The office block caught my eye for a moment. At night, all the tower lights were left on, even though no one ever went up or down the stairs, not even the security guard who sat watching television in a little cubbyhole next to the foyer.

Suddenly, I forgot about the blackbird, about the eggs, and about Julie. I thought instead of the security guard in his cubbyhole with his television screens and his flask of tea and a place to put his feet up. I'd driven by there at night and seen him. He was almost completely isolated from the outside world, no one could get to him unless he pressed buttons on his control panel. He'd got everything.

Ted Kitchen used to be a security guard at Anderson's. Anderson's was now abandoned and empty; nobody would go there ever, for any reason. Anxiously I tried to recall the conversation I'd had with Ted in the woods: I was sure he'd said something about being able to get in *under the wire* at the old factory. If he could, it would surely be a convenient place for him to stash loot – perhaps that was where he'd hidden the gold disc and the statuette. He might even have prepared a bolt hole for himself – somewhere he could hide out, if he ever had to, while his criminal contacts arranged false passports and so forth.

Supposing he was there now, and no one else had thought of looking?

12

DS Willis wasn't at his desk when I rang Tipping police station.

'He's down in the custody area, love. Assisting with an interview.'

'But this is important. It's about Ted Kitchen, the suspect in the Rick Monday murder case. I think I know where he is. I think he'll be in the old Anderson factory where he used to work as a night watchman.'

There was silence for a moment.

'How are you spelling Anderson?'

'What?'

'I'm writing out a slip. How are you spelling Anderson?'

'Look, it's Anderson, as in – Anderson! It's on the Lime Way Industrial Estate. Will you tell DS Willis that Chris Martin from the *Tipping Herald* phoned?'

There was another long silence. 'Martin? Did you say Martin? From the Tipping *what*?'

I hung up and jumped into the Mini, armed with a street map of Hudderston. If I got to Anderson's first, I could write up an eyewitness report of the arrest, and this would go some way towards putting things right with Mr Heslop. We'd be one up on Three Counties Radio and the *Hudderston Advertiser*, and if Willis didn't like it, that was just too bad.

Twenty minutes later I drove through the uninspiring portals of the Lime Way Industrial Estate, and the depressing headline of the *Hudderston Advertiser's* New Year lead story flashed before my eyes: 'Bleak New Year for Hudderston as three more firms announce closure'. A signboard beside the road displayed six blank spaces where the names of six businesses should have been, and old copies of the *Sun* and the *Herald*'s classified section drifted across the cracked road surface like tumbleweed. Yellow flowers of ragwort and dandelions sprouted from the pavements. It was the sort of scene that Ernst, our photographer, would have snapped gleefully, entitled 'Industrial Decay' or 'The Legacy of Thatcherism', and entered for a photo-journalism award.

I parked on the concrete forecourt of the complex of buildings that had once housed Anderson Electronics, and got out of the car. The door to Reception ('All visitors must first report to Reception') was barred and padlocked, and a glance through its grimy glass panel revealed a large empty space littered with wastepaper. Access to the rest of the complex was via the main gates and looked impossible: the gates were chained and padlocked, and they'd been topped off with shiny new barbed wire. I rattled them a bit, and the 'To Let' and '5 mph' notices attached to them shuddered noisily against their fixings. There didn't seem to be any way for anyone to get in.

I started back towards the car. On the forecourt of 'Veejay's Special Application Paints' were several teenage boys clustered round the rear end of an old Austin Allegro. They seemed to be intent on something in its boot. I didn't like the look of them. They had strange, aggressive haircuts and their clothes looked as if they'd been through an industrial blender, but there wasn't anyone else around, so I decided to give them a try.

'Excuse me!' I shouted, running towards them. 'I'm sorry to bother you, but I wonder if you can help me?'

There was a flurry of activity around the boot of the car. The tallest of the boys, who wore a small gold ring in his right nostril, swung round with his arms outstretched as if to conceal what was going on behind him. I tried to convince myself they were all off-duty trainee accountants checking over their golfing equipment.

'Would you mind?' I asked again, stopping a few feet short of the group. 'Have you seen a man hanging around

156

in the old Anderson factory? Someone who might be sleeping rough?'

One of the boys slammed down the boot of the Allegro and held it in place. I caught a quick glimpse of its contents – a collection of ladies' handbags and purses. It was too late to back off. I giggled, as though they were playing some sort of joke on someone and I was in on it.

'What you talking about?' demanded Nose-ring, aggressively. 'Why you asking us? What d'you think we are – social workers?'

'No, of course not! I'm a reporter. I'm on a story, but it doesn't matter, really.'

Nose-ring turned his head slightly and a look passed between the group, slipping beneath half-closed eyelids and tugging nastily at the corners of mouths. They all glanced in the direction of Anderson's forecourt. Nose-ring let his gaze fall to my feet, then climb slowly over the rest of me.

'The police'll be here any minute,' I remarked, casually.

They all laughed.

'No, really – they will!'

'Why? They after that old bloke? That pervert? That one that used to come here last winter? I don't believe you. They're not going to bother with him.' They laughed again. 'You're some sort of do-gooder, are you? Is that what you are? Well, why don't you do some good for us, eh! How much money you got?'

I decided to pretend I hadn't heard the last bit. 'Not to worry, thanks for your help.' I turned and started back towards the car. I'd taken about three steps when I was suddenly overcome by the most peculiar sensation. All the hairs on the back of my neck rose and a prickle ran down my spine like an electric charge. I don't know how, but I knew that Nose-ring was behind me, with his fist raised above my head, and that what was on his mind was not inviting me back to his place for tea and cucumber sandwiches. For once, I didn't waste time thinking how stupid I would look if I was wrong. I ducked out of the way, and the next thing I knew I was dancing a desperate tango in the dust with Nose-ring, dodging his grimy fists and Doc Marten-clad feet.

'You cow,' he panted, after we'd gone a couple of rounds. 'Me and my mates here want a cup of tea. You going to give us some money, or what?'

I was terrified. 'I've got ten pounds you can have.'

'Let's see it.'

We stopped tangoing. I reached for my credit card wallet, which had a ten-pound note in it I'd kept aside for Julie's dinner money. I pulled the note out and offered it to him at arm's length, hoping he'd take it and leave me to make a run for it, but instead he seized me by the wrist and twisted the wallet out of my hand.

'You're a bit of a tight-arsed cow, you are. You don't care if me and my mates starve to death, do you?' He let go of me, and ran his finger over my credit cards. The others barred my exit. His face slowly crumpled with disgust. 'Jesus, is this all you got? What's this – a *Debenhams* card?'

'You can have it if you want it –'

He threw the wallet back at me contemptuously, eschewing the Debenhams card and an M & S card. 'Thought you was a reporter. Ain't you got no phone?'

'No.'

''Course she's got a phone,' put in one of the others. 'They've always got phones!'

I shook my head desperately. 'No, we haven't – not on the *Herald*!'

They began nudging one another and whispering amongst themselves, pulling the ten-pound note this way and that. I couldn't hear what they were saying, but I didn't like the sound of it. When they'd finished they all looked at me and smirked.

'Right, fat bitch, we're going to give you what you want,' said Nose-ring.

And at that moment, I thought I was going to faint. It seems embarrassing now, but I could think of only one thing they might all think I'd want.

'Come on, we ain't got all day!' They began circling round

158

me, getting closer, their stubble and their acne and their tattoos brushing up against me.

'Oh, *please* . . .'

'Please? Yeah, that's better – you should've said that in the beginning: *Please can I give you some money!*' He mimicked my tone, and they all laughed. 'Come on, don't piss about – give us your car key, you bitch!'

'My car key?'

'Yeah, *your car key*, bitch.'

I don't know why, but I felt almost grateful to them. I said, 'Thank you, thank you', and thrust the keys towards him.

He smiled. He didn't take the keys. 'Good. And you've never seen me, right? Me or any of me mates.'

'No, I've never seen you!'

'And you're going to walk home – right? You see over there? That's a footpath. It goes to the station. Got it?'

'Yes!' I cast a quick glance over my shoulder in the direction he was pointing.

His fingers closed over the keys. 'And there's something else you better not forget. I know what *you* look like.'

Before he could change his mind, I let go of the keys and thanked him again and set off in the direction he'd indicated. I could hear them laughing, but I didn't care. As soon as I was out of sight, I broke into a run, and I didn't stop until I reached the railway line. They could have my car, and the jacket on the back seat, and all my cassette tapes, and I wouldn't say anything to anybody. I'd pretend my car had disappeared from Tesco's car park while I was shopping – no one would ever know. Anything so long as I never had to see Nose-ring again.

I collapsed, panting and shaking, against the rusty fence at the back of the Anderson factory. How could this have happened? I felt so guilty – it was all my fault. And it wasn't fair. I was a liberal; I'd always felt sorry for boys like Nose-ring: I'd never voted for the Conservative Party or short sharp shocks or the return of the eleven-plus or anything like that. Those boys had got the wrong person. How could they do this to *me?*

Through the fence, I could see the forecourt where I'd left the Mini. In fact, if it hadn't been for a row of storage sheds blocking the view I would have been able to watch while Nose-ring drove my car away. Except that he was probably already on the other side of Hudderston, sneering at my Simply Red tapes and cursing the window handle for jamming. And then I began to feel angry. Why *should* they get away with stealing and defiling my things? I could give a good description of them to the police; I could do a photofit. If I could only get to a phone, I stood a good chance of getting my car back and putting those creeps behind bars where they belonged.

And then I remembered something. On the drive over from Tipping, the Mini had overheated; after I had switched off, bits of it kept on vibrating and there was steam coming out of somewhere. It had briefly crossed my mind even then to wonder whether it would start again without divine intervention. With luck, Nose-ring wouldn't be able to get it started.

A train roared by on the embankment overhead. If I went back to the forecourt now, and they were still there, struggling to start my car, they might kill me – or worse. I tugged at the fence, wondering how solid it was. If I could get into the factory grounds, I'd have a better view of the forecourt, but the boys wouldn't be able to see me or get to me. Without stopping to consider the possible consequences of breaking and entering and committing criminal damage, I pulled and pushed at a damaged section of wire until I'd made a hole in it big enough to crawl through. Actually, it looked as though someone or something had already started the hole off. I wriggled through the gap and made my way cautiously across the old car park, which was littered with broken glass and plastic cups that had been thrown out of passing trains. I could see part of the forecourt now, and there was definitely something red on it just about where I'd parked the Mini. I moved stealthily along the row of storage sheds, hiding behind them, picking my way across lengths of plastic piping that were rolling about in

160

the breeze. It looked as though someone had broken into the sheds and dragged out the piping, and then for some reason dumped the whole lot on the road. They had also smashed all the windows and pulled the doors off their hinges. But when I got to the third shed, the one backing on to the forecourt, things were different. The windows had been boarded over with pieces of newish-looking hardboard, and the door had been screwed back on its hinges. Even the door knob had a shine on it, as though someone had handled it recently and quite frequently – and that was when, for the first time since the incident on the forecourt, I remembered Ted Kitchen. A shudder ran down my spine despite the heat. Ted could be in there now, lurking amongst the cobwebs with a knife in his hand. Except, Nose-ring had said he hadn't seen Ted since the previous winter. I stood up on tiptoe and tried to peer through a chink in the hardboard covering the window. It was pitch dark, no sign of life. There were dark shapes of things in there, but they didn't seem to be moving or breathing. They could be rubbish – or they could be stolen heirlooms left behind by Ted.

Curiously, I opened the door and peered round it. I could just make out bricks and tins and broken glass on the floor, and two packing cases and a dark bundle of something lying in a corner. I decided I ought to take a closer look at the dark bundle – it might turn out to be a sack stuffed with Georgian silver – and that was when I noticed the odd thing. Well, it wasn't really an odd thing: it was a very mundane thing. It was pale orange and shiny, and it was sticking out of the top of one of the packing cases. It was the sort of thing you saw every time you opened your emergency store cupboard at ten o'clock at night when all the shops were closed.

It was an unopened packet of Jacob's Cream Crackers. I don't know why, but I stepped forward to pick it up for closer inspection – and a dark shape suddenly rose up from behind the packing cases and made a dash for the door.

It was Ted. I got a brief flash of his wizened figure before the door slammed shut behind him and plunged the shed into darkness.

At first, I thought he had locked me in and run off.

'Who's that? Is that you, Terry?' he shouted, and I knew immediately that he was still *inside* the shed, right by the door. 'What you trying to do – give us an 'eart attack? Where you been? I been waiting for you for hours.'

I had no idea what I should do next.

'What you playing at? Terry? Is that you? Who's there?' He smelled like the inside of Richard's sock bag after a week at scout camp. I dropped to the floor so he wouldn't see me in the tiny shaft of light let in by the window, and picked up a brick.

'Terry?' He stepped forward. 'Terry – come on, mate, I got you the money –' Suddenly he lunged forward and grabbed the packing case I was hiding behind, pushing at it aggressively. 'Don't muck about. I can't take no more of this!' I could feel his questing hand skim the side of my face. He might not have been on to me – I wasn't sure – but I wasn't going to take any chances. I leapt up and lashed out at where I imagined his face to be with the brick. The force of the impact ran up my arm and wrenched the brick out of my hand. I heard it squish through something soft and stop with a dull thud against bone.

I made a dive for the door. I didn't care what I'd done to Ted; after all, he was a murderer. He had fallen heavily and was quite possibly unconscious. But then the door wouldn't open. He must have bolted it and I didn't know where the bolt was. Frantically I began exploring all round the door knob in search of something that felt like a bolt.

'What you doing?' He was getting up. 'What you hit me for?'

The bolt had to be at the top of the door. My fingers closed over it.

'I'm bleeding! I think you killed me!'

I wrenched open the door – and then I made my big mistake: I turned round to look at him. I'd never hit anyone with a brick before – or anything else for that matter – and

162

I suppose I wanted to see what the damage would look like. The right side of Ted's face was streaming blood and I had a nasty feeling his ear was hanging off.

I backed out of the shed in horror.

'I know you!' he shouted, his voice taut with pain. 'You've cut my ear off! Why'd you do that? I never done nothing to you. You're that reporter woman, aren't you? Help me – get me a bandage or something!'

Ted slumped to the floor, pressing to his ear something disgusting-looking that had probably once been a handkerchief. I'd read somewhere that even quite minor ear injuries bled profusely. Or at least, I thought it was ears.

'I'm telling you, missus, I never did nothing to Mr Monday. You've got it all wrong. Go on, give us an 'and.'

I shook my head, backing off still further. 'The police have been to your allotment shed. They're on their way here now.'

'But I told you, they've got it all wrong, it wasn't me that killed Mr Monday – he was dead when I got there!' He lurched dizzily to one side, the blood soaking out between his fingers. 'All right, I admit I done a few burglaries now and then – to help out with the mortgage, like – but I never hurt no one! Mr Monday was dead when I found him, missus, and that's God's own truth!'

I shook my head again. I was torn between the desire to get away from Ted as fast as I could and the fear that he might die from blood loss and it would be my fault. I went back into the shed.

'Look, I took the money – I admit it – but it wasn't in the study like you said in the paper; it was upstairs in his bedroom! Do you hear me? In his bedroom! Well, don't you get it? I could've gone up them stairs and helped meself to the money and gone back out the way I come in in two shakes of a donkey's whatsit – *but he was already dead!*'

'What do you mean, the money wasn't in his study? I saw it myself!'

He snorted weakly, splattering blood. 'No, it wasn't, I'm telling you! Look, Mr Monday used to pay me in cash, I seen where he kept his money and stuff. It was in a little cabinet next to his bed. I'm not daft! Do you think I'd have gone up against a big bloke like Mr Monday for a measly five thousand quid? I've got more than that stashed away in a Phostrogen packet behind me F1 geraniums!'

I made a mental note to pass this information on to the police.

'Listen, I know Tangley House like the back of me hand. I could've got in and out of there sweet as a nut without Mr Monday knowing a thing about it. They're all deaf, them rock stars – I read it in the papers. You've got to believe me. I done a few burglaries and I've got a dodgy MOT on me car, but that's it! I never hurt no one. Not even that silly cow who come back from her bingo early the other week. I could've biffed her one, but I didn't. It's not my fault she's got a dicky heart, is it?'

He pulled another handkerchief from his pocket. It was so encrusted with some dried fluid I'd rather not think about that it crackled when he put it to his ear. He seemed to be getting weaker.

'You listen to me,' he groaned. 'Mr Monday was dead when I found him. The murderer, the person that done it to him, he ran off while I was upstairs looking for the money –'

'Ah! – I thought you said you knew exactly where the money was?' I interrupted triumphantly.

'Yeah, but I had to make it look like I didn't.' He broke off to moan to himself. 'I had to ransack the place! Otherwise Mr Monday would've known it was me, wouldn't he? Look, I saw the light on in his study. I knew he was in there – there weren't no other lights on. I'd already watched the house for a bit to make sure he was by himself. He had his music up real loud, you could hear it miles off. I reckoned he must be doing a bit of composing. Why don't you ask Mr Fletcher if you don't believe me?'

'Why should I ask Mr Fletcher?'

''Cos he'll tell you. He was doing his nut about the noise, wasn't he? I saw him. He was going to go round and complain, but his missus stopped him. Well, I s'pose it was

164

about the noise. They had a right old barney on their front lawn. I had to wait for 'em to go in.'

'But the Fletchers were out! They told the police.'

'Oh, no, they weren't. You ask 'em about it. I'm telling you the truth, missus. Why would I lie about a thing like that? Ain't you got no elastoplast?'

I was baffled. I began rummaging absently through my handbag, even though I knew I hadn't got any elastoplast. 'I don't see how you can have seen the Fletchers on their front lawn,' I said, suspiciously, 'if you broke into the house through the back.'

''Cos I checked out the front of the house first, didn't I? I don't just go barging into things like a bloody kid! What d'you take me for? I never went round the back till I was sure the Fletchers had buggered off, then I had to go the long way – all the way round along the lane, 'cos the side gate was locked. Well, I knew I could get in through the back, no problem. And I never saw a soul, or heard nothing except the music. I goes up the stairs in the dark, with me torch battery on the blink, and that bloody racket making me head ache. It should've been sweet as a nut, like I said. I seen his watch and a couple of rings in a glass jar, but I never took 'em, 'cos I liked Mr Monday. Then I goes downstairs – and that's when I seen the study door open and Mr Monday lying there. It was *'orrible*, missus! Blood everywhere – up the walls and everything!' His eyes bulged and glinted in the semi-darkness, and he began to shiver. 'Whoever done it was a maniac. I'm right glad I never run into them. They'd have done for me, too!'

I pulled a bundle of make-up stained tissues from my bag. I was beginning to wonder if Ted might just be telling the truth.

'I reckon, whoever it was must've heard me upstairs and run off in a panic,' he went on. 'Maybe they was going through Mr Monday's pockets or his desk or something. Maybe they was after the money, too, but they didn't know where to look for it! I mean, I don't know how they could've heard me – not with all that din – but I s'pose there was gaps in the music and Mr Monday's floorboards always did creak something rotten. Anyway, they must've run out through them French doors 'cos the draught blew the study door open – and that's how I seen inside!'

'I see. Are you *sure* you didn't see anyone else hanging around? What time was it when you saw the Fletchers? D'you think someone would've been able to let themselves into the house and kill Mr Monday while you were walking round the house along Tangley Lane?'

'I don't know, do I? All I know is what I told you. It gave me a right shock. I think I wet myself. I tried to help Mr Monday, but when I seen he was dead I ran out into the garden and fell arse over tit in a flower bed!'

I glanced down at Ted's feet – his size-seven feet clad in army boots.

He sat up suddenly. 'Look, missus, you've got to help me! The police don't care who done it, they just want to pin it on someone. That's how they work. My mate Terry said he'd get me on a boat . . . Look, I pulled the knife out of him, didn't I? I did me best!'

I tried to think quickly. Ted was beginning to look deathly pale, and if someone with first-aid experience didn't attend to him soon I had a feeling I could end up on a manslaughter charge. The make-up tissues were disintegrating in my tense grasp, but at the bottom of my handbag there was a crumpled panty shield. If only I could think of some way of attaching this to Ted's ear I might be able to stem the flow of blood.

'And there's another thing,' said Ted, suddenly. 'You put in the paper that I took Mr Monday's gold record and a statue, but I never!'

And at that moment a voice shouted '*Now!*', and suddenly, everything went black. Before I could work out what had happened, I was face down in a damp, smelly and not particularly soft piece of upholstery (it was Ted's mattress), and several other things were hurtling in the same direction and landing noisily all around. One or two of them landed on top of me, including, as I realized a few seconds later, a large sweaty man who wore Brut aftershave to very little effect.

'Is it him?' demanded a voice.

'Yeah, it's him!'

I tried to open my mouth, but nothing would come out of it.

'Bastard!' said a third voice. There followed the sound of several heavy kicks being delivered to a soft object. I was sure the soft object wasn't me, but I hurt anyway. All over. And someone's foot was on top of my head.

'Edward Kitchen, I'm arresting you on suspicion of burglary, aggravated burglary, and murder. You have the right to remain silent, but if you do not mention now –'

The man with the Brut aftershave suddenly shifted his position and put a hand on my thigh.

'– something which you later rely on in your defence, *creep* –'

The hand went up towards my crotch.

'Sarge!' The word vibrated through my back.

'Shut up! I've forgotten where I bloody was now. You *disgusting* little creep, you'll just have to figure out the rest of it your bloody self!'

'Sarge –'

'What is it?'

'Sarge, there's a woman down here!'

'*What*?'

Slowly, the foot was removed from my head, the hand from my crotch, and the constable from my back. I lay still for a minute, hoping they might all go away, but it was no use. I turned over and sat up.

For a long moment, DS Willis didn't say anything. Then he kicked me. Deliberately. With his steel-tipped boot. No one said anything. The officer who'd sat on me looked away as if embarrassed and began brushing down his jeans, a train roared by on the embankment, and Ted Kitchen held his cuffed hands to his face and let the blood leak out between his fingers.

'You're dead,' said Willis. 'I hope you know that. You're dead.'

I knew I ought to complain, or explain, or ask him to,

167

but I couldn't work out how to do it, so I got up and walked out.

When I reached the forecourt, the gates were wide open. I couldn't see the Mini at first, because it was boxed in by police cars. All its doors were open and the contents of my glove compartment – two local street maps and the car's insurance documents – were blowing about in the breeze. There was no sign of the Austin Allegro, or of my jacket or the box containing my cassette tapes. Across the bonnet in vibrant blue spray paint someone had daubed what at first appeared to be a still-life depiction of two tomatoes and a cucumber. I examined it briefly, and decided the cucumber looked rather peculiar for a cucumber. It had an odd, bulbous bit at the end. The paint was still wet but, under the gaze of Tipping police, I couldn't quite bring myself to rub at it with a handkerchief.

13

Mr Heslop put down the camera and waited in embarrassed silence for me to cover my bruised shin.

'I don't like this one bit,' he remarked, unhappily. 'This is Tipping – not Los Angeles. Our police may make the odd balls-up occasionally – they're human, for God's sake – but I won't believe they go around beating people up. Not even people like you. Not in Tipping. Anyway, how do you know this burglar friend of yours was telling the truth? Just because he says he didn't commit the murder doesn't mean to say he didn't.'

'No, I know, but it's obvious when you think about it. It explains everything. Ted broke in and took the money, and the person who copied the key killed Rick. I don't know why I didn't think of it before. Look, if Ted was a killer, don't you think he'd've killed *me* when he had the chance?'

Mr Heslop sighed in an oddly wistful sort of way.

'The police haven't found the statuette or the gold disc on Ted, have they? Of course not, because he's a professional burglar, and professional burglars wouldn't touch anything like that. And I told you what he said about the Fletchers. You wait: the police will bring the Fletchers in for questioning. The whole case is wide open! Please, Mr Heslop, let me see if I can find Joanne Randall, the woman who wrote the death threat letters.'

Mr Heslop reached for a packet of Anadin Extra Strong, and began wrestling tablets out of their bubble pack.

'I've got a very old address for her in a small village in Somerset. All the letters were postmarked Somerset. Well, you know what these country places are like. Even if she's moved on from this address someone will be bound to know where she is now.'

'I see.' He considered for a moment. 'All right then. Take the camera and a tape. I'll pay travelling expenses, but not speeding tickets or hotel bills. If you can't find her quickly, or she doesn't want to talk – straight back here and forget it. Understood?'

I leapt to my feet excitedly and made for the door.

'Wait a minute. Are you sure you're up to this?'

'What do you mean?'

'Interviewing nutcases. Because that's what she is, you know.'

I thought about this. He might be right. I promised to do my best.

It was almost midday as I turned off the main road and pointed the car in the direction of a cluster of grey stone cottages huddling together in the corner of a field of young corn. A cold wind razored the corn-tops and wailed through the overhead power cables. In the distance, windscreens twinkled on the motorway. The man at the petrol station had said he was sure Buckle Cottage was *this* side of Curry Norton, and as far as I could see there were no more cottages this side of Curry Norton. In fact, apart from Curry Norton's church spire and the electricity pylons marching off into the distance across the fields, there was nothing to be seen for miles.

I cruised slowly past the cottages, none of which had a name-board attached to it, and parked on the side of the road.

A middle-aged woman wearing Carmen rollers answered my knock. She looked quite pleased to see me.

'Excuse me, I'm looking for Buckle Cottage – a Mrs Alice Randall.'

'Oh, no, dear, she's gone. Buckle Cottage is next door.'

'I see. Do you think you could give me her new address then, please? Or do you think your neighbour could?'

'No, no, dear – I mean she's *gone*. Cancer, I think it was. They buried her up at St Margaret's. Are you a relation?' Her accent was redolent of cream teas, cider, scones, jam and warm fields dotted with hay bales. 'It must've been five years ago, now. The grave'll be in the new part of the churchyard, you should be able to spot it all right.'

'Actually it's *Joanne* Randall I'm after. Would that be her daughter?'

She shook her head, and a curler dropped off. 'I don't know, dear. I'm new here, me. We all are. These used to be tied cottages, and old Alice was one of the last tenants. I don't think she had a daughter. She never had anyone come to visit her except the woman from the social.'

'Are you sure?' I gazed despondently at Buckle Cottage, with its newly painted window frames and freshly washed net curtains. 'Do you suppose it's worth me asking any of your neighbours?'

'Shouldn't think so, dear.'

Suddenly I had a brainwave. Down in the village there would be one of those little shops that sold everything from ankle socks and paraffin to freshly sliced bacon, and whose owner would know everything about everybody. 'Not to worry,' I said. 'I'll ask at the shop.'

She gave me a blank look. I hurried back to the car and drove as fast as I could to the village. It wasn't lunchtime yet and I was already hot on Joanne's trail.

A few minutes later I pulled over not far from a bus stop on the other side of Curry Norton. The village had neither shop nor pub, and its houses all looked as if someone had recently died in them and no one had noticed. I didn't know what to do next. Surely someone must know something about the Randalls. Then I had another brainwave. With difficulty, I wound down my window and reversed the car so that I was alongside the bus shelter.

'Excuse me!' I called, to the elderly couple who were huddled over their shopping bags at the back of the shelter. 'Can you tell me the way to the vicarage?'

They glanced up from their newspapers and stared at me.

'The vi-car,' I repeated, slowly and deliberately. 'I'm look-ing for the vi-car.'

The old man took a deep breath. 'We – haven't – got a vi-car,' he said slowly, enunciating his words with exaggerated care. 'He comes on a ro-ta.'

This was the last straw. No wonder Joanne had left Curry Norton – no shop, no pub, not even a vicar.

'I wonder if you could help me? It's really important. I'm looking for a woman called Joanne Randall who I think used to live at Buckle Cottage.'

The couple exchanged glances, then resumed their blank stares.

'Please, I've come all the way from London!' It was no good mentioning Tipping: no one had ever heard of it. I sighed despairingly.

'I remember Joanne,' said the woman, suddenly, and she smiled, put a finger to her temple and moved it round in a slow circle. 'As a fruitcake,' she added, in case I hadn't got the point. 'Went off to London, didn't she? I remem-ber her catching the bus. Went off with a suitcase, she did.'

'No, she didn't!' protested the old man. 'She married that Timpson boy.'

'She never did! I don't remember that!'

'Yes, you do. Don't you remember that old Ford I had that the exhaust fell off of? I took it over to Long Sheet and it was that Timpson boy that fixed it up. I told you.'

'No, you didn't! It was that Morris Oxford you had all the trouble with, not the Ford! You should've stuck to Fords, I told you –'

'Excuse me,' I interrupted. 'Are you talking about Joanne Randall who used to live at Buckle Cottage? Are you saying she married someone called Timpson and moved to a place called Long Sheet?'

The old man ignored me. 'I never had any trouble with the Morris Oxford. Go on, you daft old bat, you remember young Joanne marrying that Timpson boy. It was just after your birthday the year we had the late frost that killed all my tomatoes. You said she had one in the oven, but she didn't, though.'

I left them to it, and got out my road atlas. There was a Long Sheet about four miles away as the crow flew, and it looked bigger than Curry Norton. I decided I'd got no choice but to give it a try.

Half an hour of winding roads and tractors' backsides later, I pulled up outside a euphemistically entitled Accident Repair Centre on the outskirts of Long Sheet, got out of the car, and approached the little shack that passed for an office.

'Excuse me, I know this is an awful nuisance, but I'm trying to find someone I think once worked here. His name is Timpson, and it's really, really important that I get in touch with him.'

The woman raised an eyebrow and continued puffing dedicatedly on a cigarette.

'Owes you a lot, does he?'

I felt my pulse-rate leap. 'No! No, it's nothing like that. Actually, it's his wife I'm trying to get hold of – Joanne.'

'Oh, yeah?'

'Yes. *Honestly.*' She looked as if she didn't believe me. I leant forward confidentially. 'Look, if you tell me how I can get in touch with them, I promise I won't say it was you that told me.'

She laughed. 'I couldn't tell you where Ringo was even if I wanted to. It was Florida last time I heard.'

'*Florida?*'

'Yes – the bugger!' She carefully dropped her ash over my side of the counter. 'He was a right sod. You won't get any money out of his missus.'

'I told you, I don't want –'

'She's over at Upper Burtock.'

'Really? Do you have an address?'

'It's the big house, at the top of the street just past the church. You can't miss it. It's called the Sanctuary.' She took a deep drag on the cigarette, and chuckled hollowly.

I waited for her to explain the hollow chuckle, but she didn't seem inclined to, so I thanked her, and went back to the car at a run. *The Sanctuary*? Did this mean that Joanne Timpson/Randall had become some kind of nun? If so, it seemed highly unlikely that she would want to talk about the hate mail she'd sent to Rick. In fact, if she was a nun, it didn't seem very likely she'd have written the letters in the first place.

My heart began to sink, but I found Upper Burtock on the map and twenty minutes later I was driving slowly up its single street past the Spar shop and the church. At the top of the hill stood a large, detached, brick-built house, its walls embedded with pebbles and seashells in a garish triangular pattern. It dominated the village; as the woman in the repair shop had said, you couldn't miss it. I was sure it must be the Sanctuary, and, sure enough, nailed to a tree beside the gate was a small board proclaiming the word 'Sanctuary' in neat black lettering.

After a moment's hesitation, I pulled the car into the drive and parked it behind an ancient estate car, taking in the assortment of clothes on the washing line (female underwear, jeans in various sizes, a vast pink boiler suit). Then I got out of the car and rang the doorbell.

'Hallo. I'm sorry to bother you. I'm looking for a Joanne Timpson who used to be Joanne Randall.'

Over the heavy brass door chain, an eye flickered warily. I produced my press card and extended it towards the eye. 'I'm a reporter. I want to talk to Joanne about a letter she wrote to my paper. Are *you* Joanne?'

At this, the door slammed in my face, and footsteps scurried out of earshot across an uncarpeted hall. Joanne – if it was she – had bolted. I suppose I should have expected this. I decided to give her a few minutes to calm down, then ring again. If necessary, I would ring every five minutes for the rest of the afternoon until she relented. I lifted the letter flap and peered inside. Beside the door was a table with some dusty plastic flowers on it, and a lot of mail piled up next to an old black telephone. I tried to twist my head round so I could read the telephone number, but at that moment an elderly woman in a faded kaftan padded suddenly into view.

174

The door opened, illuminating the shabby hall with its perfect layer of undisturbed dust. 'I've spoken to Joanne,' announced the woman in an imperious tone, 'and she says she'll talk to you – but she's very busy. She's doing the sandwiches.'

There was something about her that gave me the creeps. 'Well, could she come to the door for just a minute?'

'No. Are you coming in, because I've got the goat and the chickens waiting.'

I followed her reluctantly into the house, and she ushered me into a large back room that was obviously a kitchen-cum-living room. The room contained two ancient sofas, a table piled with books and clothes, a battered television set the size of a modest starter home, an ironing board, and a sickly looking rubber plant festooned with Christmas tinsel. Like the hall, it didn't look as if anyone had ever dusted it.

'This is her,' said the woman in the kaftan irritably. 'I'm going to feed the goat.'

A woman stood at the sink. She was almost six feet tall, in her late thirties, with a short, neat haircut that did not flatter her coarse features. She wore a vibrant cerise sweatshirt and a pair of patched and faded blue jeans, and, apart from the sweatshirt, she looked perfectly sane and rather ordinary. She glanced up and stared at me without smiling.

'I'm Chris from the *Tipping Herald*. It's awfully kind of you to see me,' I began, gushingly. 'I just want to ask you a few questions about the letter you wrote to my paper.'

'What letter?' She ignored my offer of a handshake.

'The one you wrote to the *Herald* about Rick Monday.'

She stooped suddenly over the bread. 'I don't know what letter you mean. I've got to be at Asda in half an hour for my shift.'

'Asda,' I repeated, dully. 'Fine. Look, are you saying you didn't write the letter, or what? Why did you let your friend ask me in if you don't want to talk to me?'

She dropped the butter knife and glared at me. 'Well, I've changed my mind, haven't I? I don't like the look of you.' Her expression changed suddenly. 'And I don't believe you.

175

I don't think you're from the papers. It was someone from the Centre sent you here, wasn't it! I bet it was Liz!'

'What do you mean?' I was very glad she'd dropped the knife.

'You and Liz – you're peas in a pod! Standing there in all that fancy designer get-up thinking how smart you are! I'm not stupid!'

I was baffled. Everything I had on had come from Marks and Spencer.

'Look, I told you, I'm from the *Tipping Herald*,' I said, hastily revising my opinion of her mental state. 'I've seen all the letters you wrote to Rick and I traced you through your employment records. I'm sorry I've upset you. I'll leave. Don't bother to see me out –'

She was across the room before I could stop her and had hold of me by the arm.

'If you're a reporter, where's your card?'

Fortunately I'd still got the card in my hand. Joanne scrutinized it minutely as though she expected it to be a forgery, then let go of my arm.

'Oh. I thought you were from the Centre. I've got this new counsellor, see, and I don't like her. She keeps telling me I've got to put the past behind me and stop fantasizing.'

I snatched my card back and made a bolt for the door.

'Only, I'm not fantasizing! I was engaged to Will McGill and he was going to marry me! It's not a fantasy! *Rick Monday stole my life*. Do you hear me?' She followed me to the door. 'Look, you're supposed to tell the truth to your counsellor, and I told her the truth, but she doesn't believe me. She says she's never met anyone like me and she's going to look me up in a book! What good is that supposed to do me?'

I crossed the hall.

'I told her how that devil Rick killed my little baby – I never told anybody that – *and* I told her about Joe, and about all them people chasing after me for money and me not being able to pay, and she says I've got a *self-esteem problem*!'

I turned the front door knob. I'd be happier when I was on the other side of it. 'What do you mean, Rick Monday killed your baby? Was that a – you know – a metaphorical statement?'

'A what? Look, I told you, he stole my life. He poisoned Will against me. I don't know if that's metaphysical or what, but it's all because of him that I married Joe and that I was ill. If it hadn't been for him, it'd be me now in that big house with Will jetting off to places.' Her hand flew to her mouth. 'Oh, my God! It's Monday! The eggs!'

Suddenly she turned her back on me and fled to the kitchen.

'Help me, help me!' she begged, suddenly agitated and contrite. 'I've got all the eggs to do, *and* the sandwiches, and it's nearly one o'clock! It's the pills they give me at the Centre – I'd've been all right if *you* hadn't interrupted my concentration!' Biting her lips, she reached for a bucket of eggs and a stack of boxes that had been hidden under the table. 'Oh, you've got to help me! Jasmine'll go mad if I don't have everything ready! I'll tell you what you want to know if you help me – just put some eggs in these boxes!'

I followed her back to the kitchen and picked up an egg.

'You think I'm making it up, don't you?'

'I . . .'

'Well, I don't care what you think.' She picked up a handful of eggs and rammed them into a box. 'I could've shown you my engagement ring, the one Will bought me – it was a sapphire and diamond and it cost eight hundred pounds. I saw one just like it in a catalogue last week. But Joe took it away and pawned it and I never got it back.' She threw me an egg box. 'He was my soulmate, Will was. I had our charts done. I'm Aries, and he's Leo, but we were both born on the cusp, and this woman said there were exceptional astronomical events on the days of our birth – our planets were in conjunction or something. We were *meant* to be together.' Two eggs exploded in Joanne's right hand and she pushed them into a box and shut the lid on them. 'You should've seen how happy he was when I told him about the baby. He bought me two teddies: one with a pink ribbon and one with a blue one, for if it was a boy or a girl. Well, I got

177

them in Mothercare but he gave me the money for them. I told you, we were *engaged*! It was Rick who made us break up. He said I'd be in the way –' an egg dropped through Joanne's slimy fingers and smashed on the table top – 'but I wouldn't have been in their way, I loved them!' She swept the broken shell out of the way with an elbow. 'I went to every gig. I followed them round the country. Sometimes they even let me in the van with them . . .'

'Is that why you wrote the letters to Rick? Because of something that happened to your baby?'

'It wasn't something that just happened, he made me get rid of the baby, he *made* it happen. Don't you see? He didn't want Will and me to be happy. He didn't want Will marrying me! He wanted Bad Monday to be in the papers all the time with models and actresses and things. I told you, he poisoned Will against me. He *made* me have the abortion, and then he got Will a minder, and he said he'd get the police and have me sectioned if I didn't leave them alone. He said Will was going to say I'd slept with all the roadies if I caused him any trouble – but he wouldn't have, I know he wouldn't have!' She let an egg slip through her fingers, roll across the table and fall to its doom on the grimy floor. 'See, "Just for the Money" had got into the charts, and Rick wanted Bad Monday to be like Rod Stewart and the Rolling Stones and people like that. He could get Will to do anything he wanted.'

'I see. So you mean . . .'

'I wrote all those letters to him to scare him. I didn't see why he should get away with it – do you?'

'So when you said in your letter Rick was a murderer, this was what you meant?'

'Yes! Well, it's true, isn't it? The cheque they gave me for the clinic had Rick's name on it. Rick had Will round his little finger. I wrote to Will, too, but he never answered. Rick poisoned him against me, that's why he married that *awful* Aimee.'

I abandoned the eggs, opened my briefcase and pulled out the sketch of Rick with his hands round Will's throat.

'Have you seen this before?' I asked.

178

She snatched it from me contemptuously, smearing it with egg yolk. 'Course I have. It was in the papers, wasn't it? I saw it when I was in the hospital after my episode.'

'Ah.' I took the picture back hastily.

'It was all made up by newspaper people. Rick and Will were the best of mates. They only split up because Rick wanted to go to Hollywood. And anyway, Will was really strong,' she added admiringly. 'If they'd've had a fight, he would've killed Rick as easy as that.' She picked up an egg and pulped it against the tabletop with the palm of her hand. We watched it ooze and eddy towards the floor.

'Wait,' she said suddenly. 'I'm going to show you my pictures! I'll show you the pictures of Will and me, then you'll believe me!'

This was the last thing I wanted, but it was too late. Joanne dashed across the hall and disappeared up the stairs two at a time. Before I'd had a chance to get myself together and leave, she was back with a large cardboard box tucked under her arm.

'There!' She dropped the box on the floor and dived into it. 'I've got all kinds of stuff in here. Look. Here's a picture of Bad Monday's first big gig in Birmingham – that's me on the stage there. See?'

I accepted the photo gingerly.

'And here's one of Rick and Will in a car showroom when Will bought his first car. I was on the forecourt and I'd just found out I was pregnant. That's Rick looking under the bonnet.'

I groaned inwardly.

'Well, I'm not in any of these because I was taking the photos, but there *is* one of me and Will together. And this is the horoscope I told you about. Wait . . .'

In trepidation I glanced down at the box, which was packed to bursting point with dog-eared photographs, and bundles of newspaper and magazine cuttings. I decided there must be several weeks' of Bad Monday reminiscence material to be gone through, none of it of any interest to anyone except Joanne, who was of course almost exactly the kind of person

Pete and Wayne and Mr Heslop had predicted she would be. I felt very sorry for her, but not sorry enough to want to spend the rest of the afternoon looking at out-of-focus photographs and old concert programmes.

I accepted the horoscope reluctantly, and, as I did so, my eye was caught by something rather odd-looking sticking awkwardly out of the corner of her box. I wasn't sure what it was at first, so I gave it a surreptitious poke with my foot.

It was a small statuette of a guitarist wearing flared trousers.

'This is the one of me with Will!' exclaimed Joanne, excitedly. 'Look!'

I stared at her in horror.

'That medallion he's wearing – I had it engraved with both our names. I saved up for it!'

I was still staring at her in horror, and now she noticed this. And she'd seen what I was looking at.

She took her breath in sharply, and the photographs trickled through her fingers to the floor. There was an awful moment when I thought she was going to reach for the statuette and hit me with it, but then her lower lip began to quiver.

'Oh, please – I didn't take anything else, I didn't, honestly! I know it was stupid. Here!' Now she did reach for the statuette. She thrust it into my arms. 'Take it! Take it back. I don't want it.'

I recoiled hastily.

'Please, *please* take it! I'm not a thief! I told you, I didn't take anything else! I'd've put it back straight away if that woman hadn't turned up!'

I caught the statue by the plinth. It was heavy for its size, heavy enough to do severe damage to someone.

'I should never've gone to his stupid fête, I know that. Oh, thank you, thank you, you're so kind! I can't tell you how grateful I am. I should've told you about it before, shouldn't I? Thank you so, *so* much. Oh, are you going now?' I'd made a dash for the door. 'Can I have your address? I'd love to write to you and tell you all about my life – you're so kind.'

I still hadn't made up my mind whether Joanne was unhinged enough – or too unhinged – to be Rick's murderer, and the last thing in the world I wanted was to give her my address.

'I'll get you a pen. There's one here.'

I opened the front door with trembling fingers and escaped on to the step.

'You're so kind,' she said, again, pushing paper and pen towards me. 'You don't know how awful it was, seeing all of them that afternoon. I should never have gone. When I got home I had to take two of my yellow tablets.'

I took the paper and pen, and started to write down Keith's address. It was silly, but it was the first thing that came into my head. 'What time did you get home?' I asked, hoping this wouldn't sound like the loaded question it was.

'About six.'

'In the evening?'

'Yes, of course in the evening! I *had* to be back by six, didn't I, so Jasmine could have the car for delivering the eggs to the nuns for their Sunday tea. I just sort of froze up inside when I saw Will. I hadn't expected him to be there. He looked so gorgeous and everything and he didn't even *look* at me!'

'You saw Will at the fête? Are you sure it was him?'

'Yes, of course I'm sure!'

'And you didn't go back to Rick's house later – after the fête?'

'Of course I didn't. Why would I want to? Anyway, I told you, I took *two of the yellows*. Jasmine was ever so cross – she wouldn't let me go with her to deliver the eggs because she said I was walking funny. They were *all* there, you see – I couldn't cope. Rick and Rob and Will and that girlfriend of Rick's. Not Alan and Bunny, of course,' she added, referring to the two other members of Bad Monday, 'because Alan's in Australia and Bunny's dead. What's that you've written? I can't read your writing.'

I did a double-take. 'What girlfriend of Rick's?'

She gave me a blank look. 'Well, the one you showed me the picture of – you know.'

181

'What picture?'

'That one from the newspaper. The girl in it was the one that was telling people off for parking on the grass in front of the house.'

This didn't make sense. I got the picture out and looked at it. 'You mean *this* is Marianne Fletcher?' I remarked in disbelief.

She shrugged. 'I don't know. I don't know her name.'

I looked at the picture again, with the intention of pointing out how ridiculous Joanne's assertion was – and then it hit me. The high cheekbones, the heart-shaped face. Those big doe-eyes . . .

'I saw her backstage once,' Joanne said. 'She was ever so striking. Will and Rick smuggled her in under a blanket. They were giggling and carrying on as if it was some big secret, but I s'pect he dumped her like he dumped all the others.'

Now I'd seen the likeness, I couldn't understand how I hadn't spotted it before. It was so obvious, it practically screamed at you.

Suddenly I pulled myself together.

'Look, Joanne, I can't possibly take this for you.' I thrust the statuette at her, along with the piece of paper with Keith's address written on it, and fled for the Mini. 'You'll have to go to the police with it!' I jumped into the driving seat.

I'd moved so fast that she was still rooted in place on the doorstep, looking glazed-eyed and baffled. I watched her let the statuette fall into a flowerbed, where it dug a hole for itself in the soft earth. I felt pretty mean, but it was just too bad. I wound down my window and called out to her, 'Thank you so much for the information. Now you *must* go inside and ring the police about the statuette –' I started the engine, and leaned out of the window – '*before I do*!'

I headed back towards the A303 as fast as the Mini would allow. As soon as I got home I was going to have to ring Keith on some pretext and try to drop casually into the conversation the fact that I had just given his address to a lunatic.

14

Pete pulled up behind the milk float that was blocking the entrance to Yew Tree Cottage. It was ten past seven in the morning, and the road was empty apart from a postman dawdling by on his bicycle. We waited. The milkman emerged from the cottage and tossed an empty bottle carelessly into the rear of the float, then jumped into the driver's seat and whined off down the road in the direction of Hatchley Heath.

Pete turned into the entrance and slewed the car to a halt so that it was blocking both of the Fletchers' garages.

'How's your stomach?' he enquired, amiably.

'My stomach's fine.'

'I know it's fine.' He put his hand on it. 'But is it ready for this? Things could turn nasty, you know. Especially if we're wrong.'

'We're not wrong.'

'OK, then. Give me a kiss for luck.'

It seemed a bit tasteless to exchange kisses on the front doorstep of a possible murderer, so I didn't. We got out of the car and approached the house, which, in the early morning sun, looked like a location setting for a new BBC rural drama, probably about an idiosyncratic member of the medical profession. House martins darted to and fro beneath the eaves, and butterflies hovered over the honeysuckle. In the porch, a large tabby cat was sunning itself.

Pete stepped over the cat and pressed the doorbell. From an upstairs window issued the faint sound of water running and someone whistling the Coronation Street theme tune rather badly.

Pete pressed the doorbell again, then bent down and picked up the discarded note left out for the milkman. At that moment, Marianne appeared, hastily wrapped in a bathrobe of turquoise towelling.

He handed her the milk.

'Here's your extra pint of gold top.' He looked vaguely impressed by her lithe form beneath the bathrobe. 'It's Mrs Fletcher, isn't it? Hi, I'm Pete, and I think you've already met my colleague. Do you think we could just have a few quick words with you concerning your relationship with Rick Monday, if it's not too much trouble?'

'I don't believe this!' She looked as if she did. 'Look, I've already made it quite clear to all of you that my husband and I had no relationship at all with Mr Monday. Goodbye, Mr –'

'No, hang on, I'm not talking about the relationship you and your husband had with Rick – I'm talking about yours.'

'I don't know what you're talking about.'

'Well, isn't it true that the two of you had a very intimate relationship in the early seventies? Perhaps you would prefer to discuss this in my car?'

By now, Marianne was beginning to lose her cool. She juggled helplessly with the milk and tried to slam the door with her elbow, but her knee got in the way. The cat flew for cover.

'Get out!' she shrieked. '*Clifford, help me*! Call the police!'

Pete reached into his inside pocket and produced his mobile phone. 'Why don't you do it?' he suggested. 'Here, use this.'

She recoiled in panic, kicking over a yoghurt, and I began to feel a bit sorry for her, because her bathrobe was decidedly grubby and not the sort of thing you wanted to be arrested in.

'Who told you this – who made up these *lies*?' She'd gone from pink to puce. In fact, she was so upset that I suddenly got the feeling there was more to her liaison with Rick than a mere adolescent crush half-forgotten in the mists of time and pot smoke. I couldn't be sure, but it was worth a shot.

'Tina,' I replied, calmly. 'Tina told us.'

Marianne went rigid. She dropped a milk bottle on to her foot. Pete looked at me in surprise, and for a moment, no one knew what to say, but then Clifford appeared, as if on cue, clad in a grey silk dressing gown. The right side of his face was frosted with shaving cream.

'What the hell's going on? What do you think you're doing?' he demanded angrily.

'We're doing our job, sir,' said Pete. 'We –'

'Get off my property before I call the police!' He made a sudden attempt to shut the door, but Marianne was still in the way and Pete somehow managed to get his foot over the threshold. Overcome by enthusiasm, I tried to insinuate my foot into the hall, too.

'You both lied to the police!' I shouted, forcing my head in under Clifford's arm. 'And we know why! You gave the police a false statement!'

'How dare you!'

'Yes, you did! You said you were out on the night of the murder, but –'

Suddenly Clifford produced from nowhere a heavy-looking walking stick. 'Get out before I brain the pair of you!' he shouted, drawing the stick back ready to strike. 'You hear me? I'm counting three and then I'm going to let you have it!' Marianne removed a turquoise bit of herself – her elbow, I think – from the stick's path, but Pete and I were wedged too firmly in the doorway to move. We froze with the walking stick hovering above our heads. 'One . . .' said Clifford. 'Two . . .' But then Fate intervened in the form of the Fletchers' teenage sons blundering down the stairs in striped pyjamas.

'What's happening, Dad? Shall I get the airgun? Is it still in the Hoover cupboard next to the lightbulbs?'

'I know where it is! Let *me* get it!'

There was silence. I had my eyes shut by now, waiting for the 'Three'. Instead I heard Clifford say, in a slightly less irascible tone. 'Don't be ridiculous, Leo. Go back upstairs, both of you.'

I opened my eyes. Slowly, he let the walking stick fall to his side, Marianne disengaged her leg from mine, and gradually and rather shamefacedly we all extricated ourselves from the doorway.

'Mr Fletcher, I'm really sorry about this,' said Pete, brushing down his jacket, 'but I'm afraid you're in a bit of a hole. If your wife won't talk to us, my paper will only send other people, I can promise you that, and they might make nuisances of themselves.'

'Oh, really!'

'Just make them go away!' pleaded Marianne. 'Make them go away, can't you? It's *Tina*!' she added, sounding distraught. 'She's spoken to them!'

'Has she?' Clifford looked furious, but he leant the walking stick against the wall and folded his arms. 'Look, I don't like you people, I don't like what you do or how you do it, and I want you to leave my family alone.' He hesitated, an odd glint in his eye. 'So if you want a story – I'll give you one. A *proper* story that has nothing at all to do with my wife. What do you say?'

'*Clifford*!'

'Come on, what do you say?'

Pete and I exchanged baffled glances. Pete recovered first. He said, 'OK.'

'Good.' Clifford opened the door and led us inside, past the two boys in their crumpled nightclothes who were staring at us in astonishment. We followed him through the hall into a small sitting room complete with exposed beams, inglenook fireplace, and the extinct embers of last night's fire. The room smelled of woodsmoke and old-fashioned beeswax-rich furniture polish.

He didn't ask us to sit down.

'Right. Marianne, have you seen my maps?'

She gazed at him in horror. 'Clifford, you can't!'

'Yes, I can. There they are!' He strode across to an alcove that was filled with hundreds of books jostling for space on

186

uneven, overburdened shelves. 'These are all maps of the area that is now the Willow Grange Estate,' he announced, holding them up. 'I can let you have photocopies.'

Pete frowned. So did I.

'Oh, come on,' said Clifford, 'surely you know about the houses on the Willow Grange Estate, and their mysterious subsidence problems?'

Somewhere at the back of my mind, filed away with a lot of other irrelevant minutiae, were a few boring details about an equally boring story that had once appeared in the *Herald*. I couldn't be bothered to recall them. 'Well, um . . .'

'Oh, good grief! Now there's a real story for you. Twenty-one houses, less than thirty years old, and five of them cracking so badly they had to be underpinned in the last drought. And *who* built those houses – do you know?' With a flourish, he handed me a yellowed sheet of paper. 'Read this. It's a letter from the old Hatchley Heath Parish Council, written in 1942. I came across it when I was researching my book *Hatchley Heath – the War Years*.'

I took the letter and glanced at it. It was addressed to Tipping Borough Council's Public Health Department.

'Now,' went on Clifford, 'if you'll allow me to point you in the right direction on this map –'

'Hang on a minute,' interrupted Pete, snatching the letter from me and dropping it on the table. 'I'm sorry, Mr Fletcher, but my editor isn't going to be fobbed off on this one with some rumour about town-planning irregularities. You said you had a story for us, but so far the only story I can see is the one about you. It goes like this. Here you are, a respected member of the community, a leading light in village affairs, happily ensconced in this piece-of-history cottage, when suddenly –'

'Hold on, I said –'

'Suddenly, out of the blue, your wife's former lover – by whom she once had an illegitimate child – moves in next door.' Clifford's chin, beneath its coating of shaving foam, went rigid. 'So what do you do? Well, for a start, you take every opportunity to bad-mouth him. You resign from the

Committee. You make him a Christmas present of a dozen dead rats. You ask his cleaner to look out for drugs in his bathroom cabinet. In fact, you take every opportunity to stir up bad feeling against him, because the way you see it Rick Monday has ruined your peaceful, well-ordered life.'

'Now, look –'

'No, wait, I'm not finished.' In his pocket, Pete had turned on his micro-cassette recorder. I heard the little click as the tape turned over. 'You found out about Rick's latest plans for Tangley House, didn't you? I suppose you know people in the right places. And it was the last straw, wasn't it? On top of everything else you were about to have your personal space invaded by a bunch of criminals and ex-junkies!'

Clifford had turned so white it was impossible to tell where the shaving foam on his face began and ended.

'And I think,' went on Pete, 'that you saw an opportunity to put things right and you seized it. You called at Tangley House during the fête to complain about parking or noise or litter, or all three, and you spotted a front door key going begging in the kitchen. Well, you couldn't resist it, could you? It was perfect. You'd wait till Rick was on his own, preferably with his music up nice and loud, and then you'd let yourself into the house and sneak up on him. You'd use that fancy knife so the police would suspect a crazed fan or a jilted lover. The house had been crawling with people all day – no one would suspect you. And anyway, in the end it didn't matter, because after you'd finished someone else turned up to carry the can for you.'

There was a moment's silence.

'Good God,' said Clifford, weakly. 'Good God.'

'I think I'd better call the police,' Pete said softly, producing his mobile for the second time.

'You can't be serious.' Clifford was beginning to shake. Pieces of the shaving foam were detaching themselves from his chin and flying around the room. 'This is ridiculous. I didn't kill Monday! For God's sake – is that what you think? I thought the police had arrested someone. Look, all right, we lied about where we were that evening, I admit that. And I

188

admit I did resent Monday buying Tangley House – of course I did. From the moment he moved in he treated my wife as though she was nothing, did you know that? I think he hardly even remembered that they'd ever had a relationship. When Tina turned up out of the blue it only made things worse. I'm not surprised if she's taken her father's side. He welcomed her with open arms. Well, it didn't cost him anything in terms of effort, did it? He never showed the slightest regard for the suffering Marianne had gone through. Let me tell you this, when my wife got involved with Rick, she was a young girl, innocent, vulnerable –'

No one, not even someone who was too young to know better at the time, likes to hear it bandied about that they once had an affair with a complete and unmitigated shit. Marianne huddled into the bathrobe and hid her face with her hands.

'And he hadn't changed,' went on Clifford, grimly. 'He was still out for himself and to hell with everyone else. If that scheme he was cooking up with the Acorn Trust had been given the go-ahead, the whole character of the village would have changed and he wouldn't have given a brass farthing for it. The adventure centre was bad enough, but we could just about have lived with it. But you can't let loose a bunch of muggers and joy-riders on a small community without the most appalling consequences. And for what? So Mr Rick aren't-I-wonderful Monday could get his face plastered across a few glossy magazines and sell a few records? What about the rest of us? But look – I *didn't kill him*!'

Pete was looking up a number in his notebook.

'I didn't kill him!' repeated Clifford, the blood beginning to flow back to his cheeks. 'Listen. Those houses on the Willow Grange Estate. Bradman built them. John Bradman of Bradman Homes. He got the land cheap from the Council, it was his first major development. Well, he's the main mover behind the Acorn Trust, isn't he? He's the one who was backing the Mondays' schemes!'

Pete hesitated over the phone. 'I'm not with you.'

189

Clifford snatched up the letter and pushed it into his hands. 'Read this. It's the proof. It gives permission for Tipping Borough Council to dispose of waste at a site called Bell Hollow. *Bell Hollow*. Ever heard of it? Well, if I can show you on this 1898 Ordnance Survey –' He reached for a map. 'See – this deep dip to the west of Bell Copse – I'm 99 per cent certain it must be the hollow they're talking about. Well, all of this area is now the Willow Grange Estate. If I'm right, Bell Hollow must be underneath the row of houses built on the north side of Saffron Close.'

There was silence. In the hall, the grandfather clock began to chime its way through seven thirty.

'Wait a minute,' said Pete. 'John Bradman built a housing estate on top of a tip – is that what you're saying?'

'Yes. And the tip was in constant use until 1949, and it was used for both domestic *and* industrial waste. I can prove that, too.'

'I see. So if the Tangley House scheme had looked like getting off the ground you'd have tried to use this as a bargaining counter to stop it? Am I right?'

The Fletchers glanced at one another. The corner of Clifford's mouth gave an odd little twitch. He put down his maps.

'Actually, I was hoping to nip things in the bud rather more positively. I wrote to Bradman the week before the fête. I suppose some people might see it as blackmail, but honestly, these days organizations like the Acorn Trust have all the big guns on their side. I didn't sign my name to the letter, but after what happened – I mean the murder – to avoid any involvement with the police, we . . . *I* decided it would be best if we said we'd been out for the entire evening.'

I had now completely lost command of the situation. '*Why*?' I demanded.

'Because . . .' He rubbed his face tormentedly, 'because I did something that in the light of what happened . . . Well, we would've had to explain the whole thing. You see, when I wrote to Bradman, I thought he'd get the letter before the fête and would pull out – you know, at the very least cancel his personal appearance as guest of honour. But he didn't. I suppose he didn't get the letter in time. And, to cap it all, some of the Acorn Trust people were extremely rude to Marianne when she complained about the cars on our grass. Have you seen the state of it now? It's a disgrace!'

I winced, remembering the day of the fête and the note pushed underneath my windscreen wiper.

'So, later that evening,' went on Clifford reluctantly, 'at around nine o'clock, I should think, I called on Monday to put him in the picture about Bradman and the Willow Grange Estate. I know it was a mistake to lie to the police –'

'But Mr Fletcher, it wasn't *nine* o'clock when you called on Rick, it was *ten*!' I interrupted, before he could talk his way out of it. 'I told you, you and your wife were seen – in your garden on your way to Rick's – at *ten*! Rick died between nine forty and –'

Marianne leapt suddenly to her feet. 'Oh, please, I beg of you, please believe me: Clifford would never, never hurt anyone! I *swear* to you on my sons' *lives* he's told you the truth! Can't you take our word for it? Can't you see what sort of people we are? Please believe me, if –'

'Wait a minute,' interrupted Clifford. 'Let's try and stay calm. They have a point. Think, Marianne – someone might have said they saw us on our way next door around ten o'clock. We *were* in the garden then. Don't you remember?'

Pete gave an exasperated sigh and held up his phone again. 'Watering the petunias, I suppose,' he remarked, mockingly.

'No, no, you've got it all wrong, I assure you. Look, I admit I can't remember the exact time I spoke to Monday – why should I? – but I didn't kill him. I'm absolutely positive it was nearer nine than ten; I remember the grandfather clock striking nine while I was getting my maps together. Listen, I told Monday exactly what I've told you about Bell Hollow, I was only there about ten minutes, if that. He laughed at me. He said I was making the whole thing up. Until I started to get the maps out, that is – then his attitude changed. He lost his temper and called me several names I won't repeat. He flew into a rage. A real rage. I think he suddenly realized that if I

191

was right his friend Bradman would never sacrifice Bradman Homes' reputation for the sake of one rehabilitation centre, and he practically threw me out of the house. As I said, I'd hardly been there ten minutes. I was pretty shaken when I got home, but I said to Marianne, "Now the fun will start. He'll have Bradman and Rob over here in a minute." And sure enough about – oh, I don't know, forty minutes later – I heard what I thought was his front door closing. Now that must have been at around ten o'clock. I went out to have a look, but I couldn't see anything, and Marianne made me come in. We had a few words in the drive. She said I'd already done more than my fair share of damage for one night. I swear this is the truth! There's nothing more I can tell you.'

'Wait a minute,' interrupted Pete. 'You said you went outside at ten because you heard Rick's front door slam, but how can you have? He was playing music at full volume, you couldn't possibly have heard the front door, not from inside the house.' He glanced vaguely in the direction of Tangley House, which was completely hidden by apple trees and the yew hedge.

'Yes, I could. As I told you, I'm not used to being spoken to the way Monday spoke to me. I sat in our morning room at the front with a large Scotch. I opened the window and pulled a chair up to it. Well, if Bradman had turned up they might have paid us a visit, mightn't they? One wants to be prepared. The music was much quieter at the front, and I was quite sure I heard the front door, although obviously I must have been mistaken. It was probably the wind blowing something across the garden – that's what Marianne said.'

Suddenly, I realized what Clifford was saying and, to be honest, I was furious.

'But it *was* someone at the front door! Don't you realize what this means? If only you'd told the police! My God!'

Clifford looked baffled.

'My colleague has a theory,' explained Pete, giving me a hard stare. 'But we haven't got time for it now.' He put his phone away and switched off the recorder. 'Would you like to hand over those papers, please, Mr Fletcher?'

'Does this mean you believe us? That you will leave us alone?'

Pete held out his hand. 'I'll take the originals, please, Mr Fletcher.'

Clifford handed them to him reluctantly.

'Thank you.' He tucked them into his pocket. 'We'll get these checked out, but you've been very helpful and I appreciate it. Thank you.' He ducked under an overhanging beam and went out into the hall.

I was horrified. Pete had just terminated the interview, and I could think of a dozen more questions I'd like to ask the Fletchers – especially Marianne.

'Look, I feel fully justified in doing what I did,' Clifford protested, as I hesitated in the hallway. 'You have to be prepared to put your neck on the line occasionally and stand up for what's right. If you don't –'

'Oh, for God's sake, Clifford!' interrupted Marianne, snapping at last. 'Don't you understand? These people are going to ruin our lives! It's all my fault! All my fault for being so stupid!'

'They're not going to ruin our lives, Marianne, they –'

Pete took my arm and pulled me out into the garden.

'I should never have agreed to us living in this house!' she went on. 'I told you Rick wanted to buy Tangley House – I should have made you believe me!'

'Mrs Fletcher –' I began, desperately.

'You see, I'd been through the most awful time. I was *seventeen*. I saw Tina for *five* minutes and then they took her away! They told me it was for the best, and then when I met Clifford –'

Pete pushed me towards the car.

'Wait!' I begged. 'You've got to let me ask her what Will and Rick had the fight about!'

'– I was just so happy, he was so good to me. He'd spent three whole years doing up this house – that's how we met. He was researching its history and my father lent him some books. He was everything Rick wasn't: kind and gentle and thoughtful. Rick and I split up before I knew I was pregnant and I never spoke to him again or wanted to. He was living in California back then. And Clifford kept saying not to worry, he said Rick would never want to come back and live in Hatchley Heath again and he'd have forgotten about Tangley House –'

Pete pushed me into the car. 'Look, Bradman Homes are big news. Industrial pollution is much better than child abuse or corruption!' He leapt into the driving seat and thrust the key into the ignition.

Furiously I wound down my window. 'Mrs Fletcher – Marianne!' I yelled. '*Please* tell me why Rick tried to strangle Will. I want to know what started the feud between them. You do know, don't you?'

She looked aghast, so I decided to make it even easier for her by giving her some options. The only trouble was, I couldn't think of any. Pete started the engine.

'Well, it must have been jealousy, mustn't it?' I suggested desperately. I couldn't think of anything else, so I shouted, '*Over you*!'

Suddenly, against a backdrop of grinding metal and foul blue smoke, the world stood still and Marianne's face drained as white as an old bleached bone.

There was no mistaking her appalled reaction. My mouth dropped open.

'*You* and Will McGill? Something happened between you and –'

Before I could elaborate, Pete whisked us out of the drive in a storm of gravel, leaving Marianne slumped weakly in Clifford's protective arms.

15

Mr Heslop wasn't in when I got to the office – in fact, the cleaners were still at work with their disinfectant sprays – so I got out all my old photos of Bad Monday and spread them haphazardly across the desktop. Rick and Marianne and *Will*? I pored over the pictures. There wasn't one in which Rick didn't project sexiness and sultriness and desirability, while Will lurked in the background looking angular, awkward and unpleasant. Marianne was too beautiful for him, she belonged to the wrong social class – they might as well have come from different planets. What attraction could there possibly be between a cosseted convent girl who was already involved with one of the most desirable men of the moment and an ex-Borstal boy with a reputation for violence, and no style? I gathered up the photos. There was no accounting for taste, of course. Still, I had the strong feeling I was missing something.

I picked up my phone and dialled Will's number. It was early, he'd still be in bed.

Jackie answered the phone.

'Go away! I know who you are. He's not here!'

I didn't believe her. 'Look, it'll only take a minute.'

'I said he's not here!' She sounded half-asleep, or drugged, or both.

'Jackie, you didn't tell the police the truth, did you? In fact, you told them a whole pack of lies about where you and Will were the weekend Rick was murdered. They wouldn't be very pleased if I told them that, would they?'

'What are you talking about?'

'About the so-called alibi you gave Will. Look, I'm not saying I think he had anything to do with the murder, but you shouldn't have lied to the police. Are you going to let me speak to him, or shall I ring them right now?'

There was silence. 'I – I can't,' said Jackie. 'I don't know where he is. Me and Will are having a – a trial separation.'

'Oh.' I was taken aback. I wondered if there was any significance in this new situation.

'It's only temporary! It's only for a week or two. Why do you have to keep pestering us? The police've got a bloke for the murder. Can't you just leave us alone? Oh, for Christ's sake, bugger off – go and pee up against the rubber plant or something!'

Now I was even more taken aback.

'There – you've woken the bloody dogs up now! I wanted to sleep through! Go away – go away – go away!'

She was becoming increasingly hysterical. 'All right, *please*, Jackie. Just answer me one question. Did Will ever tell you anything about a relationship he had with a woman called Marianne?'

'*Who*?'

'It was a long time ago, Jackie, before –'

'Oh, stop it, stop it! I don't care! My Will would never be unfaithful to me. He could sue you! He will if I tell him about this! Why are you harassing us? The police have arrested the murderer!'

'No, they haven't. They've got the wrong man. Do you understand?' I thought desperately. 'Haven't you heard of the Birmingham Six or the Guildford Four?'

There was silence. I expected another outburst but there wasn't one. The silence went on for a long time. I could hear her breathing so I knew she was still there. I said 'Hallo' a few times, then there was a muffled click, and the phone went dead.

I replaced the receiver with the intention of redialling her number immediately, but before I could do it the phone rang again of its own volition.

It was Julie. 'I've overslept and I can't find my clean shirt
– I'm going to be late! Did you do one for me?'

'It's in the kitchen next to the ironing board.'

'It isn't. I can't find it.'

'Are you sure? I'm certain I –'

'Oh, Mum!' she interrupted, suddenly. 'I don't want to go
to school, *please* don't make me. Will you write me a note?
Please write me a note so I don't have to go to school any
more. I can't *bear* it any longer!'

'Are you all right?'

'No! No, I'm not all right, I'm going to die!'

Naturally, I was horrified at this unexpected piece of news.
'What's the matter? Shall I come home?'

She blew her nose into the phone. 'No. No, don't come
home. What good's that going to do? It won't do me any
good, will it? I'm not going to die. I wish I was, but I'm
not.'

'Why?'

'It doesn't matter, it doesn't matter. I'll get the shirt and
go.'

'Wait –' I glanced at my desk calendar, trying to work
out whether she was pre-menstrual or if I should start
worrying. 'Look, why don't we talk about this tonight? If
you're unhappy at school, let's talk about it. You can take
a break from revision for half an hour, can't you?'

'No. I can't. I can't ever stop. And *he'll* be there. I'm not
talking in front of him.'

'Oh.' I felt a twinge of guilt, but Mr Heslop was coming up
the stairs. 'Well, all right. Let's meet for lunch instead. We'll
have a pizza at that new place. I can pick you up outside
the gates.'

'I can't,' she said, resolutely negative. 'I'll have to have a
note first.'

'Oh. How about tomorrow then? I can give you a note for
tomorrow.'

There was silence, so I said, 'OK, I'll write you a note
for tomorrow. Look, you'd better go now, or you will be
late.'

Mr Heslop had emerged at the top of the stairs, and he wasn't smiling.

'Mr Heslop!' I leapt up, reaching for Clifford Fletcher's bundle of maps. 'Can I see you for a minute –' I followed him to his office. 'I've got a lot of good news and a tiny bit of bad news. The bad news is you were right about Jo. She was a waste of time – but she did tell me about Marianne Fletcher. It seems Marianne Fletcher was Rick's girlfriend before she married Clifford. She was the girl in the picture, remember? And she was the mother of Tina. Remember I told you about Tina?'

I waited politely while he put his sandwiches away and unbuttoned his jacket.

'Well, there's two bits of good news.' He was getting out his pencils. 'The first is that the Fletchers lied in their statement to the police and they've now virtually confirmed my key theory, and the second –' He was arranging the pencils in their holder. I knew the Willow Grange estate scandal would be right up his street. 'The second is to do with John Bradman and Bradman Homes.'

He looked up sharply. 'What are you talking about?'

I gestured dramatically towards the street map of Tipping that adorned his wall. 'Do you remember the last drought, when all those houses in Saffron Close started cracking? Have you heard of Bell Hollow?' I grabbed a pencil and recklessly shaded in a large blob round Saffron Close. 'Well, it's here. During the war it used to be a landfill site – for domestic rubbish *and* industrial waste. It's under these houses, and that's why they've been cracking.' I then did a very good interpretation of a three-bedroomed house plummeting into a bottomless pit, and followed it up with a heartrending impression of a small child smitten by toxic-fume induced asthma.

'And God knows what's under there, so I thought the first thing we should do – as well as checking the facts, of course – is to visit the Grange Primary School – it's here, see? – to find out if they've noticed any unexplained increase in illnesses over the last thirty years: leukaemia and asthma and that sort of thing. Who knows what's been dumped there – asbestos, old car batteries, anything. What was that stuff they used to paint on clock faces to make them glow in the dark? Wasn't there a clock factory in Tipping once?'

Mr Heslop snatched his pencil back from me and replaced it in its holder.

'I don't know what the hell you're talking about. For your information, while you were out yesterday, a representative of the Acorn Trust rang to inform me that they have now lodged an official complaint against us with the Press Complaints Commission.' He snatched Clifford's maps. 'We'll be very lucky if they don't go to court and seek damages against us.'

'Oh!' I stopped thinking about alarm clock factories.

'So I'm not in the least bit interested at the moment in some fifty-year-old rumour about people dumping their carrot peelings on a piece of waste ground. I've got an appointment with the lawyers this afternoon, which is going to cost an arm and a leg.'

'Oh!'

'I'm going to have to seriously consider suspending you, Chris.'

I was stunned. (For some reason, to this day I still feel surprise when life deals out unfair blows.) 'But you can't . . . There's the Willow Grange thing, and I'm finally getting somewhere with Rick Monday –' There was also our hefty mortgage. I began to feel sick.

'Ah, yes, I was coming to the Monday murder,' he said grimly, rummaging through his out tray. 'We've been told to expect important developments within the next twenty-four hours. I imagine the police will be charging your friend Kitchen, so that will be the end of that.'

'But . . .'

He offered me a sheaf of papers. 'I've been forced to the conclusion that you were quite simply out of your depth with Monday, and that if I hadn't sent you to interview him none of this would have happened. I have to share some of the

199

responsibility. Go on, take these. They're press releases on a YMCA keep-fit week.'

'*What*?'

'It's a national event, it's quite important. You see, I've decided to give you the benefit of the doubt for the time being. Well, actually I think our legal bods may take the view that by suspending you I'd be admitting fault on our part. And, as I say, I may be slightly to blame for some of this.' He dropped the papers on to his desk. 'I didn't take enough account of your personal circumstances. You've been through a lot lately, what with the divorce, and your son leaving home – and your daughter, of course.'

I wasn't completely speechless. 'What about my daughter?'

'Oh, come on, I know it's not easy on your own.'

'But I'm not on my own!'

He was beginning to get angry. 'Look, I hope you realize I'm bending over backwards to be fair here. You know perfectly well I put my neck on the line in employing you in the first place, which is why I feel I bear a moral responsibility for all this. Whatever happens now, I'm going to stand by you, Chris.'

'Oh!' Well, this was a relief at any rate. 'Thank you.'

'Yes. You have my word for it that if the worst comes to the worst I'll see to it your name goes forward for the next secretarial vacancy to come up.'

I let this remark sink in. There was a long and awful silence.

'You'll probably be happier anyway,' said Mr Heslop. 'Perhaps you could enrol yourself on a WP course in the meantime.'

He thrust the YMCA file into my hands with a sad smile. I took it, and began to retreat slowly from the room. Later, I'd think about all this and tell him what I thought of it. I'd say it quietly and dispassionately, employing logic and my most disarming smile.

I got as far as the threshold. Then I couldn't stand it any longer. 'If this was anyone else but me!' I shouted, in a horribly loud voice. 'If anyone else but me had done what

I've done and cost the paper as much as I'm going to cost it, you wouldn't be offering *them* a secretarial job, would you? Would you? Of course you wouldn't! Well, you can *stuff* it! You can *stuff* your pathetic secretarial job and your Word for Windows course and your *Secretary's Handbook*! Did you crawl out of the Ark, or what?'

And I slammed the door in his face before he had a chance to think of an answer.

For half an hour, I drove round Tipping with no idea where I was going, what I was doing, or why I was in the car. I forced my way into other people's lanes and roared through amber lights for no particular reason. I was so angry, I didn't care. No one was ever going to patronize me again. No one was ever going to patronize me, or put on me, or make me say sorry for things that weren't my fault – not today, not tomorrow, not ever again.

But after a while I stopped feeling angry. I tried to remember exactly what I'd said to Mr Heslop, and the more I thought about it the more I came to the conclusion that I'd made a big mistake. Mr Heslop was seeing the lawyers that very afternoon, and he was hardly likely to go out to bat for someone who had just told him to stick the *Secretary's Handbook* up his backside.

I slumped back in my seat, and gazed across the ugly skyline of Hudderston's commercial district. There was a phone box in the layby. I could apologize; I didn't have to mean it, over the phone he wouldn't be able to tell. I got out of the car, found my phonecard, and started to dial the number. But then it hit me. I was doing it again. I was about to apologize to Mr Heslop for letting him patronize me. And whatever the consequences of not apologizing, I wasn't going to.

I put down the phone. I had an awful feeling I'd been here before, on several occasions, but this time it was going to be different. Really. I picked up the phone again. I'd still got a job to do, even if not for much longer. I swallowed down a big lump of something that had come up in my throat, rang Tipping police station and asked to speak to their Press

Officer. Had there been a major development in the Rick Monday murder? I demanded. After a long pause during which I had to listen to rather more of a tinny Madonna recording than even her most ardent fans would have cared for, an assistant Press Officer came to the phone and informed me that there was a briefing in progress at that moment and that a statement would be issued later. Then he hung up. I dashed back to the car. I was still on the story, no one had told me otherwise. If something big had happened, Rob Monday would know what it was. Perhaps, now that the police had questioned Ted Kitchen, they were at last about to announce a complete change of direction in the investigation.

I cruised slowly round Eldon Park School's teachers' car park, searching for a space, but there wasn't one, so I gave up and headed for the main entrance. I spotted the police car as I rounded the side of the gymnasium building. It was a black unmarked Rover with a blue lamp on the dash, parked on yellow lines next to the front steps, and at the top of the steps stood Rob Monday and DCI Banks, deep in conversation. Rob Monday was nodding like an automaton, his head bowed, his hands thrust deep into his tracksuit pockets. I hastily steered the car up on to the kerb, switched off the engine and leapt out, just in time to see Rob and DCI Banks shake hands solemnly. DCI Banks walked briskly down the steps and got into the Rover.

'Excuse me!' I called, but he shut the door. His driver pulled smoothly away without a backward glance.

I ran after Rob. He had taken a short cut down a side path and was now heading for the gymnasium.

'Mr Monday, – can I have a word, please?'

I think he must have seen me coming.

'What do *you* want? I hope you've announced yourself properly at the school office.'

'Of course I have!' I lied easily. 'What did the police want?'

'They came to tell me they charged Ted Kitchen with Rick's murder half an hour ago.'

'Are you sure?' I couldn't believe it. 'But they can't have! How could they?'

He shook his head. 'Well, apparently the Crown Prosecution Service make the decision. The police put all their evidence in front of them, and then they –'

'No, no, no!' I interrupted angrily. He was going to explain the whole procedure to me, as though I was one of his eighth years who had failed to appreciate the niceties of the offside rule. 'What I mean is, how can they possibly have enough *evidence* to charge him?'

'They've got plenty of evidence. Look, I haven't got time for this. I've got a class waiting on the field.' He turned his back on me and began walking off towards the playing fields.

'What evidence?'

'What do you mean, what evidence?' He quickened his pace. 'He's admitted the burglary – he's admitted to fifty-seven other burglaries, as a matter of fact. And they found an imprint of a glove on my brother's body which matches the prints made by a pair of rubber gloves they found in his allotment shed . . .' He hopped lithely over a scattering of Coke cans on the path. I had to run round them. '. . . They've got fibres which match the remains of some clothes he'd tried to burn, and the clothes were *bloodstained*. What more do you want? Will you leave me alone now? I've told you, I don't want to talk to you.'

He ran up the steps to the field, two at a time.

'But Mr Monday, did you know your brother had the fête money *upstairs*, not in the study?'

He didn't answer, and I couldn't tell if he'd heard, so I carried on breathlessly: 'And did you know that, despite what he said earlier, Clifford Fletcher *was* in and he heard someone arrive at the front door of Tangley House shortly before the murder? And did you also know that Clifford –'

'Stop it!' He halted suddenly. 'Stop it! You're on school property and I can have you thrown off! Don't you know when to give up? I'm telling you, I don't want to hear any more of your theories!'

To prevent myself colliding with him when he stopped,

I'd grabbed hold of a litter bin, and I stood now hanging on to it as I caught my breath. I could tell that I'd got him worried. 'Why not?'

'Because I don't. Go away.'

The litter bin was rocking on the metal spike that held it in the soft earth, spilling crisp packets and sweet wrappers to the wind. Rob snatched at it and tried to firm it in place.

'Look, just tell me the truth about what happened between Rick and Will and Marianne. I promise I won't publish it.'

'Oh, don't be ridiculous!'

In the distance, hidden from view by a border of trees, a train thundered by on its way to Waterloo.

'Please. Look, I'm in a lot of trouble. I'm probably going to lose my job because of the complaint the Acorn Trust have made against me.'

'What complaint?'

'Didn't you know? I think your friend John Bradman intends to get me sacked.'

'That's nonsense! You're making this up. That article of yours had nothing to do with plans for the Centre being dropped. Why should John make a complaint against you?'

I did a double take.

Rob gave the bin a final shove into the upright position, and walked off.

'What do you mean?' I shouted, catching him up.

'Oh, come on, you're not going to con me into feeling sorry for you. You're an inept journalist and your paper is a waste of trees, but don't kid yourselves you were responsible for stopping the Centre. John told us the day before the fête that he was thinking of postponing the scheme. It had nothing at all to do with your pathetic article.'

'Didn't it? Did he tell you that?' My foot went down a goal-post hole. I clambered back up and ran after him. 'What did he say?'

'I've just told you what he said. Will you go away, please?'

'But what did he say exactly? Did he say anything to you about a letter?'

'What letter?' He was beginning to lose his temper. 'Look,

204

if it makes you happy – all right. Your article may have been the last straw as far as the Centre was concerned. I don't know how you'll be able to face yourself in the mirror in a few years' time when a new generation of muggers and burglars hits the streets.'

As I seriously doubted I'd be able to face up to myself in a mirror under any circumstances in a few years' time, I didn't even bother to contest this.

'You know, I hadn't thought about it before,' said Rob suddenly 'but I see now that Rick had a point. He was absolutely right when he said that John Bradman wasn't the only member of the Acorn Trust! It wouldn't have been my choice, but we *could* have got one of the others to have stepped in and taken over his projects if he couldn't go on with them. That is, until you and your friends –'

'When did Rick say that? Did he actually tell Bradman he'd get one of the other members of the Acorn Trust to take on the activity centre scheme? *And* the Tangley House project? Did they have a discussion about it?'

'How on earth do you know about the Tangley House project?' Rob stared at me open-mouthed.

'Then John Bradman must have got the letter! It's the only logical explanation. Did he come up with some story about financial commitments or falling share prices or something? 'He must have been looking for a way out without admitting the truth. It must be true about the tip!' I exclaimed excitedly.

At this, Rob quickened his pace to a lope. I don't think he had the faintest idea what I was talking about, and it didn't seem worth explaining, so this time I let him get away. He'd inadvertently given me a whole new perspective on things. Supposing John Bradman had received Fletcher's letter just before the fête? And supposing its contents were true, and he decided he had no option but to comply with Clifford Fletcher's demands . . . I closed my eyes for a moment and tried to imagine the scene. Rick is eagerly preparing for the Hatchley Heath fête, his interview with the *Sunday Times*, and the fame he hopes will follow. Bradman happens by in his canary yellow tracksuit and diffidently mentions the possibility of postponing all Acorn Trust schemes in Hatchley Heath for the next couple of years until there's a recovery in the housing market ... Rick might not spontaneously combust, but he would certainly make it clear that there was *no way* he was going to let the Acorn Trust off the hook.

I started back to the car. No wonder Bradman had cancelled his dinner engagement with Rick. The recital ticket story had probably been a complete fabrication. He would have realized the more he thought about it that talking Rob and the others into a postponement (for which, read abandonment) of the activity centre would be a piece of cake, but that Rick was going to be a problem. Now, of course, the next step in this line of reasoning was actually a leap of monumental proportions. People who own several companies and donate money and time to charity are not known for going around stabbing other people to death with ornamental knives. On the other hand, John Bradman was in deep trouble. If the tip story ever came out, there would be a number of ghastly and inevitable consequences. First, Bradman shares would take a nose-dive into the nearest black hole. Second, everybody living in a Bradman home would rush out to consult a surveyor about the cracked plaster on their living-room ceiling or the mysterious puddle on the front lawn that filled up with funny oily water every time it rained. And third, John Bradman's personal reputation as a supporter of environmental issues and all-round nice chap would evaporate faster than metered water.

I jumped into the car. Bradman Homes' head office was in Kingston, and Kingston was just off the A3. I could be there in half an hour.

16

From the phone booth, I had a good view of the entrance to the Bradman building, with its glass canopy picked out in green and its elegant sign incorporating the well-known hedgehog logo. BRADMAN was all the sign said; in seven simply-drawn letters it announced: 'You know who we are and what we stand for. You know you can trust us'.

There were three large parking bays in front of the building marked 'reserved for the directors of Bradman Homes'. Two of the bays had Daimlers parked in them, but the third, labelled 'JBH 1' was empty.

'Bradman,' announced the switchboard operator.

'Could I speak to Mr Bradman, please?'

'Putting you through . . .'

I tightened my grip on the receiver in readiness for adopting Plan B.

'. . . John Bradman's office. Can I help you?'

'Yes. Could you put me through to Mr Bradman, please?' I demanded, in my best gushy, pushy, WRVS voice. 'I'm returning his call of a few minutes ago.'

'Oh.' There was a startled pause. 'Well, he's not in, I'm afraid. May I ask who –'

I slammed the receiver back on its cradle. He wasn't in. This was what I'd hoped for, but now I was hyperventilating. Sweat started to accumulate in the palms of my hands and the pulse at the back of my neck throbbed in painful harmony with the engine of a passing petrol tanker. Before my nerve could go completely I pushed out of the booth, ran across the road and flew up the steps of the Bradman building two at a time.

The receptionist looked up from the glossy brochure she was in the process of inserting into an envelope.

'I'd like to speak to John Bradman's secretary, please,' I demanded, breathlessly.

'Do you have an appointment? I'm afraid Mr Bradman doesn't see anyone without an appointment.'

'I don't want to see Mr Bradman – I just want to talk to his secretary for *two minutes*. You see, a few weeks ago my boss sent Mr Bradman an important letter and he hasn't had a reply. Well, I've got this awful feeling I may have put the letter in the wrong envelope and sent it to a competitor. Do you see what I mean? Please, I only want to put my mind at rest that Mr Bradman received it.'

'I see.' She eyed me suspiciously. 'Well, I'll find out if Mrs Mayall is free. Please take a seat.'

I sat down obediently, and pretended to admire the framed painting of a Bradman estate entitled 'The Oaks, Harpersfield' which had been strategically placed opposite the seating area. The receptionist retreated out of earshot and began pushing buttons on her phone with long, perfect fingernails. Out of the corner of my eye I could see her tapping her free hand impatiently on the edge of the desk. If she said no, I was going to have to think of some other way of getting into John Bradman's office.

'Mrs Mayall would like you to go up,' she said, suddenly, with a pitying smile. 'Take the lift to the fourth floor and she'll meet you there. All right?'

'Yes. Thank you.'

'The lift's right behind you. It's fully automatic.'

I got into the lift and pressed the button marked 'four', scarcely able to believe my luck. Not only was John Bradman conveniently absent, but his secretary was obviously of a sympathetic and friendly turn of mind. In five minutes I'd have the proof that he'd received Fletcher's letter, and he would never know how I'd come by it.

The lift delivered me to the fourth floor with a little sigh, and a woman in a tailored beige dress stepped forward.

'Hello, I'm Mrs Mayall. I believe you have some sort of

problem. How can I help you?' she enquired with such unexpected warmth that I felt like launching into my genito-urinary history.

I resisted the temptation. 'Well, a few weeks ago I typed up a very important letter to Mr Bradman, and the thing is, I was in an awful rush and I sent it off without saving it on my machine or taking a copy . . .'

Mrs Mayall's mouth tweaked convulsively downwards, as though she knew exactly how this felt.

'. . . and now my boss is jumping up and down because Mr Bradman hasn't answered the letter. I'm almost *sure* I sent it, but I was just passing, and I thought perhaps you could confirm whether the letter ever got here and put his mind at rest. Well, mine, really.'

She nodded sympathetically. 'I will if I can. What's your boss's name?'

Behind me, the lift doors clanged shut.

'It was marked "Private and confidential" on the envelope, so I'm not sure if you'd've seen the letter itself.'

She frowned slightly. 'If you don't tell me who it was from, I don't see how I can help.'

I hesitated. 'It was from Clifford Fletcher.'

Mrs Mayall studied the ceiling for a moment. 'Hmm, that name doesn't mean anything to me. But come into the office. We keep an incoming mail book to record tender dates and so forth, and it's just possible I might have made a note of your letter. When did you say you posted it?'

I followed her into her office. If she was suspicious of me, she wasn't showing it.

'It would have been the first week in May. I wish I could give you the exact date – probably the Thursday.'

'First class?' She reached for a large red book and began riffling through the pages.

'Yes. Well, probably.' I remembered the state of Clifford's slippers. Perhaps he'd sent it second.

Mrs Mayall ran her finger down a long column of entries. 'Ah. There you are. A letter marked private and confidential arrived for Mr Bradman with the first post on the Friday. Of course, we've got no way of knowing if it was *your* letter or not, but there it is.' She turned the book round and pointed out the entry.

'Oh, great!' I glanced quickly up and down the neatly written column of entries. There was no record of any other confidential letter being received in the few days preceding or following the receipt of this one, so it had to be Clifford's.

'Thank you,' I said, gratefully. 'I wonder – do you know if Mr Bradman was in that day? I mean, would he have opened the letter immediately, do you think?'

She raised her eyebrows. She was beginning to look suspicious. 'I could look in the diary if you like.'

'Oh, would you mind? It's awfully kind of you.'

She produced another red book and began looking through it. Out in the corridor, the lift divulged a passenger, clanged shut, and hummed off again.

'Mr Bradman had an architects' meeting here at eleven. He was in most of the day, and he's always very prompt at dealing with his post. Look, why don't you leave me your number, so I can check with him and ring you?'

'Oh, no, please don't trouble yourself!' Actually, I had rather expected the arrival of Clifford's letter to have been a fairly memorable occasion; I'd thought Mrs Mayall would recall her boss turning sheet-white, clutching at his breast and cancelling all his appointments for the rest of the day. I gave her a searching look. She seemed to have no such recollection.

'Well, if that's all – let me see you out,' she suggested, suddenly appearing unnerved.

'Oh, don't worry!' I backed off across the landing and pressed the button for the lift. 'I've taken up much too much of your time already! I can't thank you enough for all your help. I really do appreciate it.'

The lift hesitated on our floor, clicked, whirred, and then sank to the floor below. I leaned on the button again, catching sight of an Acorn Trust poster pinned to the notice board next to the lift doors.

'Goodbye,' said Mrs Mayall, standing in her doorway, watching me.

'It must be nice working for someone like Mr Bradman who does so much for charity,' I remarked, casually. 'Someone who cares about people.'

She seemed to consider this. 'Well, yes, I suppose it is. He jumped out of a plane once,' she added, proudly.

'Really?' The lift had vanished. 'I don't know how he fits it all in. He's pretty keen on music too, isn't he?'

'Yes. How did you know that?'

'Oh, you know, someone mentioned it.' She must definitely be suspicious now – she'd probably got entirely the wrong idea about me and my personal letter. 'Piano, isn't it?' I went on. 'Does he play an instrument himself?'

She frowned.

The lift was now on the ground floor. I put my finger on the button and held it in place. 'So, do you often have to track down tickets for him – to recitals and things – to see his favourite pianists play?'

'What?'

'You know, at places like the Wigmore Hall.'

'What? What on earth are you talking about?' She advanced across the landing, frowning. '*I* don't organize Mr Bradman's social life. Just a minute. Who are you exactly?'

The lift was at last on its way up; it would be here any second. I could still talk my way out of this, *and* get a bit more information out of Mrs Mayall. 'I told you, your boss and my boss are friends. My boss said you once managed to get hold of a last-minute ticket to a concert for Mr Bradman – a few weeks ago, in fact. He seems to think I ought to be able to do the same sort of thing. Is it true? Was it at the Wigmore Hall?'

'What on *earth* are you talking about? Wait a minute –'

At that moment, right on cue, the lift hummed into place and the doors swished open. Someone got out, and I had to do a little dance on the spot to avoid running into him.

It was John Bradman.

I stared at him for a second, but I didn't panic. Quite often, people don't remember my face, not even when they've had fairly long conversations with me.

I got in the lift.

'John, I'm sorry, this lady – I don't know who she is, but she's been asking some awfully strange questions about you!'

I pressed the button to close the doors. I thought I'd made it, but John Bradman had got his hand in the way.

'It's Mrs Martin,' he said, tautly. 'Isn't it? Mrs Martin from the *Herald*. Oh dear, am I to take it that you didn't announce yourself properly to my secretary?'

I tried to press the button again, even though it was hopeless.

'Isn't that a breach of your code of ethics?' he went on, malevolently.

And at that point my patience snapped. I must still have been awash with adrenaline from my run-in with Mr Heslop. 'Is it? Well, so what. It isn't as bad as some of the things some people do, is it? It's not as bad as building a housing estate on top of a rubbish tip, is it!'

He blinked. Briefly, his mouth assumed the shape of one of those little squirmy lines that goes over the first 'n' in mañana.

'Oh, John, I'm so sorry!' exclaimed Mrs Mayall, blushing furiously. 'She lied to me! What have I done?'

'It's all right, Penny, you weren't to know.' He'd recovered himself already. 'Hold all my calls for the next five minutes, will you? I'm seeing Mrs Martin off the premises.' And he jumped into the lift and let go of the door.

I backed away from the control panel. It was a stupid move, but I wanted to be as far away from him as possible. I couldn't tell what he was thinking, but I had a feeling I wouldn't like it.

'Mrs Martin, I must warn you to be very careful. If you think you can threaten my company, you're making a very big mistake,' said John Bradman, pressing two buttons on the control panel and turning to face me.

I willed the lift to move.

'You and your paper had better be very sure of your facts before you print a single word concerning this company and any of our developments, or – I promise you – you are going to be very sorry.'

The lift wasn't moving, and I began to wonder what he'd done to it. The headline 'Local reporter dies in mysterious lift accident' began to put itself together before my eyes.

'We will be sure of our facts. We've got very good information and we're checking it all out,' I retorted.

'I see.' The control panel was making little clicking noises, and a red light had come on. 'Well, if you've got such good information, may I ask why you found it necessary to trick your way into my office?'

I decided not to answer this. 'Will you please let me out of this lift,' I said shakily. 'You're holding me against my will. You can't do this.'

'Can't I? I think you'll find you're not in much of a position to complain. Are you aware of the Data Protection Act and the penalties for attempting to obtain information under false pretences?'

'No.' I was sure they were horrendous. 'But the fact is –' Actually, the fact was, I was beginning to panic. 'The fact is, I don't need to obtain information about the Willow Grange Estate under false pretences. It's all on the public record!'

Suddenly, his lips drained completely of blood, twisting palely together like two earthworms that have drowned in a watering can. His fingers moved to the control panel, and the lift lurched into life, catching me off balance and unexpectedly displacing my stomach into my upper abdomen. I floundered about, grabbing helplessly at the decor.

'You stupid woman,' he muttered, in a barely audible whisper. 'You stupid, stupid woman. You don't know what you're doing. You're a pain in the neck and a bloody stupid *cow*.'

There was something in the way he said this that sent a shiver down my spine. The word 'cow' just didn't belong to him: it didn't match his elegant suit or the subtle fragrance of his skin or his clean-cut fingernails; it hung shockingly between us, like an axe raised with the intention of slicing its way through the air and embedding itself in my skull.

Before I could respond, the lift bumped to a halt, the doors slid open, and he stepped towards them. Shaking slightly, I pushed past him and jumped out into the foyer.

When I turned back, he was already pressing buttons on the control panel. 'You lied, Mr Bradman!' I shouted. 'You lied about where you were on the night of Rick's murder. You said you were at a recital, but you weren't. You –'

The doors clanged shut. I stabbed desperately at the 'call' button, but it was too late. Casting a glance at the astonished receptionist, I took a deep breath, and marched with as much dignity as I could muster out of the Bradman building.

I don't know why, but I didn't panic when I got back to the office. Mr Heslop had left a terse message on my keyboard. It said: 'Ted Kitchen charged with murder this a.m. Two paragraphs for the front page, please.' I ignored it and reached for the phone.

To my surprise, Wayne answered almost immediately.

'It's me,' I said. 'Your role model.'

'What?'

'It's me, Chris.'

'Oh. Right. How are you, love?' There seemed to be a party going on at the CID office. 'Nice to hear from you. Excuse the noise, we've got something big going down this afternoon.'

Going down – I thought of the lift in the Bradman building and shivered. 'Look, I need to have a chat with you about the Monday murder. I've got hold of a lot of new information.'

'*Jesus, did you see that one? Go on, Greg, rewind it!*' interrupted a hoarse male voice in the middle distance.

'Well, I know you've charged Ted Kitchen –' in the background, there was a staccato volley of minor explosions that sounded suspiciously like ring-pulls being ripped off cans – 'but I think . . . I think I've got a new suspect.'

'Oh.'

'Go on, rewind it in slow-mo! Let's take a look at that bit just before the other guy got his bloody knee in the way.'

'Well, how about lunch next week?' He didn't sound very interested.

'Next week?' I repeated, dismayed.

'Yes. How about –'

'Christ, look at that! I told you he was good, didn't I? Have you ever seen such incredible penetration! The man's a –'

'– Wednesday?'

'But I wanted to talk to you now.'

'What?'

'Oh, bugger me – the limp useless bastard!'

'I wanted to talk to you now, because –'

'Oh my God he's got it in again!'

'Oh, for God's sake!' I snapped, suddenly losing my temper. 'Are you watching porno videos, or something?'

'Huh? It's last night's Cup match, love. Look, you're a sweetie, but I'll have to love you and leave you. Wednesday's fine – ring me next week to confirm it.'

'But Wayne, I've got some –'

'Same time and place as before,' he interrupted. 'Here come the chapatis, I'll have to go. 'Bye, love.'

I gave up and put the phone down. It was hopeless. If Wayne wouldn't help there was nothing I could do to check out John Bradman's whereabouts at the time of the murder, or anything else about him for that matter. Not until next Wednesday at any rate. And I was beginning to suspect I'd made a bad mistake in letting him know I knew about the Willow Grange story.

I huddled dejectedly over the keyboard and hammered out a story under the heading, 'Local man charged with Monday murder and spate of burglaries'.

215

A local man, Mr Ted Kitchen, has been charged with the murder of the rock star, Rick Monday, who was best known for his seventies hit 'Just for the Money', and more recently for the song adopted to spearhead the current campaign against child abuse, 'Reaching out for No One'.

Mr Monday was found dead almost three weeks ago following a break-in at his home. Tipping police, led by DCI Kenneth Banks, have conducted a painstaking investigation into the murder, successfully linking it to an earlier series of burglaries in the area.

Mr Monday will be sadly missed by all those who benefited from his unstinting work for the community.

I didn't like the piece much, but I hoped it would cheer Mr Heslop up when he got back from seeing the lawyers. It might even keep me out of the typing pool for another week.

17

The following morning I went into the office early and started work on the YMCA keep-fit event story. I had decided to keep my head down and not to say anything to anyone about my unfortunate encounter with John Bradman yesterday. Mr Heslop was sure to find out soon enough anyway, in the form of a letter from the Press Complaints Commission. Or worse, a visit from the serious fraud squad. By eleven o'clock I had rung sixteen health clubs and asked them if they would like to participate in a survey on local fitness facilities, and I'd left messages for two prominent GPs to ring me back with their comments on the general health of Tipping people. So, when my phone rang, I leapt on it, hoping it would be the manager of Tipping Leisure Centre with his up-to-date attendance figures.

'It's me, Jackie. I've got to talk to you – it's urgent.'

'Jackie?' She was talking on a mobile phone in a bad reception area.

'Yes. Can you meet me in ten minutes in the petrol station at the bottom of Church Street?'

'Why?'

''Cos you can park in front of the car wash.'

'No – I mean, why do you want to see me? I'm working on something else at the moment and then I'm meeting someone for lunch.'

'Oh, please, it'll only take a few minutes. I've got all my luggage in the boot and I've got to be at Heathrow in an hour. I'm going to Florida.'

Church Street was only a short walk from the *Herald*

building. With luck, I could make it there and back in twenty minutes, and still be at the school by twelve. 'All right,' I said, 'I'll see you in front of the car wash.'

Jackie was sitting in the driving seat of a dark green Renault 25 – I recognized the outline of her shaggy blonde hairdo silhouetted against the garish blue wall of the car wash – and seated next to her was a platinum blonde with a scrawny neck and earrings the size of early nineteenth-century chandeliers. Although the sky was overcast, both women were wearing Ray-bans.

She wound down her window, and I caught a glimpse of her eyes behind the glasses. They were pale and puffy.

'Go on, then, Jackie,' urged her companion. 'Is that her? Blimey!'

I ignored her disparaging tone and opened the rear door.

'Shall I get in?' When neither of them replied, I began to clear a space for myself on the back seat, which was pretty much of a tip, littered with chocolate wrappers, biscuit crumbs, silk scarves.

'No!' shrieked Jackie, suddenly. 'I can't!'

'Oh, yes, you can!' shouted the older woman, lunging forward and grabbing the keys out of the ignition before Jackie could get to them. A wave of perfume too expensive for me to identify flooded from the many nooks and crannies that made up her person.

I got into the car.

'Oh, Mum!' screamed Jackie.

'It's for your own good!' Breathing heavily, Jackie's mum dropped the keys down what was left of her cleavage. 'You gotta think of your future. You're not getting any younger – you gotta get some money in the bank! Come on, tell this woman your story before she gets fed up with you and pisses off!'

I was a bit taken aback, so I offered the mother my hand. 'I'm Chris from the *Herald*,' I said nervously.

She gave my hand a brief shake, as though it was a rather loathsome dishcloth she'd prefer not to have contact with. 'I know who you are. Well, I didn't know who else to go to, did I? I'm not having my girl getting screwed. She's had a bloody hard time. That bastard threw her out after all she done for him. Best years of her life! She won't get nothing from British Airways now, you know.'

'Oh, shut up, Mum. You don't know what you're talking about!' Jackie was twisting in her seat in anguish. 'I told you, he didn't throw me out – he's paying for this bloody trip, isn't he? The minute we land he'll be on that phone begging me to come back, you wait and see if he's not –'

'Look, excuse me,' I intervened, as the decibel level started to rise unpleasantly. 'I don't know what this is all about, and I've got another appointment in twenty-five minutes . . .'

'I'll tell you what it's all about! It's about that sod McGill! Hit my girl and broke her tooth, didn't he!'

'Mum, I told you . . .'

'Gave her four years of hell. Made her do unnatural things with them dogs.'

'Mum! He never!'

'I mean, I'm all for a bit of fun, but there's a limit, isn't there? I can tell you some things! I want compensation for my girl. It's only fair, isn't it? I'm telling you, she lied for him – to the police!'

I was beginning to get the measure of Jackie's mum. I bit my lip and cursed myself for responding to Jackie's call, because even at a brisk pace it had taken more than ten minutes to get here; it would take more than ten minutes to get back. I said, 'I know all about that, I told her. She knows I know.'

She let out a nasty cackle. 'You don't know the half of it, my love. You think that sod McGill was tucked up safe in bed with my girl when that Rick Monday was murdered, don't you? Well, a lot you know. I wouldn't put nothing past him.'

'What do you mean?'

'I mean you should see some of the bruises I've seen on her. You should hear some of the things he's said to her. Sick, that's what he is! She's had her arm broke –'

'Mum, shut up, *shut up*!' screeched Jackie, beside herself, turning to me beseechingly. 'Please don't listen to her! She doesn't know what she's talking about. She's making it up! Will never laid a finger on me, I swear it . . . not on purpose, he didn't. Look, I've done something stupid, I know that, but you're not to believe a word she says! I wouldn't be talking to you at all – I still love Will – but I don't want to end up with people thinking someone went to prison because of a dreadful misunderstanding and it was my fault!'

She bit her lip, and tears began to run out from beneath her glasses and splash into her leather-clad lap.

'Mum's wrong about Will, I know she is! It's all because of the drugs thing, that's the truth of it! And I'm not saying Will's a junkie, 'cos he isn't. He just does cocaine occasionally.'

I began to lose patience. 'Look, I don't know *what* you're talking about and I've got to be somewhere else in five minutes!'

'Well, I'm trying to explain! You see, that weekend – the weekend of the, you know, murder – Modus were negotiating for a new contract. They're supposed to be, like, the elder statesmen of rock now; they're supposed to set an example. They're not supposed to do drugs.'

'So?'

'So that Sunday it was like I told you, we were going up to Mick's place at Scarcroft. We were all ready to go – we were packing up the car, in fact – when Will ups and says he can't go without some coke. He says he can't get his head round the music without it. So then he says I'm to drive on up in the Porsche, and he'll go and pick some stuff up from this guy he knows in Kensington. Or Cricklewood – or somewhere. I'm not sure. Well, I didn't want to do it – drive the Porsche, I mean – people try to race you on the motorways. But Will'd been in an awful mood since, well, lately, – so I thought I better do what he said.'

'I see.' Julie would be coming out of school in ten minutes and waiting for me under the tree by the school gate.

'He said I was to tell everyone he'd be there by eight,

latest. He knew they wouldn't like it, 'cos they couldn't start without him. And he knew it would be rotten for me, because I don't get on with the other wives. I mean, they're all models or actresses, and I don't know what to say to them, and also they were all friends of *Aimee*. They hate me. They –'

'Get on with it,' muttered her mother, impatiently.

'Shut up, Mum. I'm just trying to explain why I got in a muddle! You see, the next day we heard on the news about Rick, and everybody flipped. Well, they knew the police'd be round asking questions any minute because of all those nasty things Will said about Rick. And the record company rang up in a big panic about the Press and what Will was going to say. And Mick – you know, Modus's bass guitarist – *he* was shitting himself because the band's new deal with the record company was at a really delicate stage. Do you see what I mean? If Will had told the police he'd been with some low-life drugs dealer that evening, it'd've ended up in the papers, and the record company might've cancelled the deal!'

'I see.' I glanced frantically at my watch. 'But you said Will arrived at Mick's place at *eight*, and since the murder didn't happen until ten or eleven I don't see . . .'

'He never!' put in Jackie's mum, gleefully. 'Don't you get it? He never got to Scarcroft till the next day! And he was in a right state, an' all!'

'He *what*?' I wasn't sure if I should believe this. 'Are you now claiming that Will wasn't with you at Mick's place at the time of the murder, and that all the members of Modus *lied* to give him an alibi? I don't believe you.'

Jackie shook her head energetically. 'But they didn't lie to give Will an alibi for the murder. They lied because Will was in London getting stoned when Rick was murdered. They were worried about their contract! They're old, aren't they – this'll be their last deal! It's their bloody pension! I told you, Will got stoned and spent the night in a hotel somewhere – he told me!'

'Yeah, he *told* you!' interrupted her mother, forcefully. 'But you don't know where the lying bastard was! He could've

221

been anywhere! You told me he turned up the next morning grinning like the cat that's got the cream and wouldn't tell you nothing. You said you'd never seen him act so weird before and it scared the shit out of you, remember? You rang me up from that bloody Mick's house and told me! You said the sod wouldn't talk to you at all until the police turned up and then it's, "Go on, Jackie, get me out of a hole, tell 'em I was with you all night." That's what you told me!'

'Shut up! Shut up! It wasn't like that! Listen, please.' Jackie gripped my arm desperately. 'It was Mick's idea for us to say we'd both been there all night. *Mick's* – not Will's! I screwed it all up because I was upset. I told this detective from the local nick we'd been at Mick's since *Saturday*. Will was furious! I got confused; the last time we went to Mick's we went on a Saturday and stayed for a week, and I just got confused.'

'All right, I understand that,' I agreed. 'But . . .'

'Oh, come on!' Jackie's mum swivelled round in her seat. 'Tell her the rest of it. Tell her what you told me – all them things Will said about Rick when that song came out. And tell her about how you know he was lying when he said he had to go up to London for coke 'cos he'd got a load of it in the guest bathroom! Go on, Jackie.' She seemed to be enjoying this. 'Tell her what you found out about that stupid song.'

There was silence.

'What song?' I prompted.

The silence continued.

'"Reaching out for No one",' muttered Jackie. 'Rick didn't write it – Will did.'

'It's the truth,' put in her mother, eagerly, before I could say anything. 'Rick nicked it off him. Jackie found the manuscript in his attic, didn't you? Go on, tell her.'

'What?' I was speechless.

Jackie nodded. 'I was having a bit of a clear-out and I came across all this old stuff: school exercise books and things. There were all these songs and poems he wrote when he was a kid. And this was before Rick had made the record, about eighteen months ago. I specially remembered "Reaching out for No one" because it was so sad.'

'But . . .' I stared at her in disbelief. 'That can't be right! I mean, if it's true, why didn't Will sue Rick for copyright infringement or plagiarism or something?'

'Because he couldn't, could he? Because he'd have to admit why he wrote the song, and when, and what it meant. He wouldn't want to do that. You see, when he was about thirteen he lived in this awful Home, and something terrible happened to him there. He told me about it once when he was very, very drunk. A man, a care worker, told him he loved him and did things to him. I think he wrote "Reaching out for No one" to, you know, get things off his chest. He doesn't even know I know about it. He'd go nuts if he did!'

My eyebrows felt as if they were about to go through the roof of the Renault.

'Well, it's the truth – I don't care if you believe it or not,' retorted Jackie, who was crying and hadn't bothered to wipe her nose.

'No, it's not that exactly – I just don't see how Rick could have got hold of a copy of the song.'

'Oh, that's easy! Will and Rick used to be the best of mates. Will showed him all his stuff. And I can prove it, anyway. Do you remember a song called "Just for the Money"?'

'Of course I remember it.'

'Well, the original version of it was in the same exercise book – on the next page!'

There was silence.

'I think it was in that terrible Home that Will met his ex-wife,' volunteered Jackie, apropos of nothing, at last wiping her nose on her sleeve.

'*Wife*,' corrected her mother, crisply. She turned to me with a smug smile. 'Quite a story, eh? What do you think now, Mrs *Tipping Herald*?'

I began to fumble for the door handle. My pulse was racing like an early Beach Boys drum solo.

'Hey, hang on a minute!' Her hand came out of nowhere and clamped on my arm. 'You haven't answered my question. What you going to do for my girl?'

I managed to open the door with my free hand. At that

moment I wished I had a little black book with the names of publicity agents in it instead of school dentists. 'Well, if you'd like to give me your card or something . . .'

'Oh, God, you're not going to tell Will I told you, are you?' interrupted Jackie, frantically. 'You can't! He'll kill me!'

'If you give me your card, I'll get someone to phone you. Where can I get in touch with Will?'

'Oh, my God!' sobbed Jackie.

'He's at the house,' hissed her mother, digging her long plastic fingernails into my wrist. 'He's packing up his stuff. He's off to his villa in Alicante for a week. You're probably too late. Who're you going to put us on to?'

'I don't know! I mean . . .' I sought desperately for a way to get my arm out of her grasp. 'It's a question of choosing the right person and making the right deal.'

'Oh, I see. You know lots of people then?'

'Lots of people.'

She let go of my arm and handed me a small pink card. 'This has got the name of our hotel in Miami on the back.' The card said: 'June Day, Beautician. Your legs waxed in your own home.'

'*Please don't tell Will you've seen me!*' shrieked Jackie, dementedly.

I jumped out of the car and ran all the way back to the *Herald* building. By the time I reached the back stairs I was perspiring copiously, but my mind had risen above this and was engaged in planning my next move – a heated discussion with a secretary in Julie's school office who would (I knew) be extremely unwilling to go out to the school gates and tell Julie I wasn't coming.

On the landing I bumped into Mr Heslop.

'Good God, where have you been?' he demanded tetchily, as he bounced off, hitting the wall.

'Sorry! I . . .'

'Oh, never mind! I've been looking for you. Don't ask me why, but Bradman's been on the phone. He's dropping the complaint.'

'He's what?'

224

'He's dropping the complaint. All right? Happy now?' He began to sidle off down the stairs. 'You and I are going to have to have a talk when I get back.'

'But what do you mean? Why?' I ran after him.

'Well, I should have thought that was obvious. We've got one or two things to sort out.'

'No, I meant . . . I meant why did Bradman . . .' I decided not to bother. 'Look, Mr Heslop, I need to talk to you *now* about the Monday murder.'

'Not now, Chris.'

'But it's –'

'No. I'm going for lunch.' He side-stepped me, and disappeared out of the building without a backward glance.

I ran up the stairs two at a time and made a dash for my phone. Julie would be furious, of course, but I was sure she'd understand when she knew the reason.

The phone rang while I was looking for the school number.

'There you are!' It was Dawn in reception. 'I've been ringing you for half an hour. There's a man to see you.'

'What man?'

'His name's Mr Huntley and he's from the Mister Fixit shop or something – he's been waiting for an hour!'

'Oh, but Dawn, I can't . . .'

'You have to! You're not making me be the one to tell him he's sat here for all this time for nothing!' And she slammed the phone down on me.

Desperately I dialled the number of Julie's school, and managed to persuade the secretary to despatch a handy pupil to the school gate with a message for Julie. Then I rang Hudderston police station.

'I'd like to speak to DS Horton, please. It's very urgent.'

'Sorry, love, DS Horton's in with the guv'nor at the moment. Do you want to ring back in half an hour?'

'I'm afraid I can't. Look, it really is very urgent. Could you tell him that Chris from the *Herald* rang about the case we were discussing yesterday and that I now *definitely know who did it*. Tell him I'm on my way to this address.' I gave him

Will's address. 'Have you got that? Can you make sure he gets this message within half an hour?'

'I will if I can, love.'

'But this really is very important. Are you sure you've got my name?'

'Yes, I've got your name and I'll do my best.'

I knew I'd pushed him too far because he'd stopped calling me love.

'Thank you,' I said. '*Please* do.'

I ran down the stairs to Reception two at a time. I could see Mr Huntley, craning round the side of the photograph board to watch the back of Dawn's thighs as she watered the rubber plant.

'Hello, I'm Chris Martin. I'm so sorry you've been kept waiting. What can I do for you?'

He jumped guiltily and treated me to a sickly smile. I didn't recognize him from my earlier visit to Bangles. He was in his fifties, bald, pale, and, unlike the other members of the Angles family, plumply built. On the whole, he looked like one of those pallid, sluggy things you find living under upturned bricks.

'Have you been able to remember something about the person who had the key cut?' I demanded eagerly, offering him my hand. Then I had a brainwave. 'If I show you a photograph of the person, would you be able to recognize him, do you think?'

He looked baffled. 'What photograph?'

'Of the person who came to your booth to have the key cut!' I began searching through my file for a recent photograph of Will McGill. 'It's awfully good of you to come in, but I'm in a bit of a hurry, so –'

Mr Huntley reached suddenly into his inside jacket pocket and held something out towards me in a clenched fist.

'I've got this for you,' he said. 'Do you want it?'

I looked up nervously. 'What is it?' He was holding the whatever-it-was in exactly the same way small boys offer you daddy-longlegs.

226

He grinned and opened his fingers. Lying on the palm of his hand was a key fashioned from a dull yellow metal. It was a house key, and it looked old and worn. Engraved beneath the manufacturer's logo was a slightly irregular 'O'.

For a moment I just stared at it in astonishment. My neck began to pulse nastily.

'Where did you get this?'

'It was down behind my cash register. Is there a reward?'

'Behind your . . .' I reached excitedly for the key. Mr Huntley closed his hand on it. 'How on earth did it get there?'

'Well, I don't know. Someone must've dropped it down there, mustn't they? People are always dropping stuff down behind my cash register, and expecting me to fish it out for them. Pens, ten-pound notes, shopping lists – you name it, I've had it down the back of my cash register. Do you want it or not? I've had to shut the shop up to come in here.'

'Yes, of course I want it, but I don't understand how it got behind your cash register.' I tried to visualize the cash register at Bangles.

'Well, there's a bloody great crack in the counter where it doesn't fit together properly, isn't there? Do you know anything about franchising? Let me tell you, you have to shell out a fortune for equipment that doesn't do its job properly!'

'But I don't remember seeing a crack in your counter when I was in your store.'

Mr Huntley seemed suddenly to lose patience. He jumped to his feet and, to my horror, pocketed the key.

'Oh, don't you? And who the hell are you to tell me what I've got in my shop and what I haven't? I come here in good faith in answer to your appeal – I'm a regular reader of your paper, I'll have you know – you keep me waiting for the best part of an hour, – and *now* you've got the cheek to tell me you don't think I've got a crack in my counter! After all the trouble I've been to! Well, you can –'

'Wait a minute, please.' I outmanoeuvred him desperately

as he made a move for the door. 'Haven't you been sent here by one of the Angles family?'

'By one of the . . . I don't know what you're talking about! I told you – I told your girl –' he scowled angrily in Dawn's direction – 'I own the Mister Fixit shop in Hudderston High Street. I've lost half a morning's takings coming in here!'

'In *Hudderston*?' I was baffled.

'Yes! It's a prime site, I'll have you know. I pay through the nose in bloody business rates and I can't afford to lose income.' He produced the key again.

This time, I snatched it from him. I couldn't be a hundred per cent sure, of course, without trying it in the front door of Tangley House, but at that moment I'd've bet any amount of money that this was Mrs Jobson's missing key. And I never bet, not even on the lottery.

'Do you open on Sundays?' I demanded.

'What? Don't be silly!'

'Oh! Are you –' No, of course he was sure. But this didn't make any sense. 'Well, when did you find the key? Do you know how long it's been, er, behind your cash register?'

'No, of course I don't. I had to open up the counter this morning 'cos this wretched woman dropped her credit card down into it. I had a good clear-out, and there it was, underneath a load of rubbish people had shoved down there – sweet wrappers and lolly sticks and stuff. The crack's at the back, you see, where the customers lounge about while they're waiting for things and write out their cheques. Look, I haven't got all day – is there a reward?'

I pressed the key into the palm of my hand, and a little shiver of excitement ran through me. I got out a publicity photo of Will McGill and showed it to him.

'Do you recognize this man? Do you ever remember seeing him in your shop?'

He gave me a blank look, then fumbled a pair of spectacles on to the end of his nose and stared at the photograph through them, twisting it this way and that. He shook his head. 'I don't know. He looks like someone, doesn't he?'

'Does he? Who? Someone who's been in your shop?'

228

'I told you, I don't know. He looks a bit like that snooker player, doesn't he – the one with the eyes too close together. It's a good photo, this . . . professional,' he added, fingering it. 'I nearly took out a franchise on one of them instant processing places.'

I snatched the photograph back. 'Never mind. Look, you've been awfully helpful but I've got to catch someone before they leave the country. Let's get you sorted out with a reward, shall we? What's your chest size?'

His eyes widened. 'My what?'

'Your chest size – and your wife's, and your children. Gosh, yes!' I said excitedly, hoping enthusiasm was infectious. 'Go and see Dawn over there and she'll sort you out with some T-shirts.'

'T-shirts?'

'Yes! You really do deserve it – have as many as you like. Thank you so much for coming in!'

'*T-shirts*?'

Before he could tell me what he thought of the T-shirts, I ran out of the foyer with the missing key to Tangley House at last clutched firmly in my palm.

18

I drove slowly past the wrought-iron gates of Will McGill's house. The gates were open, and there were two cars in the drive: Will's Porsche, and a white XR3i. At first, I thought the XR3i might belong to Wayne, and I was furious that he'd gone ahead without me, but then I remembered that Wayne's Escort was a standard model, and anyway, he wouldn't have gone ahead without me, because he had not the faintest clue what this was all about. I did a U-turn and drove back to park the Mini just past the gate and, I hoped, out of sight of the house. I wouldn't do anything until Wayne arrived, but I'd keep the engine running so that if Will tried to leave, I could shoot out across his driveway to block him.

I sat in the car, craning my neck down the empty road, waiting for a glimpse of Wayne and perspiring gently in the hot May sunshine. For five long minutes punctuated only by the erratic throbbing of the Mini's engine, there was no sign of Wayne, nor of anyone else save a man in a Harrods delivery van, and the only indication of Will's presence in the house was a small suitcase on the front step with an airline tag attached to it. Through the windscreen, the sun began to curl up the edges of my notepad. A damp trickle of perspiration wended its way down my temple and dripped on to my shirt collar. And then, the inevitable happened.

The Mini's engine stalled.

I couldn't risk Will sweeping out past me in the Porsche. I began pumping urgently on the accelerator to restart the car. The engine coughed asthmatically, made a noise like a giraffe in the midst of its death rattle, then lapsed into silence.

I didn't panic; I tried again – and again. If it didn't start next time . . .

Before I could work out my contingency plan, Will McGill walked out of his house with a large suitcase. He put down the suitcase, pushed his hair back from his face, and peered in the direction of the commotion.

He'd seen me.

I got out of the car. I counted to ten, walked up the drive, retrieved Mrs Jobson's key from my pocket, and held it out to him.

'I believe I've found something you lost.'

His mouth moved into its accustomed sneer. 'What is this – a wind-up?'

'It's the key to Tangley House.'

'Really.' He stooped to pick up the suitcase. 'And here's me thinking you were just a trainee arsehole. Go on, piss off, I've got a plane to catch.'

He was good – very good – at keeping his cool. I wished fervently that I'd been able to work out exactly how he had come to mislay Mrs Jobson's key behind a cash register in a Hudderston shop so I could have told him and wiped the smug smirk off his face.

'Look, Mr McGill,' I said. 'I know all about your false alibi. The police are already on their way!'

'Oh, good.' The smirk turned to a grin. 'They can throw *you* out then! What the hell are you talking about?'

At this point, I began to panic. '"Reaching out for No one".'

'What?'

'"Reaching out for No one" – the song. You wrote it when you were living in the children's home, and Rick stole it.'

He dropped the suitcase heavily on his foot. '*What did you say?* Who told you this?' He hadn't even flinched when the suitcase landed on his toe. Either he didn't have corns or he was very, very tough.

'Get this. You tell me who it was, or I'm going to beat your brains out inch by inch!' he snarled, and he grabbed me by the shoulders and slammed me down across the bonnet of the

231

Porsche. And just in case I hadn't got the idea, he pounded my head rhythmically against his gleaming red paintwork.

It didn't take me long to work out where my loyalties lay. 'Jackie!' I whispered.

'Jackie? You're lying! Jackie knows zilch about me!'

'She saw it in a book!'

'What book?'

I was desperate. How did I know what book? He was still pounding my head against the car and I was sure my brain must be getting very close to the surface. 'Your book – an exercise book! She found it in an old box in your attic!'

He paused briefly. I could tell from the look on his face that I'd said the right thing, but he carried on banging my head against his bonnet for a few more beats anyway, as though he didn't want to break the rhythm. I hope he made plenty of dents in the metalwork. Then he let go of me and stepped backwards.

I got up. I was shaking all over, and I'd dropped the key.

'What else did she tell you?' Will demanded, frantically dusting himself down for imaginary dust he might have picked up from my clothing. 'What did she tell you about me?'

'Nothing.'

'Did she tell you what those perverts did to me? Did she tell you there's something wrong with me?'

'No.'

'Do you think I'd let some scumbag put his hands on me?'

'No! No, I don't!'

He had gone so white I thought he might faint in my direction. I took a step sideways. I was still terrified, but I'd lost the key, and it was evidence. I began to look for it on the grass next to the car.

'Jackie Day is a liar and a cow. She doesn't know her arse from her elbow!' he hissed, through clenched teeth. He was so angry he could scarcely speak. 'Are you listening to me? You better, because if I see any of this crap in print, you're dead! Stop pissing about with that grass!'

At the end of the road, a car was at last approaching. I thanked God silently.

'I'm looking for the key. The key you took from Tangley House.'

'What key?' The car was cruising, the driver obviously unsure of his exact destination. 'I'm warning you, you print anything that cow has told you, and you're dead! I mean it!' He looked as if he did, too. 'She knows nothing! What she knows about me you couldn't piss on a postage stamp! Does she think she's going to screw money out of me – is that what the game is? Jesus Christ, it's June, isn't it?' he added, almost beside himself.

The car had stopped, just beyond the hedge that screened the house from the road. At any moment Wayne's large, dependable physique would appear in the gateway.

'Mr McGill, you've got about one minute to tell me your side of the story before the police get here,' I gasped, my teeth rattling in their sockets. 'Give me a break – I'll write the true story of what really happened between you and Rick in my paper. Your fans have a right to know. The feud! Marianne! The song!'

Suddenly the car that had been parked behind the hedge accelerated into view, coasted slowly past Will's gates and disappeared on its way.

It was a gas board van.

I felt a pit of terror open up in my stomach.

'Hang on.' Will was flexing his fingers as though in readiness for a lunge at my throat. 'Hang on a minute. What is all this crap about the police? That's not the bloody police! What's the matter with you?'

If Wayne didn't turn up within the next few seconds he was going to kill me, I was sure of it. I sought desperately for a way out. 'I've called the police and told them everything, so it's no good you thinking of doing anything to me. They know I'm here!' I tried to back round the bonnet of the Porsche, to put it between me and him. He followed me. 'The police know you weren't in Yorkshire at the time of the murder, and when I give them the key . . .' And suddenly I

233

caught sight of the key, which had lodged itself on top of the Porsche's headlamp casing. I made a grab for it, but Will was faster. Before I could stop him, he picked up my finest piece of evidence and hurled it in the direction of the front gates. I watched in horror as it flew through the air, jingled across the paving and skidded out of sight into a flower bed. I knew now, too late, that I'd made a terrible tactical error.

Suddenly, a woman appeared on the front steps, a strawberry blonde with emerald green eyeshadow and spiky, malevolent features. I didn't like the look of her.

'Who's *she*?' she demanded, pointing an accusing finger at me.

He ignored her.

'You silly bitch,' he said. 'You pathetic, stupid bitch. Bloody Jackie put you up to this, didn't she? You don't know what you're talking about. It's a bloody reporter, doll,' he added, contemptuously. 'A mental retard. Don't worry, I'm going to make her leave.'

The redhead completely ignored this piece of information. 'What's *this*?' she demanded, holding up a bedraggled black thing. 'It's a Versace, you bastard! You bought that bitch a bloody Versace! You think I'm stupid, or what? You spent a *fortune* on her! You told me you never thought anything of her!'

He half-turned to look at her. 'Oh, doll . . .'

'You're not going to make me leave, I'm waiting for the police!' I interrupted. 'So don't try anything, because they'll be here any minute!'

'Shut up!' The redhead threw the dress at Will. It was still on its hanger, which caught him sharply on the back of the head. This did not improve his temper. He picked the dress up and threw it at me. 'Listen, you – I've had just about enough of this! I want you out of here, *now*! Everything that witch Jackie told you is a lie! You got that? I haven't got any exercise books in my attic. I haven't even got an attic! And I didn't kill Rick Monday either, if she told you that, 'cos if I had I'd've done it with my bare hands!' He held

234

up his hands to show them to me, as if I didn't already know how strong they were.

And at this point I began to get the nastiest feeling; it was taking shape and growing and re-forming, like a thunder-cloud on a summer's day. If Will had killed Rick; if he knew I knew everything, why had he thrown the evidence carelessly into his flowerbed instead of pocketing it?

'Oh, for God's sake call the police or security or do some-thing! What's the matter with you? Just get rid of her!' put in the woman on the step distractedly. Rather belatedly I recognized her as Aimee, his estranged wife.

Suddenly, Will lunged forward and caught me by the wrist. 'You're upsetting my wife and I'm not having that! You're spoiling the look of the place. You're putting fingermarks on my car! I don't have to tell you anything, but just so you know what an airhead that slut is, I'm telling you this: I was with Aimee when Monday was murdered. Got that? All night. You tell her that. Me and Aimee are getting back together, and she's out of here – you got that? And so are you. Go on, on your bike.' He gave me a shove in the direction of the gate and let go of my wrist.

I took several reluctant steps in the direction of the gate. Where *was* Wayne? 'Oh, come on,' I said nervously. 'First you tell the police you're with Modus, then it's some cocaine dealer. You won't get away with this, Mr McGill. You won't!' I knew I sounded about as convincing as a Tory Party pledge to support the Health Service, but I was feeling pretty desperate. Will McGill had given me a headache and pulled a button off my cuff, and I just had to be right about him. There wasn't any alternative. 'If you were really with Aimee that night, you could have said so from the start. Look, everybody knows how much you hated Rick, and you haven't got an alibi. I spoke to Marianne, I know all about the feud. What's the point of . . .'

'Oh, for Christ's sake, what's the matter with you? I warn you: I'll sue! I'm not having all that garbage written about me all over again. I'm bringing out my first solo album in the autumn and I'm not having it. Get this straight: there was no feud between me and Rick until he split the group up. It wasn't me who did Rick's legs in over Marianne – it was Rob.'

'What?' I had to do a quick rewind on this. For a moment, I couldn't think who he meant. 'Did you say *Rob*?'

'Yes. I'm counting to five, and then I'm calling security.'

I was baffled. This didn't make sense. I'd seen the picture. 'But how can it have been Rob?' Rob and Marianne? 'You mean it was *Rob* who tried to strangle Rick? But it can't have been. The picture's of you and Rick. It's definitely your car.'

'Don't be stupid! I'm telling you, it was Rob. Look, he was going out with this tart – he met her at some poxy village hall do in that crappy place they came from. She was a nice bit of stuff, out of his league, so Rick pulled her. Rick always fancied anything Rob got his hands on, that's what he was like. Those two were at each other's throats most of the time, that's why we dumped Rob as manager. And also because he was a prat.'

'But . . .'

'Oh, come on, think about it. They were like twins. You know, with the flares and the hair. Imagine, it's late, it's dark, and some shit artist sees some guy who looks like Rick pull some other guy he can't see properly out of a car with my numberplate on it . . . What do you think?'

I was speechless.

'Will, we're going to miss our plane!' roared Aimee, threateningly. 'Get rid of her!'

'No. Hang on a minute.' He glowered at me. 'Listen, I knew Rick better than anybody. We were mates. There's nothing about him I don't know. And I'm telling you, he was a complete and utter shit. That's what I liked about him – 'til he turned round and pulled the plug on me, too. Take it from me, all that stuff about wanting to save the world was bollocks. All he ever cared about was himself and being one up on everybody else. He wanted to be one up on me, on you, on Rob, on the whole bloody lot of us. He may have fooled those ponces on the Acorn Trust and on the newspapers, but he didn't fool me. Sooner or later, if somebody hadn't

236

topped him, I'm telling you, the whole boiling lot of you do-gooding pus-heads would've found out just what a shit he really was.'

Suddenly, I knew I'd made a mistake. Right back at the beginning of this whole thing. An awful mistake. A mistake of gigantic proportions.

'Rob thought the world of that Marianne,' put in Aimee. 'She had fabulous legs. Oh, come *on*, Will!'

I thought of the key lying in Will's flower bed. Whatever else happened, I'd got to get it back, because now at last I knew how it had ended up behind the cash register in Mr Huntley's shop.

Will's mood seemed to change again. 'Get out!' he snapped, taking a menacing step towards me. 'I'm calling security, I'm calling my lawyer. You haven't heard the last of this!'

I turned and fled for the gates, stopping briefly to scrabble about in the debris under a very nice hydrangea paniculata where I expected to find the key. But there was no sign of it. There was nothing under the bush except a heap of rubber bands discarded by the postman. And then, just as I was beginning to panic, I spotted Mrs Jobson's key dangling from a faded flower head.

'What the hell do you think you're doing?' shouted Will, and he'd got the remote control in his hand, ready to close the gates.

'Don't worry, I've got it!' I shouted, and I snatched the key and ran for it.

For the second time that week, I parked the Mini in the layby off Eldon Park Road overlooking the commercial district and got out of the car. In the distance, up on the school playing fields, groups of children were going through the strange ritual motions of football, rounders, hockey, and athletics practice.

Wayne sounded unabashed. 'I did get your message, but I'm finishing off a report. Is it something to do with the Monday murder? It says here you've got an absolutely definite suspect.'

237

'Yes, but . . .' His tone held a hint of sarcasm, which seemed a bit unfair – after all, he wasn't to know that my message had referred to a completely different absolutely definite suspect. I decided not to explain this. 'Listen. Can you hear me?' The mid-afternoon news was blaring at full volume from a lorry parked further down the layby. 'I've worked the whole thing out. I know who did it, and why. I've got the evidence in my hand.'

'Oh? All right. Shoot.'

I hesitated.

'. . . is believed to have expressed the view that the Minister's personal life is not a resigning issue . . .' boomed the radio.

'It was his brother, Rob. Listen, I'm at the school now –'

'Local news, now this lunchtime, and –'

'Hang on. How can it have been the brother? What do you mean, you're at the school?'

'I'm at Eldon Park School, it's where Rob teaches. Did you know he tried to kill Rick once before?'

'What?'

'Yes. That cutting I showed you from the paper –' Something was happening up on the playing field. The hockey match had stopped and the players were all running to one end of the field. 'It's a long story. Look, Rick and Rob used to fight over everything, apparently. I mean, I know most brothers do, but think about this: Rick slept with Rob's girlfriend and made her pregnant. Rick and Will dumped Rob from Bad Monday, and then Rick and the group became famous, while Rob stayed at home to become a teacher – a PE teacher!' I added, thinking of Woody Allen's famous remark about PE teachers. 'Rob's married, but I don't think they're very happy, and just recently he found out about Marianne having Rick's baby. Look, Rob hasn't been trying to protect Rick's reputation – he's been trying to protect himself! Think about it.'

'Chris, I hear what you're saying, but . . .'

I stuck my finger in my ear.

'Look, Rick bought Tangley House because Rob liked it and because they'd made some silly pact that whoever became

238

rich first would buy it – Rick told me that himself. Don't you get it? Rick was taking over the Hatchley Heath Committee and the Acorn Trust scheme – all Rob's work, his *life* –'

'Yes, but . . .'

'And there's the key! Do you remember me telling you about Mrs Jobson and how she was sure her key had gone missing and been replaced by a copy?'

'Chris, listen –'

I was too excited to listen. 'No, *you* listen . . .'

'*. . . reports are coming in of a sensational development this morning on the Willow Grange Estate . . .*'

'Hang on a minute,' interrupted Wayne. 'Of course, I remember you telling me about the key. Let's take this a step at a time. Have you really got the key?'

'Yes! It's in my hand!' Stupidly, I waved it at the receiver. On the playing field, a small group of people had detached itself from the stalled hockey match and begun moving slowly in the direction of the road.

'Is it? I see. Well, look –'

'*. . . The head of Bradman Homes, John Bradman, has announced that the company are to fund a full geological survey of the area, following suspicions that . . .*'

'– I want you to come into the station right now and bring the key with you. Have you got that?'

'* . . . Remedial work to correct the problem is expected to run into hundreds of thousands of pounds, but Bradman Homes have promised that no purchaser of a Bradman Home will . . .*'

'Chris? Are you still there?'

'*A spokesman for Willow Grange homeowners said they were stunned by the news, but added his personal thanks to Mr Bradman for . . .*'

'You're to come in *right now* and bring the key with you,' repeated Wayne. 'Are you listening?'

'I'm listening.' Oh, hell . . .

'Good. So you're on your way here then?'

'No! Sorry, Wayne, I'm not.' The three figures on the hockey field were getting closer. The taller of the three, clad in a navy tracksuit, looked very familiar.

'Chris, for God's sake, there'll have to be a full inquiry! I promise you'll be kept fully informed.'

The tall figure was definitely Rob Monday. He had his arms around the shoulders of two girls, one of whom was limping.

'I don't believe you,' I said, searching desperately for an apt turn of phrase to sum up my feelings. 'In a pig's testicles you'll keep me fully informed!'

There was a brief silence.

'Actually, Chris, the word you're looking for is "bollocks",' said Wayne, and slammed down his phone.

I leapt out of the phone box. I already had sticky wet armpits; so much for the extra-dry formulation of my deodorant. Surrounding the playing field was a sparse privet hedge that had seen better days in the early sixties before juggernauts started reversing into it, and I pushed my way through it and began walking up the hill towards the approaching trio. I could handle Rob any day of the week; after McGill he'd be a pushover, and Wayne would already be racing across the car park towards his car. Since Eldon Park School was only five minutes' drive from Hudderston Central even if you didn't have a blue flashing light on the top of your car, this time, nothing could go wrong.

I don't think Rob spotted me until we were almost face to face. He was absorbed in conversation with the two girls, and he glanced up at the last moment, just as I was about to launch into my 'Excuse me, would you like to give me a comment on why you murdered your brother' speech.

He recognized me, and frowned. 'For God's sake, I'm on my way to the hospital with an injured pupil,' he said, tetchily.

With a flourish, I took Mrs Jobson's key out of my pocket and showed it to him. 'I've just spoken to Mr Huntley from the Mister Fixit shop in Hudderston,' I said quietly. 'This is Mrs Jobson's key, which you used to let yourself out of your brother's house after you'd killed him. You accidentally swapped it for your own key. You didn't notice what had happened until *I* told you, on the Common, and then you went to the shop in Hudderston and had a copy made before

240

the police turned up to ask you about it. Isn't that right? Would you care to make a comment?'

Rob blinked. There was a short silence. And then his face changed. If I'd had any doubts about his guilt, they vanished.

'This isn't the moment to discuss this, Mrs Martin,' he muttered. 'Please go away.'

I stood my ground.

Rob studied his feet for a moment, then said, 'Samantha, I'm sorry about this. I want you to take Becky to the office by yourself and ask Mrs Fisher to arrange for her to go to the hospital, and for someone to ring her mum or dad.'

'What?'

'Come on, it's only a sprain.'

'But Mr Monday, who is this woman?' demanded Samantha, rudely. 'Is she CID? She don't look like police! She hasn't read you your rights, Mr Monday! She's got to read you your rights or you shouldn't go nowhere with her. She's got to say that bit about –'

'Samantha, that's enough! Will you go on, please,' urged Rob, desperately.

The girls looked apoplectic with curiosity, but they gave up and limped off in the direction of the school. Rob watched them go and then, without a second glance at me, turned and started walking briskly back towards the players on the hockey field.

I don't know why, but this was the last thing I'd expected him to do. I think I'd imagined he'd break down and confess everything on the spot.

I hitched up my skirt and ran after him. 'Excuse me, Mr Monday, wouldn't you like to make a statement? I mean, for God's sake –' For God's sake, if he ran off, I'd really be in the soup. 'Don't you want to tell me why you did it, Mr Monday?'

He broke into a run. The purple flashes on the backs of his trainers were vanishing in an increasing blur of speed; soon they'd be over the hill, out of sight. I did my best to catch up, but I knew it was hopeless. Rob had been in training most of his life; I'd been out of it for most of mine. My ankles felt like matchsticks; I'd never make it across the field. I panted to the top of the rise and let my knees cave in under me.

To my amazement, Rob suddenly stopped too. He watched me stagger to my feet. I couldn't tell what he was thinking, but he was waiting for me.

'All right,' he shouted, only slightly out of breath. 'I want you to write down my statement. Hurry up!'

As soon as I'd caught up, he started off again at a brisk pace.

'It was an accident,' he said. 'I don't suppose you'll believe me now, but it was an accident.'

I fumbled in my pocket for something to write on, finding an old shopping list.

'I can't tell you exactly what happened. I've been over and over it, but all I can remember is picking up the knife and feeling very, very angry . . . Will that do? Are you getting this?'

We were heading towards the perimeter fence that bordered the railway line. 'I'm getting it.'

'Good. Now I'll tell you where to find the evidence. The gold disc is buried in my herb patch under the variegated sage and you'll find the tracksuit I was wearing at the back of my wardrobe. I've put it through the washing machine three times but I expect there's still blood on it. It's the one with the orange piping.'

I wondered if he'd used biological washing powder in his machine and whether it would matter.

'And I wiped my prints off the knife, with a handkerchief which I used to wrap the gold disc in. I must have left fingerprints all over the study and on the phone – I don't know why the police didn't question me about them. I suppose they just took my prints to eliminate them from the investigation.'

Out of the corner of my eye, I could see two police cars far below in the layby. I tried to wave at them without Rob noticing.

'So there should be plenty of evidence to substantiate what

I'm telling you. Are you sure you're getting this?' I think he must have noticed the police cars, too, but he seemed not to care. 'Well, are you?'

'Yes!' He was quickening his pace. I had to run to keep up. 'I'm getting most of it.'

'And will you say I'm sorry? I want you to be sure and tell them I'm sorry.'

I realized suddenly that he was heading for the footpath which ran along the top of the railway embankment – the same footpath that meandered along the back of Hudderston's industrial estate and ended up at the railway station. I cast a horrified glance over my shoulder at the two police officers standing next to my Mini, looking baffled, not doing anything.

'I want you to say I'm sorry I've wasted police time and I'm sorry I let them waste taxpayers' money on prosecuting the wrong man, and –'

There was a gate in the hedge that enclosed the playing fields. To my relief, it was secured by an enormous padlock.

'– and I'm sorry about all the mess I'm going to leave behind.'

'All right. I've got that.'

Without warning, he broke into a run, but I didn't bother to try and catch up, because I knew any second he'd spot the padlock, and panic. He must have been planning to escape via Hudderston railway station. When he realized this was impossible, he'd probably give up and wait with me for the police. I waved frantically at Wayne.

But when I turned back, Rob had pulled a bunch of keys from his pocket and was undoing the padlock with them. He waited for me to catch up.

'Well, that's it,' he said, in an oddly matter-of-fact tone. 'That's all I've got to say. I want you to take these keys and lock the gate after me.'

'What?'

'There's a railway line down there, Mrs Martin, and there are dozens of children on the field!' He thrust the keys into my hand, his face taut with urgency, and slammed

243

the gate on me. 'It's the one with the red tag. *Don't follow me*!'

Aghast, I ignored this, dropped the keys, swung open the gate, and ran after him, managing somehow to match his speed. I don't know why, but it was beginning not to hurt any more. The pockmarked tarmac of the path was a relief after the spongy grass surface of the playing field, flying effortlessly beneath my feet like a travelator. Suddenly, I knew I could do it: I could stay with him, follow him all the way to the railway station if necessary, and call the police again from the stationmaster's office . . .

With a supreme effort, I closed in on him.

'You haven't told me why you did it, Mr Monday,' I panted.

'I have. I told you, it was an accident! Go *back*!'

'It wasn't! You can't stab someone by accident!' I gasped for breath. 'You were jealous, weren't you?'

'What?'

'I said, you were jealous. You took the gold disc because you were jealous of everything that was Rick's.'

'Don't be ridiculous!' He slowed down slightly. 'You don't get it, do you? *I* wasn't jealous of him – *he* was jealous of me! Leave me alone!'

'No, you were jealous of him! You were jealous of his success. You didn't want him muscling in on your work with the Acorn Trust.'

He gave me a sudden, angry look. 'Don't be ridiculous! You haven't the faintest idea, have you?'

At the bottom of the embankment, a train roared by on its way to the coast.

He waited for the noise to subside, slowing to a (for him) comfortable jog. 'For God's sake!' he snapped. 'You don't just walk into projects like the activity centre. Don't you realize that? John spent nearly a year laying the groundwork for it. Look, I loved my brother, but you and people like you, you didn't know him. His agenda was . . .'

Another train rolled past, drowning out the rest of this remark.

I waited for him to repeat it. He didn't.

'But you still haven't told me what happened!' I protested, sprinting to keep up with him.

'I've told you *three times* it was an accident! Can't you accept that? What difference will it make to anything now, for God's sake?' He stopped, hanging on to the railings to steady himself. I managed to stop, too. 'You can take this down, then,' he panted, 'if it'll make you leave me alone. Go on, get your paper and pencil out again.'

I rummaged desperately through my pockets.

'This is what happened. I went to the house because I thought John was having dinner with Rick.' He wasn't waiting for me to find the pencil. 'I wanted a chance to smooth things over between the two of them. As I've already told you, John had been talking about postponing the Centre and Rick made some stupid remark about finding someone else to fund it. I wondered what the hell else he might say and I didn't want him putting John's back up unnecessarily. I didn't want him chucking away several years' work just to get his face on the cover of the *Sunday Times* magazine.'

He suddenly looked very angry. I'd found my pencil, but he wasn't giving me a chance to get anything down.

'Rick saw the Acorn Trust projects as nothing more than a stepping stone to the furtherance of his career. Whatever he may have said to you, he didn't give a toss about the kids, or about Hatchley Heath. As soon as he'd got himself back in the headlines and a couple of hit records under his belt, he'd be off to pastures new and to hell with the rest of us. I'm sorry, because I loved him, but that was the truth,' he added, bitterly.

I was getting bits of it, my fingers on the pencil sticky with perspiration.

'Anyway, that's why I went to the house. I took my key with me so I could let myself in to wait for them, but when I arrived Rick was already there, by himself, and he was in a foul temper. He said he'd just found out that John was going to drop out of all the Hatchley Heath schemes we were setting up with the Acorn Trust and leave him in the shit.

I don't know where he got this from, but he said I should never have got involved with a two-faced bastard like John. I was a pathetic spineless wimp who couldn't keep his eye on the main chance, and from now on I was to stick to teaching kids to kick footballs, and growing cabbages, and leave all the important stuff to him.' Rob was now shaking slightly, and I could tell he was replaying Rick's last diatribe in his head. 'The Acorn Trust, the Hatchley Heath Committee, his career, everything. He said he'd find some other sucker to fund the Centre – and the Tangley House scheme – and he'd get them to do things his way.' He paused, clenching and unclenching the fingers of his right hand. 'We were in the study. Rick turned the volume up on the tape machine and I told him to turn it down. I was furious, but I was trying to stay calm. I didn't want to lose my temper. I went over to turn the volume down myself and Rick tried to push me out of the way. I think he hit me in the stomach – not very hard, but it knocked the wind out of me and I fell against the desk. I should have just left it, but I grabbed hold of him, and the next thing I know we were pushing each other across the top of the desk and my hands were round his throat.' Rob stared unseeingly across to the treetops on the other side of the embankment. 'I don't know where he got the knife from. Probably a drawer in the desk. He pushed it against my throat. I think he was only trying to taunt me with it, but I grabbed it – and I stabbed him.'

There was a moment's silence, broken only by the metallic clunking of the railway line below as a distant signalman changed the points.

'He died almost immediately,' said Rob. 'He said, "You've cut me," and we both got up from the desk, and then he fell over backwards. I tried to help him – I wanted to help him. I tried to press the wound together with my hand and I felt for a pulse, but it was hopeless. If the phone had still been working I'd have phoned the police there and then, but it wasn't. I sat on the floor for about – oh, I don't know – ten or fifteen minutes, in a state of shock. And then I started thinking about what would happen if I did go to the police; not just to me, but how the whole thing would have to come out. Nobody would ever think of my father again as the man who fought for a good deal for Hatchley Heath's Council tenants, he'd just be the father of two boys who had destroyed each other: Cain and Abel. I know how you people twist things,' he added bitterly.

I was transfixed. I hadn't written anything down.

Rob seemed not to have noticed this. 'Anyway, that was that. I suddenly remembered those letters I showed you – the ones from that poor groupie. I thought, if I could make it look as though Rick had been killed by some nutcase it would put the police off the track and stop them asking awkward questions. But I was in a panic, I didn't know how to do it. I cleaned my prints off the knife and off the edge of the desk. I stuffed the gold disc inside my top because I thought a crazy person would be bound to want a souvenir. I thought they might even do something awful like mutilate the body, but I couldn't do that. In the end all I could think of was to write "pig" on the wall in blood and pull Rick's papers out of the desk and rip them up. I'd started on the wall when I suddenly realized there was someone else in the house. I think there must have been a gap between tracks on the tape, because I heard the floorboards creak in the corridor overhead, twice.' He broke off, breathing heavily. 'I panicked. I hadn't thought of it before, but Rick sometimes got women sent over by this escort agency in London. I found the key for the French windows which he kept in his desk and ran out on to the terrace.'

He shook his head, rubbing his face with shaking fingers. 'You can't imagine, it was like the worst nightmare you've ever had. I've had guilt dreams before, always connected with Rick, because I resented him. I didn't want to resent him, and I tried not to, but I couldn't help it. This was like the whole bloody lot come true, ten times over. And I realized it was pointless running away, because whoever the woman was she was bound to have seen me arrive at the house and there was no way I could talk my way out of it. The best thing I could do was go back in and try to explain. I was about to –

I was on my way – when suddenly this man ran out of the French windows clutching the bags with the fête money in them. To be honest, at this point I don't think I cared whether he'd seen me or not, and God knows how he didn't. I suppose he was in a state of shock. I just wanted to get out of there and get home, and the quickest way to do that was through the front and along the top of the common.'

'So you went back in and let yourself out of the front with Mrs Jobson's key?' I interrupted eagerly.

'Yes. I knew I'd brought my own key but I couldn't find it – it must have fallen behind a fold in the bottom of my pocket, and I was in a panic. Rick's keys were on him somewhere – I knew that because I'd seen him with them when he let me in – but I didn't want to have to touch him again. And then I remembered Viv saying something about Mrs Jobson leaving her key in the kitchen, so I went and got it. I let myself out and closed the door. *Then* it occurred to me that I ought to put Mrs Jobson's key back, so I unlocked the door and put it back on her hook. Or at least, I thought I did. Of course it was really my own key I put back on the hook.'

Far below us, at the bottom of the concrete canyon, the rails of the track were humming faintly with the approach of a distant train.

Rob looked at his watch. 'Did you get all that?' he asked.

I glanced desperately over my shoulder along the path. 'Yes. Look, wait a minute. The courts will take into account all the circumstances. Please don't go!'

In the distance, the far distance, someone was approaching fast along the path.

Rob took off without a word, the purple flashes on his trainers blending into neon streaks. Pausing to wave frantically at Wayne, I took off after him, pushing the slip of paper bearing about eight words of his confession into my pocket. At the bend, Rob disappeared. When I rounded the corner, he'd stopped by a gate in the railings. The gate was old and rusted, and Rob was kicking at it with his right foot.

'What are you doing?' I yelled. 'Stop!'

The faint hum of the rails had now become a buzz. The

rattle and roar of the approaching train was beginning to echo about the cutting. I immediately made up my mind that if Rob went down the steps I wouldn't follow him across the live rails – it wasn't worth it – but I said, 'I'll come after you! You can't get away!' And as the gate tore free from the padlock I jumped in front of him, grabbing hold of the posts on either side and hanging on as though a good deal of money depended on it. 'You're staying here to wait for the police!' I shrieked.

Rob didn't say anything. Sometimes you can be wrong about people. The last thing I expected in the world was for him to raise a hand to me; I thought he was an old-fashioned gentleman. But at the end, he wasn't. He punched me on the jaw, hard; a proper punch, an uppercut, toppling me backwards off the top step of the stairway. And before I'd had a chance to recover, he took hold of me by the shoulder and heaved me violently into space. I opened my eyes in time to see a gatepost flying past my right shoulder. A gatepost, on one side of which was the footpath, on the other a fifty-foot drop into the path of the Hudderston to Waterloo express . . .

There was a tremendous crunch, and everything went black.

I don't think the blackness can have lasted for more than a fraction of a second, because when I surfaced from it, nothing had changed except that in addition to the sharp pain in my jaw, my back hurt where I'd landed on it. And I knew instantly that I was still on the top of the embankment rather than below it, because the noise of the train was still coming from the same direction. I lifted my head to look for Rob, and as I did so the train, now directly below in the cutting, suddenly began to make an awful groaning, grinding noise.

It was braking.

I sat up. The hairs on the back of my neck were beginning to rise. Why would the train stop? I began to get the most awful feeling. I turned round to look for Wayne. I could see the whiteness of his face, stark against the bushes bordering the path, as he gazed down at the line.

I didn't want to, but I levered myself up on the railings and looked down.

Far below in the cutting, one of Rob's trainers was sailing slowly into view over the roof of the still-moving train. The purple flash rotated sluggishly like a spent Catherine wheel. And I am not sure, but I think his foot was still inside it.

19

'You don't know that,' said Pete, after a long pause. 'How can you possibly know that? The steps may have been wet . . .'

'They weren't.' I hugged the receiver to my ear despondently. 'I think he jumped.'

'. . . or there may have been fallen leaves or rubbish on them. Look, if he'd got across the railway line he could've got on to the slip road to the A3 and hitched a lift anywhere in the country. You said so yourself. It makes much more sense than the railway station.'

'Yes, I know but . . .'

'Oh, hang on – bloody cones everywhere.' His engine roared unevenly through the receiver. I could hear the cones flickering past his open window. 'Look, whatever he did, he did it to himself, right? It was his decision. Are you sure you're all right?'

'I told you, I'm fine.'

'Well, there's some gin in the cupboard. Pour yourself a large one. I should be with you in forty minutes – Jesus! Why won't this *arsehole* in front stop picking his nose and pull over!'

At this point a strange crackling noise intervened, followed by an even stranger whining noise.

'Are you still there?' I prompted.

'Yes, I'm . . . Andover . . . just past the airfield. The traffic's . . .' The crackling continued.

'Hallo? Look, I'll hang up, shall I?' I examined my bruised chin in the mirror. It was strawberry-red.

'No, don't hang up.' Suddenly the line was as clear as a

251

bell. 'I don't want you to hang up. I like having you tucked under my ear. When I've got you on the phone it's the one time I can talk to you without you walking away and polishing a place mat or something.'

Hastily I put down my Mr Sheen.

'Go on, tell me your life story or something. Well, the first half. I told you, I've only got forty minutes.'

Unbidden, memories of the whispered conversations we used to have on my old phone in my old kitchen when I was still married to Keith flooded back. My stomach flipped over the way it used to.

'There is something I want to say, actually,' I said, my stomach doing another flip, but this time for a different reason. 'But I'm not sure if I should just at the moment.'

'Oh, go on. Try me.'

'It's about us getting married.' I let this sink in. 'Well, it's not that I don't love you or anything. I really do love you – very, very much.'

'Good.'

'It's just that I'm not sure if I want to get married at the moment. I mean, I'm not sure if I'm ready for it yet. I know I thought I was. I know I kept on and on about it when we were first living together and we nearly fell out over it, but I realize now that you were right. It's like you said, I wanted us to get married for all the wrong reasons – you know, because it seemed romantic and a happy ending and all that sort of thing – and that's why I'm not sure I want us to get married now, because if we ever *do* get married I want to be absolutely sure it's for the *right* reasons.'

There was silence. I waited for Pete to tell me I was talking a load of bollocks. I think I quite hoped he would. But he didn't, so I carried on.

'Of course, I'm not entirely sure what the right reasons are, but I still think we shouldn't do it unless we're both absolutely one hundred per cent sure. Just for the sake of sorting our pensions and things out, I mean. It doesn't seem right, does it? I mean, as you said yourself, we're happy the way we are, aren't we?'

Suddenly, I became aware that the phone was emitting a loud whispering noise, as though it was being held close to a waterfall, or as if it was swirling around amid the sort of wastepaper that is to be found in Pete's passenger footwell.

'Hallo?' I said, tentatively. 'Hallo? Hallo?'

The swishing noise continued unabated, accompanied by odd rasping sounds and vague thumps and creaks.

'Hallo?' I tried again, beginning to panic. 'Are you all right? What's happened? Are you there?'

'Hang on . . .' I heard him pick up the phone. 'Hallo! Is that you?'

'Yes, it's me!'

'Good. It's OK, I'm back on the road again now.'

'What happened? Are you all right?'

'Yes, I'm fine, fine! I didn't see the bastard. Big red bread lorry. Nothing to worry about – he didn't take my number or anything. He gave me two fingers and buggered off.'

'Oh, God!' Pete might be dead and I'd have killed him. 'Oh, God, Pete! I'm so sorry. Did you hear what I said?'

There was silence. 'Yes. I heard you.'

At that moment, Julie's key turned in the front door lock.

'I'm really sorry.' I tried to cuddle the phone to my chest so she wouldn't hear me. 'I knew I shouldn't have started this. I didn't mean it the way it sounded, honestly. I told you: I love you. What do you think?'

There was another short silence. 'Well,' said Pete, 'I think you're a silly bitch sometimes, but I forgive you, and don't kid yourself – I can crash my car into lorries quite adequately without any help from you.' And he hung up.

Julie threw open the front door. 'Mum!' she exclaimed in surprise. 'What are you doing home?'

'Julie!' I dropped the phone hastily. 'Thank God you're home – I've been so worried about you. I'm really sorry about lunch. What did you do? Did you manage to get something to eat?'

'To eat? Oh, God, no. It was great. I used the letter you'd given me to get out of school and meet Gavin. We went down by the river.'

'*The river*?' This was awful. I thought of the bushes where I used to meet Keith.

'Yes. It was great! Men are so *gullible*, aren't they?' She dropped her bag and jacket on the floor. 'I never had a chance to tell you, but I thought Gavin had dumped me for that tarty piece in the florists. Well, he did go out with her a couple of times when you made me stay in to revise. Still, I've got him back now so it's all right!'

'Oh . . .'

'What's that on your chin?'

'Actually, it's a –'

'It looks like a bruise! What's for tea?' She skipped off to the kitchen. 'And you needn't worry, because I've definitely decided I'm going to do A-levels after all. Even if I get lousy grades in my GCSEs I'm still going to do them, even if it means going back to school to resit my GCSEs all over again!'

'Oh!' I followed her to the kitchen. I was stunned into silence.

'And I haven't changed my mind, if that's what you think! I never ever said I wasn't going to do A-levels. I only ever said I didn't see what the point was, and I got fed up with you and *him* and Dad going on and on at me about how important they are. But now I see the point! If I've got A-levels, I won't ever have to be dependent on a man!'

I opened my mouth to query this point, but thought better of it.

She frowned. 'And don't go letting all this go to your head, but I think I want to be like you.'

I was shocked. 'Like me?'

'Yes. Well, not exactly, of course. I mean, I want a proper job doing something useful, but I'm not going to get married to some man who'll treat me like crap. That's what you did of course, but you had the guts to put it right and that's what I admire about you. You got married and you wasted twenty years – twenty whole years – with one man, just because that man was . . .'

'Your father?' I put in quickly.

254

She dropped a packet of Cadbury's finger biscuits on to the worktop, spilling its entire contents. 'Oh, what's that got to do with anything? Women can have babies and look after them themselves without any help from men. Fathers are just sort of . . . biological accidents.'

'Really. Rather like grass stains, you mean?'

'Hmm,' agreed Julie, absently. 'Anyway, that's what I want to do: choose for myself what *I* do with *my* life. I hate kids and I'm not going to have any.'

'Oh. I see.' I reached for the kettle. 'Hot chocolate?'

'Yes.' She collected up the biscuits, cramming two into her mouth at once. 'Look, what's the matter with you today? You're not going soft, are you? I'm not going to have to tell all my friends you're getting me a step-dad, am I?'

I rested the kettle against the sink and turned off the tap. 'Now, look,' I said grimly. 'I'm sorry, but I've just about had enough of people telling me what to do. I don't care whether you want to be like me or not. I don't particularly care what you think of me. I don't want to be anyone's role model. And it's got nothing to do with you whether I marry Pete or not. What the hell do you know about it? You know absolutely zilch! Perhaps I will marry Pete one day – I think I may – and perhaps if I do it'll be because I don't want him getting run off the road by a big rude man in a big red lorry when he's tired and upset and too old to concentrate – or because I want to be sure of getting a share of his pension – or because we both need someone to rub Ralgex into our shoulders after a hard day struggling with our walking frames . . .'

Her mouth fell open.

'But I'll tell you this: whatever I do, I won't be doing it because you, or some plastic-faced Californian mutant in an overpriced paperback, tells me it's the right way for women to go!'

'A plastic-faced what?'

'Californian mutant. You know what I mean. Have you got the picture?'

She gave me a hard stare. 'Why? I thought you just said

you don't care what I think. Are you going to make me that hot chocolate, or what?'

'Chocolate? Who said anything about chocolate? Is that all you can think about?' I was still holding the kettle. 'Oh, forget it. Yes, I'll make you a hot chocolate. Do you want extra sugar?' I refilled the kettle and reached for a mug.